THE OXFORD BROTHERHOOD

Also by Guillermo Martínez

The Book of Murder
The Oxford Murders

THE OXFORD BROTHERHOOD

GUILLERMO MARTÍNEZ

PEGASUS CRIME
NEW YORK LONDON

THE OXFORD BROTHERHOOD

Pegasus Crime is an imprint of
Pegasus Books, Ltd.
148 West 37th Street, 13th Floor
New York, NY 10018

ISBN: 978-1-64313-877-0

10 9 8 7 6 5 4 3 2 1

Printed in the United States of America
Distributed by Simon & Schuster
www.pegasusbooks.com

To Brenda, who made my DEAD LIVE.

Chapter 1

Shortly before the turn of the century, fresh out of college, I travelled to England on a scholarship to study mathematical logic at Oxford. During my first year there I had the good fortune of getting to know the great Arthur Seldom, author of *The Aesthetics of Reason* and of the philosophical extension of Gödel's theorems. Far more unexpectedly, in the blurred middle ground between chance and fate, I became his fellow witness in a series of baffling deaths, all stealthy, phantom-like, almost immaterial, which the papers called *The Oxford Murders*. Perhaps one day I'll decide to reveal the secret clue to these events; in the meantime, I can only repeat a pronouncement I heard from Seldom himself: 'The perfect crime is not the one that remains unsolved but the one that is solved with the wrong culprit.'

In June 1994, at the beginning of my second year in Oxford, the last echoes of these events had quietened down, everything had returned to normal and, during the long summer days, I had no other plans than to catch up with my studies in order to keep the imperative deadline for my scholarship report. My academic supervisor, Emily Bronson, who had generously excused my unproductive months and the many times she'd seen me in tennis kit in the company of a cute redheaded girl, demanded, with a firm Anglo-Saxon

attitude, that I make up my mind and choose one of the
several subjects she had suggested for my thesis. I chose the
one that had, however remotely, something akin to my secret
literary aspirations: the development of a program that, from
a fragment of handwriting, might recover the physical function of the act, that is to say, the movement of the arm and
the pen in the actual time of writing. It concerned the still
hypothetical application of a certain theorem of topological
duality that she had thought up, and that seemed a sufficiently original and difficult challenge for me to suggest a
joint paper if I were to succeed.

Soon, and earlier than I would have imagined, I felt I
had advanced enough in the project to knock on Seldom's
door. After the murders, there had remained between us
something like a tenuous friendship and though formally
my adviser was Emily Bronson, I preferred to try out my
ideas on Seldom first, perhaps because under his patient
and somewhat amused gaze I felt more at liberty to risk a
hypothesis, fill up blackboards and, almost always, take
a wrong turn. We had discussed Bertrand Russell's veiled
criticism to Wittgenstein's *Tractatus* in his foreword to the
book, the hidden mathematical explanation in the phenomenon of essential incompleteness, the relationship between
Borges' story 'Pierre Menard, Author of *Don Quixote*' and
the impossibility of establishing meaning from syntax alone,
the search for a perfect artificial language, the attempts to
capture chance in a mathematical formula ... I had just
turned twenty-three and believed I had my own solutions
to these problems, solutions that were always both naive
and megalomaniacal. And yet, when I'd knock at his door,
Seldom would push aside his own papers, lean back in his
chair and, with a slight smile, allow me to speak, fuelled by
my own enthusiasm, before pointing out another paper in

which my theory had already been set out or, rather, refuted. Against Wittgenstein's laconic assertion on what cannot be spoken, I tried to say too much.

But this time it was different: the problem seemed to him sensible, interesting, approachable. Also, he said somewhat mysteriously, it was not too far removed from the others we had considered. After all, it meant inferring from a still image – a set of symbols captured graphically – a possible reconstruction, a probable past. I agreed, enthused by his approval, and drew on the blackboard a quick and capricious curve, followed by a second one very close to the first that intended to follow its path in order to copy it.

'I imagine a scribe holding his hand in mid-air, trying to control his pulse and replicate every detail, following as carefully as an ant every step of the way. But the original manuscript was written with a certain rhythm, lightly, with a different timing. What I intend to do is to recover some-thing of that previous physical movement, the *generative act* of writing. Or, at the very least, produce a register that will mark the difference between the speed of each. It's similar to what we discussed regarding "Pierre Menard". Cervantes, as Borges imagines it, wrote *Don Quixote* somewhat hap-hazardly, collaborating with chance, following his impulses and whims. Pierre Menard, in his attempt of writing *Don Quixote* once more, but this time as a theorem, is forced to reproduce it slowly, bit by bit, like a logical tortoise, tied down by inexorable laws and strict reasoning. He does produce a text of identical words, but not with the same invisible mental operations at work behind it.'

Seldom remained thoughtful for a moment, as if consider-ing the problem from a different point of view or weighing its possible difficulties, and he wrote out for me the name of Leyton Howard, a mathematician who had once been his student and who, he told me, worked in the area of calligraphic expertise in the scientific section of the Oxford police.

'I'm sure you've seen him a number of times because he never missed our four o'clock tea, though he never took part in the conversations. He's Australian and, winter or summer, he always goes about barefoot. You couldn't have helped noticing him. He keeps to himself, but I'll write to him suggesting that you might work together: that will help you ground yourself in concrete problems.'

Seldom's suggestion, as usual, proved to be the right one, and I spent many hours over the next month in the tiny office that Leyton had been given in the attic of the police station, where he studied in the archives and case notes the tricks of the cheque forgers, Poincaré's statistical arguments during his unexpected role as mathematical expert in the Dreyfus case, the chemical subtleties of inks and papers, and historical examples of false wills. I had managed to borrow a bicycle for my second summer, and going down St Aldate's to reach the police station I would wave to the girl working at the Alice shop, who, at that time, was in charge of opening the place, small and sparkling like a doll's house with its profusion of rabbits, watches, teapots and Queens of Hearts. Sometimes, arriving at the entrance to the police station, I would also see Inspector Petersen. The first time, I hesitated to acknowledge him because I wondered whether he might still harbour a certain resentment towards Seldom (and consequently towards me) after the events in which we had crossed paths during the investigation of the murders. Fortunately he didn't seem bitter about it at all and would attempt, as if repeating a bad joke, to greet me in broken Spanish.

Every time I reached the attic, Leyton would already be there, a mug of coffee on his desk, acknowledging my presence with a mere nod. He was extremely pale, covered in freckles, with a long red beard that he'd twirl in his fingers while thinking. He was some fifteen years older than I was, and he reminded me both of an ageing hippy and of one of those beggars in proud rags that sit reading philosophy tomes at the gates of the colleges. He did not speak more than was necessary and never unless I asked him a direct question. On the rare occasions on which he decided to open his mouth, he first seemed to ponder carefully what he was about to say before uttering a pared-down sentence that, like mathematical conditions, was at the same time sufficient and necessary. I imagined that in those preliminary seconds, he would feverishly compare, in a fit of private and useless pride, different ways of saying the same thing before choosing the briefest and the most precise. Much to my distress, as soon as I told him of my project, he showed me a program that had been in use for years by the police and that employed each one of the ideas that I had come up with: the thickness of the ink and the difference of density as parameters of the speed, the gaps between words as indicators of the rhythm, the angle of the stroke as gradient of the acceleration ... The program, however, proceeded through sheer brute force, based on simulations, with an algorithm of successive approximations. Leyton, seeing my disappointment, tried to encourage me with a whole spendthrift sentence, telling me to examine it nevertheless in detail, with the hope that perhaps my supervisor's theorem (which I attempted to explain to him) could render the program more efficient. I decided to follow his advice. As soon as he realised that I meant to work in earnest, he generously opened for me his box of tricks and even allowed me to accompany him to a couple of sessions at the courts. In the dock, facing the judges, perhaps because they forced him to wear shoes, for a brief moment Leyton underwent a transformation: his a moment, as if there were something he didn't dare say or a last obstacle in his mind that he felt unable to overcome.

'But it'll be, obviously, a restricted program. And there'll be a record of every time someone uses it.'

I shrugged.

'I don't think that's the case. I myself have a copy here in the Institute, and I ran it several times on one of the computers in the basement. As to secrecy ... ' I gave him a knowing look. 'I don't know, no one told me I was commanded by the Queen to keep it a secret.'

Seldom smiled and nodded quietly.

'In that case, maybe you can do us an immense favour.' He leaned towards me and lowered his voice. 'Have you ever heard of the Lewis Carroll Brotherhood?'

I shook my head.

'So much the better,' he said. 'Come this evening at seven thirty to Merton College. There's someone I want you to meet.'

Chapter 2

As I gave my name at the entrance to Merton College it was still light, with that persistent and peaceful quality of summer days in England. While I waited for Seldom to come and get me, I peered into the grassy quadrangle of the first courtyard and became once more ensnared by the mystery of these interior gardens. There was something, whether a certain proportion in the height of the walls or perhaps the neatness with which the crests of the roofs made their appearance, that succeeded (was it a trick of the eyes or was it simply the peace and quiet of the place?) in bringing the sky miraculously close, as if the Platonic image of the rectangle, cut high above a celestial pane, were brought almost at arm's reach. I saw, halfway across the lawn, a few shiny and symmetrical beds of poppies. An oblique ray of sunshine fell on the stone galleries, and the angle at which it lit up the centuries-old stone brought to mind the sundials of ancient civilisations and the infinitesimal rotation of a time beyond human measure. Seldom appeared at a corner and led me along a second gallery to the fellows' garden. We saw a number of dons hurry across in the opposite direction, like a murder of crows in their stiff black robes.

'Everyone will now be busy with dinner in the cafeteria,' Seldom said. 'We'll be able to talk in the garden without anyone disturbing us.'

He pointed to a lonely table in one of the corners of the gallery. A very old man glanced up at us, carefully placed his cigar on the table and moved back his chair in order to lift himself slowly with the aid of his stick.

'That's Sir Richard Ranelagh,' Seldom whispered. 'He was deputy minister of defence for many years and now, since his retirement, he's president of our Brotherhood. He's a very well-known writer of spy novels as well. I don't need to tell you that what you are about to hear must be kept in the strictest confidence.'

I nodded and we approached the table. I shook a fragile hand that still preserved a surprisingly firm grip, told him my name and we exchanged a few polite words. Under his wrinkled skin and his tortoise eyelids, Sir Richard gave the appearance of a vivacious personality, with cold and piercing eyes; while nodding slightly at the words with which Seldom introduced me, he never stopped studying me behind a cautious smile, as if he wished to see for himself and suspend his judgement for the time being. That he had been Number Two at the Ministry of Defence didn't diminish him in my view, rather the contrary. I had read enough le Carré novels to know that in the realm of Intelligence, as in so many others, Number Two was in fact Number One. On the table were three glasses and a bottle of whisky, of which Sir Richard had obviously partaken a fair amount. Seldom poured equal measures into his glass and mine. After the preliminary small talk, Sir Richard picked up his cigar and gave it a lengthy puff.

'Arthur must have told you that we have a long and sad tale to tell.' He exchanged glances with Seldom, as if preparing for a difficult task for which he needed Seldom's help. 'In any case, we'll both share in the telling. But where to begin?'

'As the King would advise,' said Seldom, '"Begin at the beginning and go on till you come to the end: then stop."'

'But perhaps we should begin *before* the beginning,'
Sir Richard said and he leaned back in his chair as if
about to examine me. 'What do you know about Lewis
Carroll's diaries?'

'I didn't even know such a thing existed,' I said. 'In fact, I
know almost nothing of his life.'

I felt at fault, as if I were back at the examination tables
of my student years. I had only read, in the mists of my
distant childhood, a hesitant Spanish translation of *Alice
in Wonderland* and *The Hunting of the Snark*. And though
I had once visited Christ Church, where Carroll had both
lectured on mathematics and given sermons, and had seen in
passing his portrait in the Dining Hall, I had never become
interested enough to track his footsteps. Also, I cultivated
at the time a certain voluntary indifference, quite healthy in
fact, towards the writers behind the books, and I preferred to
pay more attention to the creatures of fiction than to the cre-
ators of flesh and blood. But of course, this last I couldn't say
out loud in front of two members of a Carroll Brotherhood.

'The diaries exist, certainly,' Ranelagh said, 'and in the
most disturbing state: they are incomplete. Throughout his
life, Carroll filled some thirteen notebooks, and perhaps
only his first biographer, his nephew Stuart Dodgson, was
fortunate enough to be able to read them in their entirety.
We know this because he quotes from all of the notebooks
in his inaugural biography of 1898. The notebooks were left
to gather dust in the family home for thirty silent years, but
the centenary of Carroll's birth sparked a renewed interest
in him and his family decided to exhume and collect all his
scattered papers. When they attempted to recover the diaries
they discovered that four of the original notebooks had disappeared. Was it due to carelessness, were they mislaid during a
move, was it a mere lack of interest? Or did someone else in

those three decades, a relative excessively anxious to protect Carroll's reputation, read the notebooks, every one of them, apply his own censorious judgement, and eliminate these four because they contained entries felt to be too compromising? We don't know. Fortunately, the notebooks that covered the period in which he met Alice Liddell and wrote *Alice in Wonderland* survived. But here, too, the scholars who went through them with a fine-tooth comb found a maddening detail, a speck of incertitude, which led to all kinds of speculation and conjecture. In the 1863 notebook a few pages are missing, and in particular there are traces of one that has been clearly torn out and that corresponds to a very delicate moment in Carroll's relationship with Alice's parents.'

'Delicate ... in what sense?' I brought myself to interrupt.

'I would say in the most delicate sense imaginable.'

Ranelagh puffed again on his cigar and slightly changed his tone, as if he were about to venture into a mined territory. 'You must no doubt know something of the story behind the Alice books. At least, allow me to refresh your memory. In that summer of 1863, the thirty-something-year-old Lewis Carroll was living in bachelor rooms at Christ Church, lecturing in mathematics and debating whether or not to enter a religious order. Eight years earlier, the new dean of Christ Church, Henry Liddell, had established himself in Oxford with his wife and four children: Harry, Ina, Alice and Edith. Carroll would cross paths with the children every day in the library gardens; when he first met Alice, she was barely three years old. At first he befriended and subsequently, at Liddell's request, tutored the dean's eldest son, Harry, in mathematics. Later, Carroll began to record in his diaries his increasingly frequent meetings and walks with Ina, the eldest of the Liddell girls, always accompanied by the governess, Miss Prickett, a singularly unattractive woman, of whom he secretly made fun together with the girls. As Alice and Edith grew older, they began to take part in the games and songs that Lewis Carroll invented and join the group on its summer outings on the river, always in the inevitable company of Miss Prickett, as he infallibly set down in his diary. By then he had developed his interest in photography; he had bought his first equipment and he had frequent sessions with all three girls, having them pose in all kinds of situations and disguises, sometimes half-naked, as in the famous picture of Alice as a beggar-maid. However odd it might seem to us now, whether because of the aura of respectability granted by his double role as Oxford professor and as clergyman, or because he seemed nothing but an eccentric yet harmless character, or simply because in those bygone days people were more trusting and more innocent, neither the dean nor his wife objected to those entertainments and outings. Lewis Carroll had merely to send them a note, and he was allowed to carry the girls off to the river for an entire afternoon. A year earlier, in 1862, on one of these outings, he told them the story of Alice underground, and the Alice Liddell of flesh and blood had made him promise to write it down as a book just for her. Lewis Carroll waited six months before setting himself down to the task and, in this summer of 1863, he still hadn't finished it. But he doubtlessly remained on excellent terms with the Liddell family. We arrive then at June the twenty-fourth. In the morning, Alice and Edith go to Lewis Carroll's rooms to drag him off on an excursion to Nuneham, and are joined by the dean, Mrs Liddell and several others. They are a group of ten, and Lewis Carroll jots down all of their names. Exceptionally, the governess, Miss Prickett, does not go with them, perhaps because the girls were accompanied by their parents. They rent a large boat, take turns rowing across the river, partake of tea under the trees on the other side and, at dusk, while the rest of the group goes home in a carriage, Lewis Carroll returns on his own with the three girls by train. In his diary, recording the moment in which he's left alone with them, he writes in brackets *"Mirabile dictu!"*, an expression he used when things unexpectedly went his way. Then he added: "A very pleasant excursion with a *very* pleasant ending." He himself underlined "very" in the notebook.' Here Ranelagh paused, perhaps also to underline the effect of these words.

'How old were the girls?' I asked.

'A very pertinent question, though I'm afraid that ages meant something different in those days. "The past is a foreign country", as Hartley noted, and that is true also for what is considered proper. We only need recall, as a piece of the conundrum, that women could be legally married at the age of twelve; however, in other aspects they were much more childish than girls are today. Lewis Carroll himself on several occasions uses the expression "child-wife" to refer to the pubescent spouses of other characters of that time. Ina was fourteen, and she was already a blossoming adolescent, tall and beautiful according to the pictures of her. She had been Lewis Carroll's first child friend, and her name appears very frequently in the diaries. That summer was the last in which she could go out unchaperoned. Alice was eleven and the previous year she had become his favourite. Several contemporary witnesses agree in pointing out the special devotion he showed towards her, though curiously there are hardly any explicit traces of this in the diaries. She was heading towards twelve, the age at which Lewis Carroll would lose or replace his child friends. Edith was nine.' Ranelagh looked at us as if expecting another question, and poured himself another glass of whisky before carrying on. 'At the end of that day, Lewis Carroll goes to bed peacefully and on the next day requests again the girls' company, but this time Mrs Liddell calls on him at his rooms and the famous conversation takes place, in which she asks him to stay away from her family. What had happened during the outing, or perhaps during the return trip on the train? What had Mrs Liddell noticed in the behaviour of Lewis Carroll towards her daughters? What had the girls told their mother upon returning home? Whatever Lewis Carroll had to say about this, however much or however little, was doubtlessly that torn-out page. What is certain is that Lewis Carroll's relationship with the family becomes distant, and this state of affairs lasts for several months. When he makes an attempt to ask again for permission to meet up with the girls, Mrs Liddell's refusal is forthright. And when at last he finishes writing the book, he cannot bring it to Alice in person; he must resign himself to sending it in the post. And yet, in spite of all this (and this is a curious fact in and of itself), the relationship is not wholly severed. After a time, he's welcomed again in the house, even though he's still kept away from the girls. And later on, Lewis Carroll will have friendly encounters with Mrs Liddell and he will continue to send his books to her daughters until well into their adulthood. He even takes Alice's picture once more, when she turns eighteen.'

'That would suggest that whatever he did wasn't considered all that serious,' I said. 'Or that he was given the benefit of the doubt.'

'This, in fact, is the only question. Did Lewis Carroll actually do something untoward during that train ride? What I mean is: did he overstep the self-imposed limits to which he himself held in his relationship with the girls during his entire life? Did a transgression of some kind take place during that journey, in the nature of a, shall we say, *physical* contact? Something that the girls perhaps recounted in an innocent manner, without fully understanding it; something that awoke in the mother a sense of alarm? Or was it merely a vague feeling of danger that the mother perceived during the excursion, perhaps an excessive familiarity, observing him in the company of her daughters? Or did the warning come from another of the adults in the group, as Lewis Carroll left to accompany the girls? Or was it, as some have suggested, something entirely different? One of the most distinguished members of our Brotherhood, Thornton Reeves, recently published the most exhaustive biography we have to date, and upon reaching that black hole he offered the conjecture that it was perhaps during that conversation that Lewis Carroll asked for Alice's hand in marriage, and it was this that alarmed Mrs Liddell and made her see him in an entirely different light.'

'The thunder of sex at the idyllic Victorian boating-picnic,' pronounced Seldom.

'Exactly,' Ranelagh concurred. 'Or rather a full electric storm above Lewis Carroll's head, suspended in time. And raging also over the battling contenders of our Brotherhood.'

'A battle? Between what factions?' I asked. Ranelagh seemed to consider my question carefully, as if he had exceeded himself and would prefer to fall back on a different formulation.

'It's a debate, still open, to determine the nature, whether culpable or innocent, of his feelings for the girls. Lewis Carroll had dozens of relationships with children throughout his life, and none of them, nor their parents, ever mentioned any improper behaviour. His predilection for young girls, and his friendships with them, was always in the open, for all the world to see. There is not, in any of the documents and correspondence related to Lewis Carroll, a single concrete proof that would allow us to draw a line, however thin, between thought and action. However, we know through the diaries he kept during the years of his relationship with the Liddell children, that Lewis Carroll underwent his deepest spiritual crisis, and there are a fair number of prayers and entreaties to God to help him make amends and leave his sins behind once and for all. But what were these sins? Were they, once again, sins of commission or merely of thought? He's never sufficiently explicit when writing about these things, as if he didn't allow himself to confide fully even in his diaries. Lewis Carroll's father was an archdeacon, and as a child his upbringing was strictly religious: the slightest equivocal thought, the least embarrassment, would suffice to make him pray for guidance. In the end, every biographical attempt to capture Lewis Carroll's persona skirts the edge of this uncertain abyss, and is based on a presumption of innocence until evidence to the contrary. And even though there are many in our suspicious times who prefer automatically to imagine the contrary, even those who are out to catch a paedophile Lewis Carroll have never yet succeeded in giving definitive proof.'

'Although they could allege,' Seldom observed, 'that the pictures he took of those girls are more than condemnatory.'

'We've been through all that already, Arthur.' Sir Richard shook his head and carried on, his eyes fixed on me alone, as if it were up to him to defend equanimity in a difficult case set before an imaginary tribunal. 'Nothing is as easy or clear as that. In those days, children were considered angelic and the nakedness of a child was part of an Edenic ideal. Lewis Carroll took his pictures under the approving eyes of the children's parents, never as something shameful that he had to practise in secret. His nudes were taken to be exhibited at a time when the art of photography was in its infancy. It's very probable that he considered himself not unlike a painter who has his models pose dressed up or stripped of all clothing.

When his young friends entered adulthood, he punctually sent their mothers the negatives so that they could destroy them if the girls felt at all ashamed in any way. Those were different times, prior to Freud and Humbert. And if it's true that human nature, like the other, abhors a vacuum, in the immense variety of human types, we should not discard the idea that in those days, and even now, there were and are individuals who love children in the purest way, and restrain from touching them improperly.'

Ranelagh turned towards Seldom once more, as if this were a subject on which they couldn't reach an agreement, and had settled on a sort of tie through the repetition of the same moves.

'But to return to the main question: I hope you now understand why that torn-out page has become a most powerful magnet, a touchstone for all biographers. Perhaps on that page, and only on that page, there appeared in writing the decisive proof, the fatal event, the explicit recognition of an infamous act. Since the sixties, when the notebooks were made public, the ghost of that page never ceased to whisper possibilities in our ears. As the poet might have said, there's no keener murmuring source than the unspoken word, nor book more voluminous than the one that's lost a page. However, until very recently, there was nothing but that: mere conjectures. None of the researchers were able to go beyond these suppositions, which, as is often the case, tended to reflect whatever portrait each of them had imagined for the character. Only Josephine Grey, another of the founders of our Brotherhood, succeeded, some fifteen years ago, in taking a step forward in the research. She managed to prove, in an ingenious and incontrovertible manner, that the page had not been ripped out by Lewis Carroll but in all probability by one of his two grand-nieces, Menella or Violet Dodgson, the daughters of Stuart, who had remained custodians of the papers. What's more, this tells us indirectly something else: that Lewis Carroll was not necessarily ashamed of or even sorry about whatever was written there. But in any case, once again, what was it that the sisters read between those lines? What did they conclude from their perusing that led them to tear out the page? What did that page, perhaps unintentionally, reveal? And so we reach the beginning of this year, when we, the members of the Brotherhood, decided we would publish an annotated edition of the surviving diaries of Lewis Carroll. They are, as I've told you, nine handwritten notebooks, kept in the house that Lewis Carroll bought in Guildford towards the end of his life, and now converted into a small museum. As none of the members of the Brotherhood could travel to Guildford and stay there long enough to go through all the papers, in the last meeting in July, a few days ago, it was decided that we'd send an intern, Kristen Hill, a marvellously devoted and meticulous young lady who is help-ing us with assorted tasks. We asked her to stay in Guildford for a few days in order to assess the condition of the diaries. She was instructed to photocopy every page, one by one, as well as all related papers she might be able to find. Her mother lives in the outskirts of Guildford and that allowed us to save on lodging expenses. And then, on the second day, we received a most extraordinary piece of news.'

'She found the page?' I couldn't refrain from asking.

'She found something that could be very . . . disturbing. But that's something that Arthur should tell you, since it was he who received the girl's phone call from Guildford.'

Chapter 3

Seldom had, in the meantime, rolled one of his cigarettes, and as the slow tentacles of smoke reached my chair I became aware of the unmistakable scent of his Indian tobacco. Unlike Ranelagh's fast and snappy speech, Seldom's deep Scottish accent seemed to echo heavily in the leafy silence of the garden.

'Kristen Hill was my doctorate student until last year. An extremely shy young lady. Diligent and studious, and highly intelligent, she graduated at nineteen. However, she never finished her thesis. At a certain point, through a reference in some old paper, she discovered a remarkably innovative work on determinants calculus published by Lewis Carroll under his mathematician's hat, and obviously using his real name, Charles Dodgson. That was how Kristen arrived at Lewis Carroll's diaries, indirectly, searching for the correspondence he had maintained on this question with other mathematicians of the time. I put her in touch with the members of the Brotherhood who were working on the diaries, and that was how we lost her for the realm of mathematics, because every biographer and every researcher wanted to have her working for them. She's an ideal research partner: quick, efficient, discreet, always on the alert. In fact, right now she's working under Thornton Reeves with a grant, and that's

why I was a bit taken aback that she should call me. It was
the day before yesterday, in the morning. On the phone, she
seemed quite unlike her usual self: I had never heard her go
on like that; I would say she sounded euphoric. She spoke
to me in an anxious tone, as if she were burning with joy
and pride, but at the same time somewhat frightened. She
told me that, as she was going through the Lewis Carroll
papers, she had found something extraordinary, something
that would provide a definitive answer to the question of the
lost page. Apparently, it's a piece of paper that, according to
her, had been always in plain sight but that no one had discovered until now. Then she explained that in the Guildford
house, together with the diaries, the family had prepared a
catalogue of all the writings and personal effects of Lewis
Carroll, gathered throughout the years. According to her, in
that catalogue, however incredible this may sound, was an
item listed as "Cut Pages in Diary".'

'That is indeed so,' Ranelagh interjected. 'I must confess
that I had never looked carefully at that catalogue, but this
morning I went to Guildford to check it in person. I cannot
understand how it escaped the attention of all of us.'

'Kristen had only to go to the corresponding file and there,
perfectly in its place, filed between two sheets of paper,
she found a crumpled page with writing on both sides. On
one side, as she described it, were dates corresponding to
Alice Liddell's life as she entered adulthood: her marriage,
the birth of her children, her death. On the other side is an
inscription, written no doubt by whoever tore out the page,
summing up the main facts of what Lewis Carroll had jotted
down on that day. Kristen told me it was in a hand she
knew well, that of Menella Dodgson, the eldest of the two
grand-nieces. She has always suspected Menella to be the
secret censor of the diaries, and this piece of paper seems to

confirm it. Menella was an extremely religious person and Kristen supposes that, before or after tearing out that page from the diary, she felt a certain compunction and decided to make a separate note of the contents. It's a single sentence, she said, but it's decisive. She believes that this sentence can answer the question that hangs over Lewis Carroll, but in a totally unexpected way. Of course, I asked at once what that sentence was. She remained silent for a moment and then she said that she couldn't tell anyone, not even me, in spite of my being the only person within the Brotherhood she could trust. That she wanted to keep it a secret until she felt sure that she would be credited with the discovery. She told me that what she had found was something almost "ridiculously logical" that no one had thought of, and she feared above all that Thornton Reeves might want to claim the honours of the discovery for himself, because she was only a graduate student and he could be selfish in ways that I couldn't begin to imagine. I asked her how she'd manage to keep it under cover, since she herself had told me that it was a piece of paper visible to everyone, that anyone could read it simply by travelling to Guildford. Here Kristen paused once more, and then confessed to me that she had stolen the paper. She didn't say this in these exact words, and yet I understood that she had taken it with her and that she was keeping it hidden, but she promised that she'd return it as soon as she managed to have an article published giving her the credit. Then I asked her why she'd called me, and, above all, why she was telling me all this. I wasn't at all pleased with the idea of being made an accomplice in something she knew perfectly well was not right. She told me that after she had taken the page, the thought had struck her that it seemed very strange that no one should have seen it before. Every biographer had at a certain point visited the Guildford house. Almost all had examined the same catalogue. How was it possible that she alone had discovered that piece of paper? Somehow, as soon as all this became known, she'd make them all look ridiculous. But perhaps, she said, there was another explanation. Perhaps someone else had seen it and had chosen not to say anything. Because that paper, with that single sentence, shattered most of the theories written about Lewis Carroll. And she imagined a further possibility, which I believe is the one she fears the most: that the paper is simply a fake, an imitation of Menella's handwriting, something placed between those two folder sheets as an apocryphal antiquity, a joke or trap set up for academics. That at least would explain why no one has discovered it before now. And it would be a shameful blunder for her if that were finally the case. That is why, she said, she thought about phoning me. She knew, because of our seminars, that Leyton Howard works as a calligraphy expert, and that I am the only person who has dealings with him. She asked me, after much beating around the bush, if I could arrange a meeting with him to verify the authenticity of the handwriting. I told her she was putting me in a difficult position, but that I would think about it and call her back. After I hung up, I spent the rest of the morning turning the information over in my head. I didn't want to hush up the disappearance and concealment of the document, something that goes against all the principles on which the Brotherhood was founded. At the same time, I didn't want to be too hard on Kristen, and certainly not be her betrayer. I resolved at last to confide only in Richard, because there's another very important question that the Brotherhood will have to decide on imminently, and in which, I realised, the discovery of that piece of paper could have some impact.'

'A huge impact,' interrupted Ranelagh. 'The edition we

are preparing of Lewis Carroll's diaries is to be the definitive one, what we like to call the Authoritative Edition. It will be annotated by all the biographers of the Brotherhood, and we are now about to divide the notebooks so that each one of us can deal exclusively with a certain volume and a certain period. It's a colossal enterprise, and whatever is written on that page cannot, obviously, be absent from it. I dare say that that particular page will be the most consulted of the entire book. Even more: that page, if what the young lady says is true, could force us to rethink a fair portion of our system of annotations. We cannot risk for it to appear at some later date, and contradict or put in doubt the general logic of the notes. We need to see the page, and sooner rather than later. What that girl did is inadmissible but, much as Arthur, I'm inclined to give her the chance of restoring it in an ... elegant way. We've agreed to offer her a chance to do so.'

'I called her yesterday – without telling her, of course, that I had consulted Richard – and suggested that, if we proved the authenticity of the handwriting, I would call a special meeting of the Brotherhood for this coming Friday. She would then show the paper to everyone, it would appear with her name attached in the minutes, and then she'd return it to its proper place. In that way, she'd be assured of being given credit for her discovery and later, after some time, she'd be able to pub-lish her article. I thought she'd agree at once, but she seemed nervous and afraid: she told me that since she'd got hold of the piece of paper, she couldn't manage to sleep at night. However, when I told her we had to go to the police sta-tion, she backed down. She didn't know that Leyton worked there and I think the place terrified her, as if she feared a trap. I wasn't able to convince her, in spite of explaining that Leyton worked in the attic, in a separate office, and that we wouldn't meet anyone else. After hanging up, I felt obviously very concerned. I was pondering all this when I went down to the Common Room and met you so providentially. As soon as I left you, I phoned her up again and told her about your program, and she finally agreed: she'll come tomorrow to the Mathematical Institute with a photocopy of the first half of the sentence. I hope it will be sufficient to verify the handwriting. She told me that she would certainly not bring the original with her, and that she wouldn't reveal more than the first few words.'

'Four or five words will suffice,' I said, 'but of course, we need to have letters or handwritten notes from that woman, Menella, ideally from about the same time, to be able to make the comparison.'

'Indeed, Kristen had already thought of that. In the archives of the Brotherhood there's a large number of letters written by Menella throughout her life. She'll bring them with her.'

'As you can understand,' Ranelagh said, 'this whole situation is highly irregular and we require the utmost discretion on your part.'

'I was also thinking,' Seldom said, 'that if it's not inconvenient for you, it might be best for us to meet at night, directly in the basement where the computers are, to make sure that there's no one around. I have a key.'

'Fine by me,' I said. 'I hope that by tomorrow at least some of the mystery will be cleared up. Maybe all this is true precisely because it's so unbelievable, as if Poe's purloined letter were not only visible to everyone but also displayed in an envelope marked "Purloined Letter". Do you think it's possible that none of the biographers has seen it earlier on?'

'I don't know,' Ranelagh said. 'I felt rather ashamed when

I found out. I confess that I at least had overlooked it. And if the piece of paper is authentic, others will feel even more ashamed. I suppose no one will be very happy when it's finally revealed.'

Chapter 4

Next day I waited patiently in the attic for Leyton to gather his paperwork. As soon as he had left, I carefully disconnected the plaque he had fixed on to the photocopying machine. It was a highly ingenious contraption that his mentor had invented before being recruited by Microtek. In essence, it allowed you to display on the computer screen the photocopied image: the prototype of what only a few years later would be called a scanner. At sunset, I went to the Mathematical Institute and sat down to wait in the computer-room until everyone had left. I fixed the plaque on to the photocopier next to the computers. I did a few try-outs to assure myself that everything was working, and waited. Punctually at nine, Seldom and Kristen came down the stairs. Seeing her, I recalled what Seldom and Ranelagh had told me about her: intelligent, conscientious, always attentive. But with typical British reserve, neither of them had hinted, not even with a wink, anything about her physical appearance. I understood immediately why the members of the Brotherhood would fight over her. She was, quite simply, a beauty, in spite of what seemed like an almost morbid shyness that made her bow her head and hunch her shoulders ever so slightly, in order to hide, perhaps unconsciously, a more prominent bosom than even she might have wished for. She was wearing thickly rimmed glasses, and when Seldom introduced us and I shook her hand, I caught a glimmer of her elusive and intensely blue eyes, somewhat enlarged by the lenses. I held on to her hand a fraction longer than necessary but she didn't seem to mind or, maybe so as not to make me feel uncomfortable, she also took a certain time before letting go of mine. The brief ritual of introduction made her blush slightly, and I, too, unable to prevent it, as if it were an instance of propagation of Fourier's waves, felt hot under the collar. I offered her one of the coaster armchairs. As soon as she sat down, she opened a folder and pulled out a sample of handwritten correspondence.

'Arthur told me you'd be needing a few of Menella Dodgson's letters. They're all dated,' she said, 'and I've sorted them out chronologically.'

I set them out under the lamp next to the monitor, trying to look as professional as possible, and began to inspect them carefully, one after the other.

'What would be ideal,' I said, 'is to find one that coincides with the date at which she made the annotation. I see that her writing changes quite a bit as time goes by.'

'But we have no way of knowing *when* she made that annotation. And she was the custodian of the diaries for almost thirty years.'

I pondered this for a moment.

'In fact, I think we might have a clue.' I glanced at Seldom. 'From what I've heard, I believe there are certain dates written on the other side of the paper, corresponding to important moments in Alice Liddell's life. If this woman scribbled those dates in chronological order, we could compare each entry with the handwriting of the annotation. And if she made them all at the same time, we'd at least know that they were made on a date following Alice Liddell's death. In any case, I think it would be helpful to have a look at the other side of that page. Have you brought it with you?'

Kristen shook her head and seemed to become even more withdrawn and wary. She cast a glance at Seldom, as if to reproach him for having told me too much; then she looked back at me.

'Of course not,' she said. 'The piece of paper is securely kept. I only brought what I told Arthur I'd bring: a copy of the first half of the sentence. Six words. And all this correspondence. I thought that would suffice.'

'I hope so,' I said to calm her down. 'May I see those first words, then?'

Kristen nodded, opened her string purse and pulled out a narrow strip of paper. The gesture of handing over the paper seemed to demand a great effort and her hand was trembling a little. Seldom and I, almost at the same time, read the beginning of the sentence:

L.C. learns from Mrs Liddell that . . .

That was all. The handwriting was rounded and somewhat disconnected, including several hiatuses within a single word. I laid the paper face down on the photocopier's glass plaque. When the light scrolled beneath the paper we saw the handwritten words appear as insects under a microscope, large and clear.

The *L* and the *C* of the initials had the same top loop, small and tightly curled. The dot on the *i* of *Liddell* had been omitted. The *r* and the *s* of *Mrs* seemed to float diagonally. The double *d* in the surname leaned left, as if written by someone left-handed. As a curious detail, the horizontal line crossing the *t* stretched to cover the entire word *that* as if she had wished to save herself a stroke even at the expense of crossing the middle *h*. I picked up again the bundle of letters and I held them up to the light one after the other. Only in one of the letters of the last period there appeared that same impatient stroke crossing the word *that* from *t* to *t*. I pointed out this detail to Seldom and Kristen, and placed the letter on the glass plaque. As soon as the words appeared enlarged on the screen, I had the vivid impression that they were by the same hand. I adjusted the size of the two samples and I showed them the perfect fit of the superimposed strokes, the similarity at the start and finish of each word, the concordance of the angles and the characteristic separation between letters. However, since I preferred not to risk a definitive opinion, I told them I'd extrapolate separately the movement of each stroke for a final crucial verification. At the time, the computers were, of course, agonisingly slow and though the Mathematical Institute was proud of the processing power its researchers had achieved by parallel connections between several machines, we had to wait several seconds while the cursor displayed its waiting signal, the lights blinked on and off, and the asthmatic wheeze of the small interior fans were heard, as if I'd set an army of bit-carrying gnomes to a colossal muscular task. However, at long last, the parallel lines appeared accompanied by the two tiny pencils at the top of the screen, ready for the race. I asked them to think of any possible extension of the sentence, so that we might have a common text to compare, written in actual time by both functions. I looked first at Kristen but

I gave Kristen back the bundle of correspondence and the photocopy of her paper. As I was detaching the plaque to take it back, I heard them whispering to one another behind my back, and I thought I heard them agree on calling a special meeting of the Brotherhood. Kristen said something that I wasn't able to make out, and Seldom answered as if to reassure her: 'Of course, certainly. I won't mention the paper; I'll only say that you'll announce an unexpected discovery at the Guildford house.'

We went back up together and switched off the lights. To go out into the street we were obliged to use the side door of the Institute. St Giles was deserted and now, at night, all activity seemed to have ceased. The distant street lights shone like blurred foggy wreaths, barely allowing us to make out in the shadows the uncanny whitish tombstones on the lawn next to the church. Only a solitary cyclist sped by from time to time. Kristen said she'd walk up to Magdalene Street and wait for her bus to Kidlington, and Seldom offered to accompany her. As we were saying our goodbyes, Seldom turned towards me and asked rhetorically how they could ever thank me.

'Well, I too would like to know what follows in the sentence!' I said. 'Might I be invited to Friday's meeting? Like a wild card at a tennis tournament? Or does one have to undergo some sort of blood ritual or perform a secret test before being admitted? I think that with a bit of practice I could produce a sample of Lewis Carroll's mirror-writing.'

Kristen laughed with her recently acquired confidence. Some of her shyness seemed to have vanished.

'You only have to cut a few heads off, isn't that right, Arthur? It's OK by me, and it seems only fair.'

We exchanged brief glances with the facile complicity of youth. Seldom smiled, as if resigned to the demands of his

Chapter 5

Next morning I woke up somewhat earlier than usual: I wanted to arrive in the office before Leyton got there to put the plaque back in its place without having to give him an explanation. But as I was coming down St Aldate's, I saw the girl at the Alice shop struggling to lift the shutter over the door, and I stopped to help her. We stood on either side, huffing and puffing, and we managed at last to lift the iron fasteners and clear the entrance. What I had seen of her as I sped past her shop every day on my bicycle was happily confirmed now that I stood by her side. She thanked me in the most charming and effusive way, all smiles and dimples, and she lifted a loose strand of her chestnut hair and tucked it behind her ear. She had quick, sparkling brown eyes and a small, intriguingly shaped piercing on one of her eyebrows. Something in her very slight expectant stare made me stay a moment longer and ask her if there was any biography of Lewis Carroll in the store.

'There's a shelf full of them!' And she pointed to the lower row in the small bookcase stuffed with books about Oxford.

The most voluminous and the one I first picked up was that by Thornton Reeves, whom Sir Richard Ranelagh, I remembered, had mentioned. The girl knelt down by my side and we remained there, knees almost touching.

'That's one of the latest ones, supposedly the most detailed one, but we also have a facsimile of the first, the one by his nephew, Stuart Dodgson. And there are several others. There's the one by Josephine Grey, my favourite. And there's the one the tourists buy, full of pictures of the places he visited. And on that other shelf there's one by a psychologist who analyses the symbols in his books based on events in his life. And we even have one by a mathematician, Raymond Martin, with a compilation of logic puzzles.'

I stared at her with unfeigned surprise.

'Raymond Martin?'

The name brought back the memory of several of his books that I'd read in my adolescence, in cheap editions, on logic paradoxes, magic and mathematics, and on mathematics and literature. Up to now, he had been only a name on a title page. I opened the book and on the flap I saw, for the first time, a photo of the man, quite old now, but still with a rebellious and slightly mocking look in his eye, his long white hair gathered in a ponytail.

'I knew that he lived in Oxford for a time,' I said.

'They all live around here, between Oxford and Cambridge. Martin's is a very entertaining book. It also collects Lewis Carroll's word games and even an encrypting code that he invented.'

'You'll make me believe that you've read the entire shelf,' I said in an admiring tone.

'In fact, I have,' she admitted, almost embarrassed. 'The mornings are quite boring here until the herds of tourists arrive. By the way,' she said suddenly, stretching out her hand, 'my name is Sharon.'

I told her mine and, as we stared into one another's eyes, she tried repeating it several times, without success.

'Is it a Spanish name? Or Italian?'

'Actually, I'm Argentinian,' I said. 'I've been here a year now, studying mathematical logic.'

'Of course,' she said, as she suddenly realised something. 'I saw you go by a couple of times last summer, in a convertible, with a red-haired girl.'

'Yes, Lorna,' and immediately I explained. 'She was my tennis partner. But she went back to Ireland after her holidays and married someone big in the IRA. I suppose that now they'll be throwing fire-bombs together.'

She smiled, somewhat taken aback. I remembered once again that until I improved my accent considerably, everything I said would be taken with dead seriousness. I picked up a few more books from the shelf that were together as part of the same series. On the spine they all had a logo with a spiral of fading words and the name 'Vanished Tale'.

'That's the imprint of the Lewis Carroll Brotherhood,' she said.

'Tomorrow I'm invited to a meeting of the Brotherhood,' I said to impress her. 'And I'm ashamed to say that I know nothing about Lewis Carroll.'

'How about that! Now I'm jealous!' she said, her smile deepening. 'I was born in Daresbury. I know everything about him, and I've never received an invitation like that. I imagine they're all a bunch of stiff-upper-lip old codgers who wear pocket watches and for whom it's always teatime. But still, I'd love to be able to peek at them through a keyhole.'

'I'd ask you to come with me,' I said, 'but it's supposed to be a closed meeting. I should not even be saying all this to you now. However, I might be allowed to drop by on Saturday and tell you all about it.'

'Aha! A secret gathering! I wonder what will be uncovered. That Lewis Carroll had a thing for little girls?' She laughed. 'I won't be here on Saturday; another colleague opens the shop on the weekends. But I would love to hear about it on Monday.'

'And what about having a beer tomorrow night, after the meeting's over?' I added. 'I'm sure you won't be able to contain your curiosity until Monday.'

She looked at me with an amused look.

'Argentinian: yes, I can see it now.' She paused, as if trying to find a polite way of saying no and, at the same time, leaving a door open. 'Tonight and on weekends I'm busy with a film series we organise at the Odeon, a Frankenheimer retrospective.' And she gave me a flyer from a stack next to the cash register. 'I'll be curious, of course, but I think I'll be able to restrain myself until Monday.'

We heard the tinkle of the bell and the first customer came into the store. Sharon adopted a stern look and pointed to the books on the shelf.

'So, are you buying any?'

I was holding in my hand the earliest biography, that of Stuart Dodgson, and the one promising riddles, puzzles and codes, by Raymond Martin.

'For now, I'll take these two,' I said. 'And I'll come for more next week.'

I got on my bike and pedalled as fast as I could to arrive before Leyton if that was still possible. On the way, I tried to decipher that other code of social contact and instinctive calculus encrypted in our species, the ancient vocabulary of hieroglyphs made up of added and subtracted gestures, smiles and looks, and concluded that the results of my combinatorial analysis gave me a fair chance. I glanced once more, as if it were the slip inside a fortune cookie, at the flyer listing the films in the Frankenheimer retrospective, and I climbed the stairs to the attic feeling expectantly happy. As I opened the office door, I discovered Leyton having his first cup of coffee. When he saw me, he uncrossed his feet from the desk and nodded towards the corridor.

'The computer plaque has disappeared,' he said.

There was not the slightest hint of suspicion or concern in his tone, merely the statement of an unexpected fact, a minimal alteration in the panorama observable through the window pane of his door: something that didn't seem to worry him much.

'No, I have it here,' I said with as much nonchalance as I could muster. I took the plaque out of my backpack, together with a Phillips screwdriver, and started putting it back in its place. 'Yesterday I stayed until late and it suddenly stopped working, so I took it home to fix it. I think it will be OK now.'

Leyton, of course, didn't say anything nor did he show the slightest interest in checking out the plaque. I wondered if, later, standing in a court room with his shoes back on, he would even remember that for a few hours the plaque had vanished. I considered the immense number of tiny substitutions and replacements that occurred in the world every day, adding up to zero in the final count. The theory of the butterfly effect, with its stifling power of seduction (as Seldom would say), together with Chinese proverbs and all the literature weighing in its favour, existed side by side with another phenomenon, anodyne and prosaic but no less frequent, one that ruled over the infinite number of substitutions and replacements that nobody noticed, half-accomplished impulses, cancellations, changes of heart, moments of pulling back that caused no whirlwinds at all on the other side of the world. Even Kristen's theft, which had set in motion a few wheels and cogs, would be seen after Friday as a short-term loan. The document would return to its place, the universe would settle back into its identical self, the tiny incision would heal without leaving a mark. And, after all, wasn't that the very problem of the copy we were attempting to study? Perhaps there was no such thing as an authentic universe. The universe could be imagined as pockmarked with small scars of infinitesimal substitutions, sutured by perfect copies that held, each one of them, a jealously guarded secret.

I went down at lunchtime and got a sandwich at my habitual café on Little Clarendon Street. On the way back, I met Seldom. He told me he had spoken with Sir Richard and that he had his consent for me to attend the first half of the meeting. He had already emailed the other members of the Brotherhood. A couple were coming from London the next day, and he himself was going now to Josephine Grey's place to tell her. He explained that she was quite elderly, and that she didn't have a computer nor did she use email. He was afraid she was becoming a little deaf and that she wouldn't hear him clearly over the phone.

I told him that that very morning I had held her book on Lewis Carroll in my hands.

'Nowadays she can barely walk,' Seldom said. 'But I think she wouldn't miss this for the world. She has her own theories about that torn-out page. I'm hoping that her driver can take her.'

That afternoon, I started to leaf distractedly through Stuart Dodgson's biography. The book was dedicated, with a sort of initial statement, 'to the child friends of Lewis Carroll'. Stuart himself had been one of those children, and had known first-hand the tricks and games of the Pied Piper that Lewis Carroll had become. Soon I began to understand the point that Ranelagh had wanted to make about the age in which Lewis Carroll had lived. Not only was the nephew untroubled by his uncle's devotion to young children, but he laid it out in all its details, praising it with disarming and frank pride. He even gave it a religious dimension with an interesting argument: 'I believe that he understood children even better than he understood men and women; civilisation has made adult humanity very incomprehensible, for convention is as a veil which hides the divine spark that is in each of us, and so this strange thing has come to be, that the Imperfect mirrors Perfection more completely than the Perfected, that we see more of God in the child than in the man.' I stopped to underline the passage: *the Imperfect mirrors Perfection more completely than the Perfected*. I thought that not even Witold Gombrowicz, so many years later, would have said it better. Far from concealing the subject or trying to minimise it, Stuart had two whole later chapters dedicated to his uncle's relationship with children: the photos, the letters and, he explained with somewhat chilling ease, the box of puzzles that Lewis Carroll always carried with him when he travelled to attract whatever young companions he might encounter. And when he went to the beach, he never forgot to take with him a number of safety pins, so that if a young girl wanted to venture into the water without getting her dress wet, he could approach her with his salvaging gift and start a conversation, while he pinned her hem high above her knees.

I kept reading backwards and forwards, stopping from time to time to consider the many interspersed drawings by Lewis Carroll himself, as if they could tell me something more about the character, until I realised it was too late to get to the eight o'clock show. I wanted, however, to give myself another chance of seeing Sharon that evening. I took a shower, prepared myself a light dinner, and set out through the already empty streets of the town centre to arrive at the last showing, at ten o'clock. While I waited in the queue for *The Manchurian Candidate*, trying to find Sharon, the doors of the other cinema opened, where *Seconds* was being shown at the same time and, among the people coming out, I suddenly saw Kristen, walking alone slowly, as if somewhat stunned from returning to the real world. I went up to her to say hello, but she took a moment to recognise me. I could see that her glasses were fogged up.

'Are you all right?' I asked. 'Was the film that sad?'

She forced herself to smile as she took off her glasses and allowed me to see for the first time her very clear naked eyes, filled with tears. She dried them with a small moan of shame.

'It was sad, yes it was, but I'm a fool, I always cry at the movies. And especially today . . . I shouldn't have gone to see it. But please, don't pay any attention to me. The film's excellent.' She put her glasses back on, looked up at me and, as if unable to hold back, as if affirming a principle or making an impassioned statement, she said: 'I believe that everyone deserves to choose a second life, like that poor man, without it all ending so terribly badly.'

She kept on staring at me, as if looking for my approval, and I had the intuition that she was in fact speaking, from somewhere deep down inside, about herself.

'Maybe that piece of paper you found,' I said, 'is the beginning of something like that in your own future.'

'Maybe,' she said, and tried to smile through her tears. 'You'll go to the meeting tomorrow, then?' she asked me.

'Of course,' I said. 'I wouldn't miss it for the world.'

She smiled again, as if my decision had made her proud, and she turned to leave, holding a hand up high. I went back to my queue, watching her wander off alone into the night.

references I was still missing. While I was taking notes and leafing through random publications, I couldn't stop thinking about Kristen. I realised, observing time slowly ticking away on the clock, that I was as anxious to see her again as I was to know the second half of the sentence. A duality, certainly not topological, opened up in me or, rather, split me in two. If a week earlier I could only think nostalgically of Lorna, seeing in the distance the green tennis courts of University Park, now the faces of Sharon and of Kristen appeared before me as a sharp quandary, confronting one another more intimately than Hegel's opposites, both with powerful and convincing arguments. I saw Kristen's raised hand almost as a promise as she said goodbye at the cinema, and also Sharon's knees and face so close to mine while she was showing me the books. The two of them seemed equally attractive, and all my logical discriminants (and Lewis Carroll's as well) couldn't help me decide on one or the other. At quarter to six, I walked down St Giles towards Christ Church College. Halfway there, I saw Seldom come out of the Taylor Library and was about to call out to him, but I didn't and chose instead to follow him so as to observe him from a distance. I thought that I knew very little about Seldom and that it was enough to observe from afar someone unawares, even someone very familiar to us, for that person to become in some sense enigmatic. Seldom was walking with his typical gait, head held low, a long stride, his torso pushed forward, one hand inside the pocket of his trousers and in the other a book that looked thick and heavy. Above his neck, among the greyish hairs, I saw the beginnings of a bald patch that I hadn't noticed before. Even so, he preserved an energetic step, giving the impression of a quiet physical strength that he had never had to resort to, equivalent to the strength that burst from his mind when leading a discussion at a seminar, or when writing with quick strokes the crucial steps of a logic demonstration. I wondered if the female students still found him attractive. Above all, I wondered what had been his relationship with Kristen when she'd been his doctorate student. It had not surprised me that he had offered to accompany her to the bus stop, but something about her immediate agreement had. It was obviously not the first time that they'd walked together. And I had also noticed that she called him by his Christian name. Of course, all this might have been entirely innocent. I knew that in England, on Fridays, teachers got drunk at the pubs with their students, and all the puzzling levels of cordiality could intermingle there after a third beer. But come Monday, when they met again in the hallways, they would revert to keeping their distance. The teachers I got to know – at least the small sample at the Mathematical Institute – were simultaneously closer and more distant from their students than in the Argentinian universities. And I imagined that it was the British tutorial system, but above all the drunk parties on Friday nights, that explained the paradox. When I reached Magdalen Street, I decided to hurry on and call out to him. He turned and, caught off guard, he smiled with his habitual cordiality. I felt somewhat ashamed, and surreptitiously peeked at the book he was carrying. Oddly enough, it was the same first edition of Stuart Dodgson's biography that I had been studying. I wondered why he would have wanted to consult it, but I didn't dare say anything about the coincidence. Reaching the entrance of Christ Church we noticed a shiny old-fashioned Bentley that looked as if it had been polished especially for the extraordinary occasion of being taken out into the streets. An Indian or Pakistani driver got out to open one of the back doors and help a very old lady who leaned laboriously on both his arm and her cane.

'That's Josephine Grey,' Seldom said. 'Come and I'll introduce you.'

The woman, upon seeing us, gave a cry of delight and seemed to straighten up and become younger with the flash of enthusiasm that lit up her face. The wrinkles on her cheeks, like a vector field, oriented themselves upwards, and something of the beautiful woman that she no doubt had been seemed about to rise to the surface.

'And so, Arthur? The great day has at last dawned? Even though you're forbidden to tell me you *must* do so. We're here now, and I couldn't sleep a wink all night. Did the purloined page appear at last? I was convinced I'd die without learning anything more about this. I've had the car brought out especially, no taxis for me today! Even so, would you believe it?' she said, pointing to the driver. 'Mahmud's son took the car out last night without my permission, and made *a dent* in it. Has the girl arrived? And who's this young man?'

The woman grabbed hold of both Seldom and me, one arm each, as we entered the hall together, her sparkling eyes jumping gaily from one to the other.

'I feel better accompanied than Debbie Reynolds in *Singing in the Rain*! So he's Argentinian, how interesting, like your first wife, Arthur, if I remember correctly. I've known many Argentinians in my life. They have the same accent as Italians, don't you agree, Arthur? And they wave their hands about with all those funny gestures, *ma che cosa dire!* I should shut up now because this young man will think I'm mad as a hatter. You'll have to come and visit me sometime with Arthur and we'll talk about – what's the expression you use down there? Lost cows? *Bueyes perdidos*, lost oxen! Oh, whatever! Lost oxen, lost pages ... You really won't tell me, Arthur?'

We had managed to reach the first floor, almost lifting her off the ground, and we entered a meeting room with a long table around which a number of people were already gathered, most of them standing next to a tray of pastries and several urns of hot water and coffee. Seldom introduced me to a very thin, short man, shrunk to almost Lilliputian proportions, who had remained close to the door. He was wearing a wrinkled and discoloured jacket, bought, I imagined, in a children's clothing store, which gave him the aspect of a shy and wizened Peter Pan. When I leaned towards him, he told me his name, Henry Haas, almost in a whisper and without lifting his eyes, stretching out a furtive hand that he pulled back as soon as I touched it.

'Henry's published an invaluable book compiling Lewis Carroll's correspondence with all the young girls who were his friends,' Seldom explained, and the little man nodded, with a faint blush of pride.

'And he also organised the archive of all the pictures Lewis Carroll took of them,' Josephine added. 'An exhausting labour, selfless and *ad honorem*, even though Henry said it was a work of pure pleasure.'

The man nodded once again and blushed a little deeper, as if he perceived in her words a secret mockery shared by everyone else, and from which he was unable to protect himself. I looked around and immediately noticed that Kristen had not yet arrived. On three walls, in horseshoe formation, were portraits of Lewis Carroll at various ages, from a first picture as a baby in his mother's arms up to what I supposed was the last, with wisps of white hair sprouting from his temples, taken shortly before his death. I also saw, in a low bookshelf, first editions of his books and the originals of many of his drawings and his correspondence. On one of the walls, there was a photo of what seemed like a meeting of the Brotherhood from long ago. A very young Seldom appeared at one end of the group, with the Royal Patron, dressed in white, standing in front of everyone. I pointed out the regal figure in the picture to Seldom and he smiled.

'He's the honorary president of the Brotherhood, even though, quite understandably, he's never attended a single meeting. He was only here for the photo, at the inaugural assembly. But we always keep a chair empty for him at the head of the table.'

'We think that Lewis Carroll would have enjoyed that gesture,' Josephine said to me. 'He was devoted to royalty.'

We placed our venerable burden on a chair and Seldom, in a solicitous tone, asked her what she'd have.

'My seventh cup of milky coffee,' Josephine answered. 'Are you forgetting that I'm about to defeat you all? Young man,' she said, pulling a silk handkerchief out of her bag, 'would you please blindfold me?'

Hearing her request, I became afraid that the old lady had really taken leave of her senses. But Seldom, seeing me hesitate with the handkerchief in my hand, nodded at me to do as I was asked.

'Henry Haas once served her the coffee and committed the sin of pouring the milk into the cup afterwards and not before,' he explained. 'Josephine refused it, and we all made fun of her: none of us believed that she could tell the difference between the sequence coffee–milk or milk–coffee if it were served to her when she was blindfolded. And so she challenged us to the test. We recalled Fisher's statistical experiment, and decided to serve her eight cups with different combinations, in aleatory order.'

'Up to now, she beats us six to nothing,' Henry said in an almost inaudible voice.

Josephine assented proudly under the blindfold, and when at last I managed to tie the knot, I went to stand behind Seldom by the table with the drinks. A tall and energetic man with a shiny bald spot approached Seldom with an imperious gesture, brandishing a cupcake.

'What's up with this girl, Arthur? I haven't been able to get in touch with her since she left for Guildford; I believe that she's decided not to answer my calls. I don't understand what all the mystery is about. Whatever she's discovered, I think I was entitled to have been informed immediately. It was I who suggested we send her there.'

I understood that this was Thornton Reeves. He was speaking to Seldom in an indignant tone that seemed somewhat feigned, as if they knew one another well enough not to be ever truly annoyed, or as if Reeves felt more hurt than upset by the situation. 'I trusted her entirely. And when the moment came, she chose not to communicate with anyone but her ex-tutor. Whatever she's discovered I expect to be strictly concerned with mathematics, or else she'll have to deal with me.'

Seldom tried to introduce me, but Reeves didn't seem inclined to relinquish either his cup or his cupcake, and he barely raised his eyebrows before going off in search of a seat at the table.

'I, however, don't think it's got anything to do with mathematics,' said a very elderly man in a very soft voice, almost as if speaking to himself, as we finally reached the hot drinks. He was helping himself to coffee with a shaky hand, and seemed as concentrated in balancing his spoonful of sugar as in carefully enunciating a logical argument. I realised, transporting in my mind the author's cover photo along the evil arrow of time, but mainly thanks to his ponytail, that the frail old man I had before me was the legendary Raymond Martin. He was wearing sagging Bermudas, sandals and a white T-shirt with the words 'TOO LATE TO DIE YOUNG'. He was glancing sideways at Seldom, unwilling to turn his head completely, as if he feared that a straightforward look would upset the delicate balance of his cup and the unsteady trajectory of his spoon.

'As soon as I got your message, my dear Arthur, I asked myself what could be important enough to justify calling an extraordinary meeting. At first, I felt hopeful, because it came from the Mathematical Institute and carried your illustrious name. Might it be that an answer had been discovered to one of the hundreds of puzzles and riddles that Lewis Carroll made up throughout his life? Might it be an unearthed sketch of one of those inventions of which he was so proud: the nyctograph, the speedometer for tricycles, the wordplay that foreshadowed Scrabble? Or a new, hitherto unknown, list of Pillow Problems? Or yet another of his humorous analyses of syllogisms? The first draft, perhaps, of his oh-so-clever paper on determinants? But then I realised that you had not wanted to anticipate anything at all. Innocent me! Who in our sad times would be interested in the slightest in Lewis Carroll's brains? And then I thought further: what kind of discovery cannot be anticipated even briefly without revealing all? It had to be, again, the usual conundrum. And so, without having to resort to *modus ponens* or *tollens*, I could at once infer the subject, and I could have written it out myself in the minutes were it not for my hand that no longer obeys my full instructions. For the time being, I maintain what I have always maintained on the subject, and I hope I won't have too much to rewrite after the meeting.'

Seldom first filled Josephine's cup in the order milk–coffee, and then his own straight black. The cup was put in front of Josephine and for an instant everyone already seated around the table looked expectantly to see the result of the test. Josephine took a sip and nodded with satisfaction.

'Ah, luckily this time you chose to proceed in the correct order, so now I can drink it.' She took off her blindfold and looked at Seldom for corroboration of her latest victory. 'Please, Richard,' she said with childish glee, 'before anything else, let it be stated in the minutes that the score is now seven to nil.'

When I arrived with my own cup at the table I found myself seated across from an odd-looking couple. The man was small, and his hair was raven black, as if he had recently dyed it. He wore it in separate strands crossed from one side of his head to the other, in what was perhaps an unsubtle way of covering up his baldness, as if a recent capillary implant were struggling to cover the shiny skull. His face also had something of that clash between the young and the old: the skin of his cheeks was smooth and pink, as if miraculously preserved from decay, but around the eyes it darkened in a concentric tangle of yellowish wrinkles, and it was difficult to tell if he had undergone incomplete aesthetic surgery, or if old age was creeping down his face at a slow pace and had reserved until last, as an act of mercy, the youthful cheeks. He was thin and restless, and his eyes seemed to want to control everything around them. He hastened to offer me his hand across the table and gripped mine with a quick electric gesture. Seldom introduced him to me as Dr Albert Raggio and added: 'A real doctor. I mean, he treats people.'

'I'm a psychiatrist with a degree from Heidelberg,' said Raggio in a slightly boastful tone, 'but I left the consulting room quite some time ago and since then I've been more interested in chronomedicine. I'm delighted to know that you're Argentinian, because it was thanks to your one great writer that I entered the Brotherhood. He published a very thoughtful essay on the distortion of time in the Alice books. Time running backwards, in which the Messenger is imprisoned before being judged for a crime he *might* commit after the judge's sentence. And Time stopped at five o'clock in the afternoon at the Mad Hatter's table. I felt it was something like a visionary's glimpse, or, as he himself would say, an observation made for others "to pursue and justify". And to pursue and justify it I've dedicated myself from then on. But not only in writing,' he said with cryptic pride.

'Indeed,' Raymond Martin said mockingly. 'He's our Father Time. Now, if you only kept on good terms with him, he'd do almost anything you like with the clock.'

The woman next to us took advantage of the brief interruption to give me her hand as well, and she told me her name, Laura, with a warm tremor in her voice. She hadn't stopped smiling while her husband spoke, as if accustomed to waiting patiently during his peacock displays. She seemed to be at least a couple of decades younger than he, and though her beauty already had that fragile twilight look of late maturity, at first glance she was still dazzling. I wondered if the patient preservation of that marvellous face was the result of the secret practice of her husband's experiments. Perhaps he was too late when he started on himself, and perfected his craft by rescuing the woman by his side. She seemed pleased by my reverently admiring look.

'Laura is a psychologist,' Seldom said. 'She's published an astonishing book on the logic of dreams and the symbolic significance of every animal in the Alice books.'

I knew Seldom well enough to guess what the word 'astonishing' might mean on his lips, but that didn't diminish in the least my resolve to speak with her whenever the occasion might arise. Unfortunately, Albert Raggio would not leave the smallest gap for anyone else to speak, let alone his wife.

'I suggested the subject for her doctoral thesis after reading various debates in the learned journals about the dog in Chapter Four, the only animal in the books that doesn't speak with Alice. In fact, he doesn't speak with anyone.'

'Wise beast,' Raymond Martin said with a resigned sigh, stretching out his hand to help himself to a second spoonful

of sugar from the bowl that someone had moved to the centre
of the table.

'*Touché*, my dear Raymond,' Raggio said. 'But I've
warned you many times: with that amount of sugar you'll
deprive us sooner than later of your enchanting irony.' He
looked at me once more, as if pleased to have a new inter-
locutor with whom to pursue his campaign. 'I don't know
how to make him realise that sugar is poison. Pure poison!
I'm tempted to say that sugar is the arch-enemy of our
species. It's been proven in mice: it is the oxidant *par excel-
lence* of our molecules, the hidden trigger of old age. Look
at him and at me. Who would you say is the eldest?' And
he pushed his face forward so that I could see them next to
each other. I tried to find an answer that wouldn't be hurtful
to either. Raymond helped himself to yet another spoonful,
as if on purpose, and his eyes sparkled with mischievous
amusement.

'For God's sake, Albert,' he said. 'If you gave me the brand
of your hair dye, I'd catch up with you immediately.'

From the other side of the table came the crackling of a
paper wrapper. A burly, wheezing man who had arrived later
than all the others was unwrapping a chocolate and popping
it into his mouth. Seeing our faces, he shrugged.

'Everything that kills you also cures you. Or is it the other
way round?' he said, looking at me, as if he felt the need to
apologise. 'I'm diabetic and I need my sweets every time my
sugar level is low.'

'What he means,' Raymond Martin translated for my benefit, 'is that you should never expect to be offered a chocolate.
At least, none of us has ever succeeded.'

The man seemed about to answer, but he was forestalled
by Josephine Grey, who launched into a flurry of simultaneous questions and complaints, as if she hadn't seen him in a

very long time and had a list of queries that she unfurled in a disorderly fashion.

'That's Leonard Hinch,' Seldom whispered to me, 'the publisher of *Vanishing Tale* and of all the Brotherhood writings. But he shouldn't be here, he's not a plenary member. I wonder how he found out.' He cast a worried look around him. 'It's ten past six. It's odd that Kristen should be so late.'

From the head of the table, Ranelagh too exchanged glances with him.

'We're all here now, Arthur. In your considered opinion, do you think she'll be much later? Perhaps Henry could do the roll-call while we're waiting.'

Henry Haas, sitting next to him, opened a large black book, but before he could write anything in it, there was a knock on the door and we saw one of the college porters come in.

'There's a call downstairs for Professor Arthur Seldom,' he said.

Seldom rose with a preoccupied look and followed the porter outside. A long uncomfortable silence fell on the assembly.

'I only hope that this young lady hasn't changed her mind and the meeting was called in vain,' Thornton Reeves said with annoyance. 'I had to cancel one of my classes.'

'And we returned from London early,' Albert Raggio added.

I looked around the muttering assembly and at each of their faces. I recalled what Sharon had told me on the previous day: a bunch of stiff-upper-lip codgers who wear pocket watches and for whom it's always teatime. She had only got one thing wrong: most of them, judging by their cups, had a preference for coffee.

Two or three minutes went by before Seldom reappeared at the door. He looked deathly pale.

'That was Kristen's mother,' he said in a loud voice. 'She's just told me that Kristen is in hospital, in a very serious condition. She was run over by a car yesterday when she was returning from the cinema, and was left lying in the street. She's now at Radcliffe Hospital, in intensive care. They're taking her into the operating theatre for a second procedure. I promised her that I'd go to the hospital at once.'

There was an appalled silence while Seldom went round the table to get his raincoat from the back of his chair. Without thinking, I too got up and followed him out of the room. He didn't object.

Chapter 7

Just as we were leaving, Josephine grabbed Seldom by the arm: 'Mahmud is downstairs. You can tell him that I said he should take you and then come back to get me. I'll wave to him from the window. That way you'll get there quicker.'

Seldom nodded. When we got to the street he approached the driver and, in a low voice, pointed towards the window where Josephine was gesturing her consent. We climbed into the Bentley and set off at once, but at such a measured pace, respectful of all traffic signals and pedestrian crossings, that I began to long for my bicycle and to ask myself whether we would not have been quicker on foot.

When at last we got out at the door of the Radcliffe and threaded our way through the maze of corridors, Kristen had been wheeled into the operating theatre. She had several fractures and a broken rib that had punctured one of her lungs, but more worrying was a blood clot on the brain that hadn't been entirely reabsorbed. That was the reason for the second operation. A trepanation of the skull was deemed necessary, according to what Kristen's mother told us in the waiting room. She was a woman of small stature, with an innocent-looking sunburnt face, like that of a peasant woman. The only resemblance to Kristen was the deep blue of her eyes, and I asked myself whether Kristen might not have done everything possible in her life to differentiate herself from her mother. While the woman spoke, she twisted a tiny lace handkerchief in her hands. She had come up from Guildford as soon as she had received the call from the hospital. She told us she had to leave her house on the outskirts of the town, with its orchard and its cats, in the care of the nearest neighbour, in order to catch the first train. When she arrived, a police officer was waiting for her. They had no clue yet about the car that had run Kristen over. The woman burst into tears as she told us. No pity, they had left her lying there, Kristen had almost bled to death. The incident had taken place at about eleven on the previous night, as she was returning from the cinema. She had got off the bus at the Kidlington roundabout and had been run over on her way home, at the bend of a street with little or no traffic. The mother had been told that in all probability it had been the fault of a drunken undergraduate; they sometimes went to the outskirts of Oxford to race their cars and compete with each other.

Seldom asked who had found her. It had been almost a miracle: a neighbour who was walking his dog. In fact, it was the dog who had discovered her, because the impact had rolled her body into the grass where it had remained hidden. The mother then told us that Kristen had briefly woken up from the anaesthesia a few hours earlier. Kristen didn't recognise her, staring at her without seeing her, but she had cried out Seldom's name. The mother then looked in the bag Kristen was carrying that evening, and found no phone book, only an agenda in which the meeting with the Brotherhood had been jotted down, and she decided to call Christ Church.

We stayed with her until the operation was over, and we saw in the distance the stretcher carrying Kristen back to the glassed-in walls of the intensive care unit. I could only make out the naked tips of her feet, the plastic tubes of serum,

and the white bulge of the bandages around her head. A
doctor approached us and the mother stood up trembling,
and gripped my arm to steady herself. They had done everything that could be done, the doctor said cautiously, and
now we had to wait and see how things evolved over the next
twenty-four hours. The doctor said that, above all, the next
hours were crucial, until Kristen came out of her coma. The
mother crossed herself and told us she'd stay with her and
maybe sleep in the waiting room. She thanked us again for
coming, but Seldom didn't seem eager to leave. He asked me
to accompany him to one of the inside courtyards to have
a smoke, and, wrapped in thought, he slowly started to go
down the stairs towards a square of bare tiles between high
walls pierced with windows. It had started to grow dark and
Seldom rolled his cigarette with unhurried gestures that I
found exasperating. As he lowered his face to the lighter, I
noticed the telling furrow in his brow and the look of deep
concentration in his eyes, chasing something within himself
that had escaped his grasp.

'Are you thinking what I'm thinking?' he asked, turning
round suddenly to face me. He immediately added, as if to
correct himself: 'But no, it's too absurd, I can't even imagine
such a thing ... It makes no sense at all that someone might
want to commit a murder because of a few words from a
diary stashed away for more than a century. Don't you agree?
And you saw them: they're eccentric, each in his own way, of
course, but certainly harmless. And yet ... '

I decided then to tell him about seeing Kristen the previous
night coming out of the cinema, and that it surprised me to
find her in such a sorrowful mood. I repeated as best I could
our brief conversation. Seldom listened to me, tapping on his
cigarette. He nodded sternly and then seemed to will himself
to gather the few clues we had in order to reason out loud.

'The likeliest explanation, of course, is that it was really an accident. But there's something I can't stop thinking about, and I'd like to share it with you even though it's not supposed to be known by anyone outside the Brotherhood. I thought Richard Ranelagh would mention it to you when we met at Merton, but I realised that he chose to avoid the subject. He told you that we would divide Lewis Carroll's notebooks amongst ourselves so that each of us would deal with a certain period. But what he didn't tell you was that since we decided to prepare the annotated edition of the diaries, a number of publishers have expressed interest in the project. The initial idea, perhaps out of habit, was to entrust the project to Leonard Hinch, our traditional publisher. He's always done an impeccable job with our books, and we have an agreement by which he cedes a portion of the rights to pay for the Brotherhood's expenses. However, when the news leaked out that we were preparing this edition, we received an offer, difficult to refuse, from one of the largest publishing companies in the United States. For the same work that we were willing to do *ad honorem*, each one of us in our spare time, we were now offered a small fortune and also, perhaps more significantly, a percentage of future royalties, something like a stipend for life.'

'I would never have imagined that there'd be so many potential readers for these diaries,' I said with astonishment.

'There aren't. I was surprised too. But what does exist is an increasingly large number of universities in every country, and each one has its own library, and a budget allotted for the purchase of books. And the diaries, we were told by the snake charmer that came to tempt us, was bound to be a book that all the librarians in the world would want, to place proudly on a shelf where it would be allowed to gather dust. So we called a special meeting to which Hinch was *not* invited, in which both alternatives were put to the vote. The discussion was a heated one and a few unpleasant things were said. I recalled a phrase that my mother liked to repeat: Money is an excellent servant, but a terrible master. For the first time, I saw in these people, whom I've known for years and years, an unexpected side, opposed to everything that we've held as true about the Brotherhood's altruistic purposes. In an attempt to refuse Hinch's offer, there were even certain comments made about him concerning personal matters of which I had no idea.'

Seldom paused for a moment and let out a long puff of smoke, as if he couldn't decide how far to go with his story.

'What kind of comments?' I asked.

'As a general rule, I refuse to repeat gossip. Because where does the power of a wave of gossip come from? One of the three conditions required according to the traditional theory is that the rumour be plausible. But I rather think that people will believe a rumour to be true if, on the contrary, it sounds implausible or sordid. And there's another unwritten condition that favours the spreading of a rumour: impunity. You only have to shrug your shoulders and say that you're just repeating what you've heard. *You're just repeating something*. And this is all you have to do: repeat it until everyone has heard it. I've written quite a bit about the attractions of rumour and its oscillations between truth and falsehood in my *Aesthetics of Reason*. That's why I try to believe, at least to start off with, that a rumour can also be false. However, I think I can trust you. It had to do with the apparently objectionable treatment of his female employees in the publishing company, and his rather insistent advances with a few of the female scholarship students. There wasn't a formal accusation, just vague insinuations, but all were in agreement: they had all "heard about it". It was enough to mention this for the vote to split. Suddenly there was a good excuse that allowed many of them to vote against Hinch, not because of plain and simple greed, but for far loftier concerns.' Seldom pulled a sarcastic face. 'Like that posh lady who used to say that she also went to the toilet, but for other reasons.'

'And how did the vote turn out in the end?'

'It didn't. It was carried on to the following ordinary session. I suspect that Hinch somehow found out that he might be left out of the project, the only one in all these years that could have made him some real money. I believe that was the reason why he came to the meeting this afternoon even though he hadn't been invited: to find out how many votes he could count on, and who voted against him. Oh well, I really don't know why I'm telling you all this. Perhaps because for the first time, ever since the Brotherhood was founded, I saw something come to the surface, something that I would never have suspected. Still, it seems totally out of proportion, if I may put it this way, that one of us should have attempted something as brutal as that against Kristen. I can't even see a connection ... And yet, I don't feel I can simply go away and leave her here alone with her mother.'

I told him that I sometimes crossed paths with Inspector Petersen on my way to the office, and that I was sure that the inspector didn't hold a grudge against him.

'But what could I tell him?' Seldom asked. 'Even I find the idea excessive, a false alarm. And above all, you know why I'm reluctant to call in the police.'

I recalled what he had confessed to me once: the reason why he had chosen mathematics, a world in which slates and hypotheses could be wiped clean without any trace other than some chalk dust on the fingers. Hence his drastic decision, taken in his early youth, of cutting himself off as far as possible from the real world in which every action and every conjecture persisted all by themselves and wove unforesee-able webs of tragic consequences. He had acknowledged that his was an odd superstition, something that he had dragged along with him ever since his adolescence through a suc-cession of unfortunate events, but that it had fulfilled itself relentlessly, again and again, like a law made for one man only, whenever he left the calm black chess square and ven-tured to move a piece on the irreversible three-dimensional chessboard of life. And once again, as I could myself attest, he had been proven right, in the cruellest possible fashion, during the events we had shared a year ago.

'You mean ...' I started to say.

'Yes,' he answered, as if following my train of thought. 'I'm afraid that if we call the police there'll be a murder.'

Chapter 8

Nevertheless, we called the police. I must say that it was I who stupidly insisted that we call them. Of course, what Seldom had told me in confidence about the squabbles at the Brotherhood meeting, and also his own unease, had given me a rational foothold, a justification as it were, but I believe that what had been foremost in my mind, as well as in Seldom's, had been a first intuitive glimmer. Many times I'd discussed with Seldom the intriguing articulation in the field of mathematics between first intuitions and the following logical steps of a demonstration. In his *Aesthetics of Reason* he had compared those sudden intuitive flashes with the movements of the knight in a game of chess, as dazzling abbreviations that erased in their sudden light all traces of previous connections. For me, it was the feeling of a self-imposed truth, as if the heaven of Platonic objects had revealed itself for an instant, and remained from then onwards present as a persistent call, a secret beat. In my case, as soon as I heard that Kristen had been run over, I recalled the helpless, vulnerable look on her face coming out of the cinema, and the curious words about a second life that had no doubt unconsciously escaped her. Something had taken place that day, something that had changed her euphoric and triumphant mood of the previous evening.

We asked at the reception desk where the phone booth was, and we were directed to a public phone at the end of a hallway. I gave Seldom all my coins but even with the receiver in his hand he still seemed to hesitate.

'But whatever could I say that would make him believe me?'

'Keep as close as possible to the truth,' I said, because I knew that what Seldom deeply hated, and what made him waver now, was having to lie. 'Tell him you have reason to believe that someone ran her over deliberately, but that you can't say more than that for the time being. And that you'll explain everything tomorrow.'

Seldom sighed and dialled a number he knew by heart. I heard on the other end a woman's voice and I remembered that Inspector Petersen had a daughter with whom Seldom had once discussed the subjects of Scottish ancestry and Highland horses. I wondered if that was the reason why he'd memorised the number. I heard a voice raised in an imperious tone. Seldom, increasingly uncomfortable, had begun to stutter and seemed unable to reply. I stepped away to allow him some privacy and pretended to read the signs along the hallway. After a while, I realised by the change in his voice that at last he was speaking with the inspector. The conversation was brief, but I noticed that Seldom seemed relieved as he hung up and came towards me.

'Done,' he said. 'He'll send one of his men to stay here all night. I begged him to be discreet and not to say anything to Kristen's mother. I don't want her to worry even more than she does already. Now I'd like to say goodbye to her.'

We went up once again to the first floor. Seldom moved through the maze of deserted hallways with the confidence of an old resident, and I, too, seeing a nurse peek out from behind one of the glass doors, had a dizzying déjà vu, the impossible and mistaken feeling in my body that, behind one of those doors, I would come across Lorna again, dressed in a nurse's uniform. The intensive care unit was utterly silent. Kristen's mother saw us through one of the glass partitions and surreptitiously motioned us to join her. She was wearing a hair net as if about to go to bed, and when we approached she seemed embarrassed at being seen like that, but had no time to take it off. From the narrow corridor between the rooms we could observe, through the partition, Kristen's bed. Her body was covered almost to the neck with a sheet, with two transparent tubes cruelly fitted into her neck and nostrils. One side of her face, of a bluish purple colour, was puffed up and unrecognisable. Seldom left his phone number with Kristen's mother, and we offered to take her place on the following day, so as to give her a chance to rest. The woman thanked us and once again her eyes filled with tears of pain and gratitude.

'I'll tell her. I'll tell her as soon as she wakes up, how wonderful you've all been to me! To me, to her ...'

She clasped her hands to her chest, then she pulled them away and clasped them again, in an attempted gesture of thanks beyond words. Seldom placed a hand on her shoulder with that uncomfortable and inexperienced attitude with which Anglo-Saxons consent to physical contact.

'If you see that during the night she makes any movement whatsoever,' he said, almost as if asking for a personal favour, 'even if it's only a twitch of the eyelids, please touch her, hold her hand or pat her brow.'

The woman agreed, somewhat surprised. We said goodbye and left the room, but Seldom remained for a moment, watching through the glass the motionless figure of Kristen in bed.

'I think I told you about the car accident I had once,' he said, 'when I lost my first wife and my two best friends. I was in a coma for several days, lying like Kristen in one of those fishbowls. But there's something I didn't tell you, something I haven't told anyone. I was at the time already studying the possible philosophical extension of Gödel's theorem, and especially the question of self-reference in mathematical language. It had occurred to me that in the mathematical formulae that are self-referential there could be a clue to a possible mathematical definition of consciousness. For a time, I set myself out to study various books on the brain and to discuss the subject with neurologists and psychiatrists. I imagined that in the neuronal functions there might be some sort of copy of Gödel's mathematical loop. In fact, I was looking, like Roger Penrose does now, for some kind of clue, some physiological parallel of the organic trace of the most elementary recognition of oneself. Around that time I met Albert Raggio (his hair had its natural colour then) and he thought I might be interested in a lecture by a certain neurologist who was proposing a quasi-virtual model of human consciousness. I went to the lecture and unfortunately I sat in the front row. This man was soon to become a world eminence. He was from somewhere in the United States, but I no longer remember his name. What I do remember is that at first sight he seemed to me like a Sunday preacher, a sort of Mormon priest, perhaps because he was clean-shaven and wore a closed collar tied with a ribbon, like a clergyman. And I also remember that he had a soft, Mephistophelean smile; he was one of those people who manage to grin and talk at the same time. He said he needed a volunteer for the beginning of his talk, and he pointed at me to come and join him. He asked me what my occupation was and his grin intensified when I told him that I was a professor of Logic. He had me sit in a chair facing the audience. He had something of a mysterious conjurer about him and made a few opening remarks about the mind-body dichotomy. He then proposed a mental experiment. "Imagine that we're in an operating theatre," he said, and lifted one of my legs. He pretended to use his hand as a saw, and for a moment I felt the edge of the blade on my knee. Everyone laughed. "If we cut off one of the legs of our friend here, obviously he wouldn't stop being who is," he said. "He'd feel perhaps one of those imaginary itches in the phantom limb, but essentially he'd still be the same person you all know, except that he'd be hopping around on one foot." He lifted my other leg and made the same sawing gesture, as if he were cutting that one off as well. "Now he's not as tall as before," he said, "'and he no longer needs to spend money on shoes, but for the rest, deep inside, he's still the person he's always been." He lifted my arms and made two chopping gestures in the air, as if cutting off my arms. "Now he doesn't have any arms, and he'll find it more difficult to wield his cutlery, but he's still, of course, himself and he'll acknowledge us with a nod if we say his name." He stood behind me, touched my spine and made the gesture of zipping up a long jacket. "Now we rip out his spinal cord," he said, "and he won't be able to make the slightest movement; but in spite of all this, though he can't even blink, deep down inside he's still the same." He then grabbed hold of my head and twisted it back and forth as if he were to unscrew it from my body. I suppose he was making funny faces behind my back because everyone was laughing. "And even if I managed to separate his head from his neck," he said, "this little head, even on its own, if we irrigated it a bit, especially because our friend is a professor of Logic, it would still be able to carry on teaching, like in the trick of the bodiless woman in the freak show." All of a sudden, I felt his hands with the tips of his nails like claws on my skull, and I imagined he was performing for the audience the gesture of splitting it apart like an egg. "We open the skull," he said, "and we keep the brain, the holy

come from outside and touch me. I wouldn't want Kristen, when she wakes, to suffer an experience like mine.'

We heard the heavy steps of boots climbing the marble stairs and saw a very fat policeman coming towards us down the hallway, breathing heavily and carrying a plastic chair.

'Now, yes, I think that we can leave,' Seldom said.

Chapter 9

All next morning I was on tenterhooks. It was raining again, somewhat heavier now, and I felt unable to do anything other than pace my room like a prisoner, staring from time to time out of the window, as if a signal could reach me through the downpour. I tried leafing through Raymond Martin's book, but I didn't go beyond the first chapter. I couldn't concentrate sufficiently on any of the puzzles he set out, even though the first one in the book, proposed by Carroll himself, turned round in my head like the refrain of an obnoxious song: 'To make the DEAD LIVE'. The meaning was far more modest: it meant writing out a succession of four-letter words, each different from the previous one by one single letter, until 'DEAD' was turned into 'LIVE'. I made several attempts but my English vocabulary was frustratingly limited, and my sequences never went beyond three or four words before coming to a hopeless stop. Even so, I kept on trying for almost an hour, and I filled several sheets of paper, as if something far more important were at stake for me between these two words. I couldn't stop wondering if during the night a certain propitious combination of words might have allowed Kristen to live. Close to midday, I crossed over to the Institute under the protection of my umbrella and climbed up to the visitors' room to send Seldom an email. Did he have any news about

Kristen? Had he been able to speak again with her mother? A couple of hours later, before leaving, I received his reply. Kristen had woken up and it seemed that she was fairly lucid, but she wasn't allowed to receive visitors for the time being. She was still undergoing all sorts of examinations and having more X-rays taken. The doctors had told her mother that there might be consequences because of a lesion in the spine. He'd let me know if he had any other news. In a postscript, he added that he had received a call from Petersen, but that he hadn't yet made up his mind whether or not to answer.

The following day was Sunday and I had no news from Seldom, and I decided not to email him again. But on Monday morning, when I came by the Mathematical Institute, I found in my pigeonhole a folded sheet of paper that Seldom had left for me: Kristen wanted to see us. Seldom suggested that I come by his office after lunch and we'd go together to the hospital.

After two days of rain the sky was clear once more and the air was full with the intense smell of the damp earth of the flower beds, of the mistletoe bushes along the sidewalks and the trees in bloom. There was also the insistent and noisy buzz of bees and other insects hovering above the remains of the blackberries the rain had caused to fall on the ground. As we walked, Seldom told me that he had only just managed to avoid another of Petersen's calls, and confessed that over the weekend he had watched all the news on television, expecting some information on the car to appear, confirming that it had been nothing more than an unfortunate accident.

When we asked at reception for Kristen's room, we were sent to the second floor, to the acute care unit, which seemed like a good sign. I still remembered Seldom's story about his own descent into Hell at Radcliffe's and the sentence he quoted from a Dino Buzzati story about the fateful first floor:

'Only the priest worked there.' I told myself that Kristen had at least managed to climb up one step.

The mother, as soon as she saw us, came out into the hallway to meet us. Kristen was still confined to complete bed rest and could barely say a few words. But she had insisted on seeing us and that's why her mother had decided to trouble the professor once again. She told us that Kristen did not yet know about the spinal lesion: she might never walk again. She seemed on the point of collapsing as she told us this, and she begged us to be careful not to say anything that might alert her daughter: the doctors were still hopeful of a miracle. She said that Kristen had asked to speak to us privately and that she'd take advantage of this to go rest a little and change her clothes. She had not left the hospital all weekend.

When we walked into the room, Kristen was lying on her back. Hearing us, she slowly turned and tried to sit up against the iron frame of the bed. She was unrecognisable, with her head bandaged up and her face still swollen, the skin of her forehead an ugly purple, and both her eyes bloodied. One of her arms was in a cast, and a tube in her throat was connected to a bottle of serum. She looked at us as if she didn't know exactly who we were, and she fingered the bedside table searching for her glasses. She placed them as well as she could over her bandages, and her mouth, as if it too became focused, stretched into a brave and painful smile. When she spoke, her voice sounded dulled but clear, as if she were gradually recovering the ability to speak and was surprised by her own diction.

'Thank you for coming,' she said. 'I think that in a while someone from the police will come to talk with me, an Inspector Petersen. My mother told me that a car ran me over, and I'm trying to remember whatever I can about that night, but everything becomes blurred. I thought that if I saw you both something would come back to me. I've a picture of you in the queue at the cinema,' she said, looking at me.

'Yes,' I said. 'You had gone to see *Seconds* and we met on your way out.'

'True,' she said, as if she could see through the fog snatches of a scene. She seemed retrospectively ashamed. 'I was crying like a fool.'

For a moment, she became lost in thought.

'I left the cinema. It was about to rain. I remember thinking that I hadn't brought an umbrella. And then ...'

She looked up towards the ceiling and shook her head, as if unable to go further.

'You must have walked to the Kidlington bus stop,' Seldom tried to help her. 'Don't you have any memory of the ride? And you got off to walk home shortly after the roundabout. Or at least, that was where they found you.'

Kristen stared at us now with no expression in her eyes, as if trying to collect herself and plunge into a dark pool of moving waters. She shook her head again: once more, she had come up with nothing.

'And the car that ran you over? The moment it hit you? Lights, the honking of the horn, the screeching of brakes?' Seldom asked. 'If at least you remembered any of this ...' And he stopped. I thought I could follow his reasoning: if she had seen the lights of the car, or heard the brakes, we could still imagine it had been an accident.

Kristen shook her head in silence.

'All I know is something comes at me like a jack-in-the-box, and up I goes like a sky-rocket! Just like poor Bill in Wonderland,' she said in a low voice. 'I can't recall anything about the accident itself.'

'But you remember the paper, I trust,' Seldom said, somewhat alarmed.

'Of course,' Kristen said. And she smiled a faint triumphant smile. 'That's the first thing I remembered upon waking and, luckily, I also remembered where I'd hidden it.'

She tried pulling herself up higher against the bedrest.

'Strange,' she said. 'I don't feel my legs at all.'

She made an effort, and managed to sit up a little further with only her hand as a lever. I wanted to help her but she stopped me with a look and turned once more towards Seldom.

'When did you send the emails for Friday's meeting?' she asked him. 'The night we three met?'

Seldom nodded.

'Yes, that same night, when I got home. I wrote a general email to all except Josephine. I went to see her in person the next morning.'

'And in the email, you said nothing about the paper?'

'Of course not,' Seldom said.

'But my name, surely, did appear?'

'Yes, of course, I wrote that you'd informed us about a discovery in the Guildford house, just as we'd agreed. Nothing more. I can resend it to you.' And Seldom looked at her with a curious expression on his face.

Kristen then made a gesture with her only free hand, indicating that she wanted us to bring her the bag that was on the chair, and open it. She stretched her neck towards it as best she could to peer inside, and pulled out with two fingers a tiny disturbing photograph: a stark-naked girl about ten years old looking straight into the camera, sitting with her back against a tree on the edge of a river, the right leg folded against the line that divided the breast, and one of her hands cupped over her left foot that was crossed as in a knot under the folded leg. The pose left a triangular opening that allowed one to imagine the pubis within. One could not avoid thinking of the photographer's instructions and the successive angles he would have tried out for the leg, so that the opening caught the viewer's eye without frankly revealing anything. Or did it?

Kristen asked Seldom if he recognised the image. Seldom glanced at it once more with disgust and shook his head.

'It's Lewis Carroll's,' Kristen said.

Seldom passed it to me as if he were ridding himself of something evil.

'This aspect of Carroll's life,' he said apologetically, 'has always repulsed me: I never looked carefully at his collection of pictures of little girls. Not even when Henry Haas published his book.'

Now that I had in my hand the photograph I too gave it a second look. The image seemed to have been hand-coloured long ago, somewhat clumsily, and the girl's face, maybe because of the darkened hues, had a somewhat sinister, strangely adult look. Her expression was serious, inscrutable, and her outline, even though it seemed cut out with care and pasted on to the bucolic background painting, revealed on one side of the hair the snip of scissors.

'This was one of a series of photos that Lewis Carroll took of a girl called Beatrice Hatch and then sent to be coloured by a London artist, Anne Bond, to achieve the effect of a pastoral scene. I found it in a plain white envelope in my pigeonhole on Friday, the day I was run over. I was somewhat puzzled, but in the beginning I didn't give it any importance: as Thornton Reeves' assistant and because of my own research, I constantly receive Lewis Carroll material. Now I can't stop wondering whether this photo wasn't in the nature of a warning of what would happen to me later. But at the same time, I can't quite believe that someone would want to *kill* me. My mother told me that it had been an accident and that the police would certainly find the person responsible very soon.'

'In any case, we shouldn't be handling it,' Seldom said, 'maybe there're still fingerprints. You should give it to Petersen when you see him.'

Kristen remained thoughtful.

'I wonder,' she said, 'how much I'm really obliged to tell the inspector. Of course I'll hand over the photo, and I can tell him about the paper, but I certainly would not want to show it to him, nor reveal to him the sentence. I suppose he can't force me to do *that*.'

'As soon as you show him the paper, if we know Petersen at all, he'll want to know what the sentence is, even more than we do.'

Kristen looked up at us and her eyes took on, somewhat alarmingly, a glassy hardness, like the one I'd sometimes seen in crazed mathematicians.

'I've been thinking about all this ever since I recovered consciousness, and I'm convinced that rather than a single article, I could write a whole book from the new perspective that the sentence opens up. I remembered a number of sections and phrases in the diaries that should now be read differently.' She smiled to herself, as if she were already imagining something of that future opus, and I thought that Seldom could also perceive that new euphoric gleam in her eyes. 'I think that sentence will be like the spark that sets the prairie on fire – or rather than prairie, I should say, the Wood of Wrong Books. You can't imagine it, because it's unimaginable. But I need some time to do that. And I need to leave this place. Arthur, I'll tell the inspector everything I remember, but perhaps I shan't remember much about the paper. Perhaps the shock and the operation made me forget all about it. And it wouldn't be something illegal, I hope. After all, what would the piece of paper have to do with what happened? Only we three know of its existence. And I know that neither of you would have wished to do something like this to me, right?' And she smiled to show us her trust, as if to seal our agreement. I asked myself whether this was not the real reason she had called us to her bedside. After all, she couldn't be aware that Sir Richard Ranelagh also was in the know. Seldom tried to convince her.

'I don't think you're doing the right thing,' he said. 'If what happened to you was not an accident, I believe you'd be in a much safer position if you revealed to everyone the contents of that sentence.'

For the first time, Kristen seemed doubtful. Maybe until that moment, this was something that she'd refused to believe, and hearing of that other possibility from Seldom's lips she felt no longer able to brush it aside so easily. After all, he had been her research adviser and Kristen surely had, as I did, the disciple's reflex, and even more so because Seldom's conjectures were almost always proven to be right. I could see she was struggling with herself to keep the paper in a private version of Pascal's wager: the probability that someone would have wanted to murder her was too low to warrant letting go of something that seemed to her increasingly valuable.

'According to what the doctors told me,' she said in a slow, steady voice, 'it was a miracle I survived. I was clinically dead in the operating room and everyone thought I was a goner. This is my second life that begins now and I'm not prepared to repeat the same fears I had in my previous one. Also, and this is hard to explain, I feel I'm being protected by something higher. There's a woman on the first floor, Sister Rosaura, who consoles those about to die. My mother has prayed with her all this time, and I too, in a certain way, turned to God. I'm no longer ashamed of saying it: I know I'm being protected. I know that Someone mightier watches over me.'

Seldom glanced at me hopelessly, as if there were nothing more for us to do there. I knew very well what he was thinking: when God appears, reason vanishes. He maintained, as did almost all the logicians I have known, that the hypothesis was so strong that it reduced to trivial any system of rational thought, and even any attempt of further thought. Once I had heard him discuss jokingly the argument 'If God doesn't exist, everything is possible'. He had said: 'But if God does exist, everything is also possible.' He watched Kristen as she spoke and yet I had the impression that he had stopped listening. He had partly withdrawn his attention and I could see in his face the struggle between disappointment, horror and pity.

We heard several knocks on the door and through the glass we saw a hand held up in a greeting. Kristen too lifted her arm as far as she could and made a gesture with her finger, instructing the visitor to come back later.

'That's Sister Rosaura, the woman I told you about. She goes through all the rooms in case someone wants to share a prayer.'

'I think that perhaps we should leave,' Seldom said. 'I promised your mother that the visit would be a short one.' And he started to get off his chair. He looked stern and somewhat uncomfortable. 'What should I say, then, at the next meeting of the Brotherhood? We had agreed that you would return the paper.'

'I will, Arthur. I promise I will. I only ask you for some time till I leave the hospital and check on all the cross-references in the bibliography. I feel I've come upon the tip of an iceberg and that I can manage to bring the rest to the surface if only I'm allowed sufficient time.'

Seldom seemed to come to a final decision.

'I can only wait till you are out of hospital. I wouldn't be able to excuse you any longer, there, within the Brotherhood, nor would I be able to lie to Inspector Petersen if he were to question me.'

'But why would he question you?' Kristen said. 'I won't tell him anything about the paper, and only we three know of its existence, right?' And she looked up at us again trustingly, without a shadow of a doubt.

The door opened and a nurse put in her head long enough to stare at us disapprovingly.

'There's a police inspector wanting to talk to you,' she said to Kristen. 'Are you ready to see him?'

'I think I am now,' Kristen said and, once more, she made a brave attempt to smile at us.

Chapter 10

'Let's take the stairs,' Seldom said. 'I don't want to run into Petersen just yet.'

We walked to the end of the hallway, but as we pushed the swinging doors that led to the ground floor, we saw, huffing and puffing, the stout figure of the inspector appear in the doorway.

'Professor Seldom, what a surprise!' he said ironically. 'It seems that neither of us likes to use the lift. Downstairs I spoke with the young woman's mother and she said that if I hurried I might still find you here. We have a little chat pending, don't we? Why don't you both wait for me in the cafeteria on the seventh floor? I'll have a few words with your student and then I'll come upstairs for a coffee.'

Seldom seemed about to excuse himself, but at the last moment he pursed his lips in a gesture of agreement. We walked back down the hallway to the lift and, resigned and somewhat upset, he pressed the button for the seventh floor. I had been only once before in that cafeteria, waiting for Lorna to finish her shift, and I couldn't help glancing over each of the nurses at the tables, as if I could still find her among them. The place had since been refurbished with colourful lamps and curtains to try to infuse it with a cheerful touch, but the result wasn't entirely successful. Perhaps the wheelchairs of

the patients, the chinstraps and the catheters were difficult
to counteract. Instinctively, I took my tray and looked for a
seat next to the furthest window. Seldom sipped his coffee
in silence; he seemed worried or saddened by something. We
saw two women come in wearing the same kind of long grey
skirt that the one waiting at Kristen's door had worn.

'These women,' Seldom said, 'give me the shivers. They
belong to some Methodist branch. I had them hovering over
me as soon as I was out of intensive care. Isn't it incredible
what they've done to Kristen in just two days? They know
how to strike at the moment of greatest weakness, when death
is at the door. But I would never have thought that Kristen
would allow herself to be dragged along like that. How is
it possible that a mind mathematically trained in axiomatic
systems, in the subtleties of paradoxes, in the consistency of
logical postulates, can cast everything aside and embrace the
god of the children's catechism? You heard her: she says she
isn't afraid because she believes that there's Someone up there
who protects her.'

Seldom seemed both perplexed and disappointed, as if a
disciple were being taken away from him for evermore.

'Maybe it's a passing thing,' I said. 'I imagine it's a natural
reaction in those who've survived an accident: they feel there's
been a miracle that was destined for them in some special
way. Didn't you yourself write about that in your *Aesthetics
of Reason*? No one enjoys being an aleatory example in
an ocean of statistics, a random number in Gauss's bell.
Everyone prefers to believe in a predestined miracle, that
they have been touched by something greater. Maybe when
she leaves the hospital she'll go back to being who she was.'

'I'm not so sure,' Seldom said. 'Do you know what Kristen's
subject was for her doctoral thesis? Gödel's last lecture.'

'The Gibbs lecture? But in that lecture Gödel seemed to

leave an opening for a certain mysticism: the possibility of an a priori existence of certain mathematical patterns and objects, like the Platonic archetypes. The existence of a heaven always beyond human rational constructions. And didn't you yourself once tell me that Platonism is the true secret religion of all mathematicians? That they are all Platonists from Monday to Friday, independently from the church they might attend at the weekend?

'I told you that was a practical way of thinking,' Seldom said somewhat impatiently. 'And up to a certain point, unavoidable. In the same way that when you estimate a stroll you don't take into account the curvature of the Earth. But even though we walk *as if* the Earth were flat, we know it isn't. And in Kristen's case, she was certainly an atheist in all the discussions I had with her at the time; she intended to uphold the thesis contrary to that of Gödel's. She was studying the axiom of choice, Brouwer's free elective acts, the oracles of Turing's non-deterministic machines, non-Euclidean geometries. In fact, all those mathematical constructions that require a deliberate human choice. Naturally, we spoke about religion a number of times, and I would say that she was actually against it. Religion reminded her of her mother and everything she hated in the small conservative village in which she was born. Anyway, I could understand if Kristen were to embrace an idea of universal harmony, of pre-human cosmic order, like Einstein did. But to regress to childhood, to a personal God looking after her ...'

He looked at me as if he wanted me to share his astonishment, and I had to bite my tongue not to remind him that, after all, he too held a similar sort of private superstition, but of a contrary sort: that of a fate that held for him inexorable misfortunes.

'And I'm sure you noticed the fanatical glint in her eyes

when she spoke of the paper. That was perhaps what worried me the most. It reminded me of something I'd quite forgotten. You know, since we are talking about religions: in my youth I was a member of the British Communist Party, which was clandestine at the time. And I had someone who was a sort of Marxist tutor to me and my friends. He was a young biologist who explained to us the laws of dialectic materialism, the discussion about the origins and creation of life in Engels' *Anti-Dühring*, the economic key to added value in the spread of poverty, the primacy of scientific materialism in every field. He spoke with unquenchable fervour. He had secretly travelled to the Soviet Union and, upon his return, he seemed convinced he could singlehandedly rouse the English working class to arms. He was a brilliant speaker and I had no doubts that he would soon clamber up the ranks of the Party and become one of the leaders. I went to do my postgraduate degree in Germany and lost sight of him, and only when I came back I learned that he had left the Party. Two years later, we met again in a pub. He had already had a few beers and he had a couple more with me. When I asked him what had happened, he said he had had a revelation and told me, with the same spark in his eyes that I saw today in Kristen's, that he had become a member of the Raëlian Movement. With the same exalted determination, with the same conviction, he now spoke to me of extra-terrestrials that would bring us the secret of immortality, of flying saucers that would land on Earth, and of the church for which they were soliciting funds, which they would set up in Jerusalem to welcome the Elohim of other worlds. I was deeply impressed, as if I were listening to a talking machine that had been gutted but that retained the same features, gestures and tone of voice that I had once known. In an instant, he pulled out lottery tickets with the Raëlian star and monogram, much as when he used

taken to one of the junk yards up north. Unfortunately, there were no traces left on the sidewalk either. It was the evening when the rain started. I asked the girl whether she remembered anything at all, any detail that might assist us. But she's wiped out completely the moment of the impact. The last thing she remembers is meeting you in the cinema,' he said to me with a piercing look. 'How well did you know each other?'

I stared at him with astonishment.

'Hardly at all. It was the second time in my life that I saw her.'

'And therefore, don't you think it's strange to find yourself here?'

I felt confused, and didn't know how much more I was allowed to tell.

'Kristen asked to see both of us,' Seldom came to my assistance. 'She remembered having seen him in the cinema and she thought that his presence might help trigger something to recall the rest. She knew she had to speak with you and wanted to remember as much as possible.'

The inspector acknowledged this with a grimace.

'Yes, that's what she told me. I asked her if she could think of someone who might want to hurt her; she said she couldn't. I asked then if on the preceding days she had noticed anything unusual, something that might have seemed threatening to her. She thought for a while and then she showed me this.'

He carefully pulled out of his pocket the photo Kristen had shown us and laid it on the table. In contact with the rough, mottled hand of the inspector, the photo seemed now to take on a life of its own, even more insidious and perverse.

'She told me she had found this inside a blank envelope in her pigeonhole on the morning of the accident.'

'Yes,' Seldom said. 'She showed it to us as well.'

'What drew her attention as an afterthought, she said, was

not as much the photo itself but that the envelope was blank. At
the time, it seemed to her of very little importance. Apparently
she's accustomed to receiving and exchanging all sorts of material on Lewis Carroll. Nor has she had a chance yet to find out
who might have sent it. She told me that perhaps there was a
perfectly reasonable explanation for this as well. Her tutor, for
instance, leaves envelopes like this one for her all the time, but
always with his initials. But perhaps that day he didn't have a
pen at hand. I asked her for the name of this professor, and
also of the various other librarians and Lewis Carroll scholars
with whom she exchanges documents. I asked her again if she
had any idea, however absurd it might seem, of why someone
might have done this on purpose, and I told her that you, in
fact, believed that someone might have wanted to harm her,
since you had called to ask for police protection at the hospital.
She said she was aware of your call but that she thought it was
an unwarranted precaution. She told me she was working on
some papers that she'd found in the Lewis Carroll archives in
Guildford and she was going to show them to the Brotherhood
the following day. However, she said, those papers could not be
of danger to anyone. In no way did she believe that she might
have been attacked because of them. She didn't quite understand why you imagined that someone would want to murder
her. And that, in any case, I should be speaking with you.'

He lapsed into silence and looked at Seldom as if his unavoidable turn had come at last.

'Everything she told you is true, and it's possible that my
concern was out of proportion. As I said to you, I only wanted
to apologise to you for the call. I might still have to do that,
if the question of the photo and the envelope is resolved. But
until then, I'd rather tell you why I called you and why I still
think she might be in danger.'

I wondered how much, and in what detail, Seldom would

tell Petersen. As we were leaving Kristen's room, I was left with the impression that he'd accepted, however reluctantly, to protect her until she left the hospital, and I realised that if he told the whole story now, he would inevitably have to explain about the paper, something we had promised Kristen not to divulge. I think Seldom also found himself caught in the horns of the dilemma. According to what the inspector had told us, Kristen had apparently found a way of not going into the details of the Guildford paper. Was it so? Seldom seemed to be asking himself the same question.

'How much did Kristen tell you about the Guildford documents?' he asked.

'She tried to tell me everything,' the inspector said, 'something about Lewis Carroll's diaries, pages cut out by some relatives or conveniently stained with ink. I wasn't able to follow the particulars. But, good heavens, it seems to be a subject that she's really passionate about! I had to stop her because my head was spinning. I asked her if the papers she had found might prove valuable for a collector, if someone might be willing to pay a large sum of money for them. She said no. Do you agree?'

Seldom appeared relieved. Kristen had chosen the strategy of telling almost all the truth but in a torrential and meticulous way, so that at a certain point Petersen had given up following her. In this way, before she had to mention the paper itself, the inspector had himself cut corners to ask whether the document was financially valuable. I remembered what Seldom had once told me: in terms of police logic, only two things carried any weight: money and jealousy, the two basic forms of possession. Seldom shook his head and, in his own way, also told the truth.

'No, the papers Kristen discovered don't have, per se, any material value. The greatest harm they could do is to amend or contradict certain paragraphs in some of the Lewis Carroll biographies. And slightly undermine a few reputations. Nevertheless, there is a considerable sum of money involved, but for a different reason.'

He then repeated what he had told me about the sordid dispute within the Brotherhood concerning the publication of the diaries. Petersen nodded from time to time, as if he had at last found in the problem fodder to his taste.

'It's nothing more than an impression,' Seldom tried to justify himself, 'but during that discussion I had for the first time the feeling that I didn't know these people with whom I had met for so many years.'

'But these papers that Kristen was going to show,' the inspector said, 'how would they have complicated or ruined the deal?'

'They could . . . delay it,' Seldom said. 'If the documents, as we believe to be the case, reveal a contradictory facet of what we surmised about Lewis Carroll, they might force us to revise the entire corpus of what has been written and believed about him. And perhaps someone needs the money really urgently.'

Petersen thought for a moment.

'But even then, why would they attack her? It's like attacking the messenger. I suppose there must be copies of those papers. They weren't even on her, as far as I know.'

I wondered how Seldom would manage to tread on this sheet of ever-thinner ice.

'I don't know why,' Seldom answered, sliding on to firmer ground. 'It makes no sense to me either. I suppose I was influenced by what might have been a mere coincidence. We were all waiting for her when we heard that she'd been hit by a car. Yes, it must have been an accident and therefore a coincidence. And yet, there remains the question of the photo to be explained.'

Petersen sighed, as if he was forced to share, much against his will, some of Seldom's misgivings.

'Perhaps someone saw who it was that left the envelope,' he said. 'I'll send one of my men to the Institute.'

'Perhaps,' Seldom said sceptically, 'but it would be odd if someone had paid attention. The pigeonholes are very close to the entrance gate. During the latest changes it was thought that placing them there would make the postman's life easier. The secretary's office was left further inside down the hallway. Anyone can come in from the street and leave a letter without anyone noticing. Unless the secretary happened to turn up just at that very moment, or another professor was checking his pigeonhole right then ... But of course, it's worth enquiring.'

'What is your theory about the photo?'

'I don't know,' Seldom said. 'Perhaps it's someone who wants to remind us of that unsavoury side of Lewis Carroll's life.'

'Someone who's on some sort of anti-paedophile crusade and wanted to prevent the diaries from reaching the bookshops?'

'Perhaps,' Seldom repeated. 'But according to what I saw at the meeting, when the sum that they would pay us was mentioned, they'd have to kill us all for the diaries not to be published.'

Chapter 11

I took the lift down with Seldom but waited until we got to the ground floor to speak to him, as if the inspector might hear us at a distance.

'That was a close shave,' I said. 'What would you have said if he'd asked you more precisely about the papers?'

'I don't know,' Seldom said. 'Probably, the truth. Unfortunately it's the first thing that usually comes to my mind. But he didn't ask. Although it doesn't mean that he won't ask next time round. Isn't it curious that sometimes, in daily life, truth is only a step away, but a step we don't take? They say of us mathematicians that we're obsessive. But did you ever consider how many theorems have been left unproven because one small step further wasn't taken, because we weren't exhaustive enough? How much of what we think and surmise and cast aside lies merely a small intuitive jump away, one more turn, one more calculating trick? That was what made me despair when I tried to prove my first results: that what I had conjectured was true but that, in the forking branches of the tree of reasoning, in the maze of possibilities, I had missed the branch leading to the *via regia*, the right little door, or at least the knowledge that we'd tried all the locks. But at least Petersen didn't cancel the surveillance of her room.'

We came down the hospital's stairs and into the street.

Outside, normal life was surfacing once again: trees, cars, sounds, colours. Seldom didn't seem quite ready to leave.

'I'll call for another meeting of the Brotherhood,' he said, 'and I want to ask you to come this time as well. My intention is to tell them everything we know about the paper. I don't want to have to carry this load on my own. But above all, I want to see their faces when I tell them, the reaction of each one of them. And I'd like you to be with me at that moment. Maybe there's one of them who won't look surprised.'

I nodded. 'Perhaps one of them will only pretend to be surprised and we may notice it.'

'Several of them have asked me already about Kristen, hopefully with the best intentions.' As if lamenting this last comment, he added: 'How dreadful ... I never imagined that I'd be thinking about them in this way. I'm hoping that Petersen will find the car at last, and everything will return to normal.'

At that very moment we saw someone come stumbling down the stairs, with her head down, weeping uncontrollably. It was Kristen's mother, wrapped in a cloud of sorrow. She took a couple of steps towards us.

'They've just told me that Kristen will never walk again. And that she'll never have children. I don't think I have the strength to go back up there again. How can I tell her?' And she looked at us as if expecting an answer. 'How can I ever tell her?'

Some of her pain seemed to overcome Seldom as well, like a wave threatening to swallow him. Perhaps he felt that his secret law of misfortunes was manifesting itself once again. He lowered his head with a defenceless gesture. Kristen's mother grabbed him by the arm, in despair.

'Please tell me you'll help me find whoever did this. Just bring me the name and I'll deal with the rest myself.'

With her flushed imploring face bathed in tears, she looked

like the medieval depiction of a peasant woman beseeching with blind faith an Oxford don. Seldom muttered something that I couldn't make out and brusquely took his leave, his expression transfigured, as if he were not able to stand being there for even another moment.

Seldom's email with the new summons reached me that same afternoon. The meeting was called for Friday – just three days away – as if the matter were burning his hands, and I asked myself if he'd manage to gather them all at such short notice. On Tuesday morning, as I was again cycling towards Leyton's office, I saw Sharon struggling once more with the shutter. I stopped to say hello and even though she thanked me with a nice smile, I noticed that her attitude was some-what withdrawn. I asked myself what might be the matter and tried to guess the cause.

'I went to the Frankenheimer series on Thursday,' I said. 'I thought I'd see you there.'

'Yes, I know. I was there but you didn't notice me.'

'How is that possible? I was standing for a long while in the queue at the entrance hall.'

'I was the usher in the screen that was showing *Seconds*. I saw you from inside, talking to Kristen Hill.'

So that's what all this is about, I thought to myself.

'I didn't know you knew Kristen,' I said.

'And I didn't know that you two knew one another. Kristen is the one who opens the shop at weekends. You didn't know that either?' And she stared at me incredulously.

'To tell you the truth, no, I didn't. I met her less than a week ago at the Mathematical Institute.'

She made a caustic grimace.

'How fortunate for you to know so many girls in so many

places,' she said. 'I suppose you keep them apart according to separate timetables.'

'Not at all,' I protested. 'In fact, I hardly know her; I've spoken to her only a few times.'

'Come on,' she said, seemingly bothered. 'I saw you both. I saw how you looked at each other and how she was crying. Even I would have lent her my shoulder.'

'She was crying because of the film,' I said, bewildered.

'*Pleeease!*' she said. 'I know what I saw and I know Kristen sufficiently well. She wouldn't cry like that because of a film.'

What could I say to her? There was only one detail that was true in everything she had imagined: the way in which I looked at Kristen that night. Unfortunately, even though the entire scene she'd imagined was untrue, she had seen that single true moment with her own eyes, and I realised that it was hopeless. I drew away from her to get back on my bicycle.

'You know, of course, that she was hit by a car that very night as she was coming back from the cinema? She's in the hospital now. She was at death's door,' I said.

'Yes, I saw the news and yesterday she asked her mother to call me to ask me to cover her shifts. I was thinking of going to visit her this afternoon. I hope it wasn't something she did herself ... on purpose, out of desperation,' she said, and looked at me again with faint suspicion in her eyes.

'What do you mean?' I said, angry now myself. 'You're very, very mistaken, and I'm sorry I can't tell you what I know, even though I don't think you'd believe me.'

I went off, pedalling furiously. I suspected that there was a lesson for me in all this, but I wasn't sure what it was. I couldn't resign myself to think that it was a sad moral about restraint, or some principle of sexual economy *à la* Wilhelm Reich advising to have only one girl at a time. Life, already so brief, couldn't be that stingy. Didn't it seem more fair that our pathetic, inconsolable finitude, our minimal spark of the Delta function between two eternal nils, might favour at least a multiplicity of love affairs? And above all, was I to blame if I'd felt equally attracted to both? Even now, after I'd seen Kristen wrapped up in bandages and disabled for life, and had felt Sharon's chestnut eyes on me, burning with angry scorn (and in spite of that, so beautiful), could I have chosen one over the other? But chance had decided, all on its own, to leave me suddenly without either.

Chapter 12

Even though Seldom had taken care not to mention in his second email to the Brotherhood anything more than 'the Guildford discovery', not giving away anything relating to the first message, the members' curiosity seemed to have notably increased, and when I arrived that Friday in the room at Christ Church, they were almost all there already, sitting around the table in exactly the same places they had occupied on the previous occasion, as if they had never moved away. Only a few changes in their attire (which I noticed at once seeing Laura Raggio's interesting dress, since I too chose the same seat as before, facing her) proved that at the table time hadn't stopped. I hadn't seen Seldom nor received any communication from him for the past few days. I imagined he'd gone to Leeds to give one of his seminars, or perhaps to Cambridge, to where he had travelled quite frequently in the recent past. When he appeared at the door, there were some chalk marks on his forehead: he seemed to have come directly from a class. As soon as he took his place next to me, we saw Leonard Hinch come in. This seemed to unnerve Seldom. I saw him gesture discreetly to Sir Richard, and then the two got together to exchange a few words by the coffee urn.

When he returned to his place, he whispered to me: 'They'll let Hinch take part in the meeting because he's bringing a new proposal for publishing the diaries. It will be added to the agenda. He's mortgaged his house to match the other publisher's offer.'

As Seldom lifted his eyes, he saw that the others had fallen silent and were concentrating their attention on him.

'And how's the girl?' Josephine asked. 'Is it true that she won't be able to walk again?'

'Yes, Arthur, tell us, how's poor little Kristen?' Laura Raggio added in a mellifluous voice.

Seldom glanced at Ranelagh, as if to ask for formal permission to begin to speak, and he in turn glanced at Henry Haas, who was hurrying to finish writing the names in the ledger.

'Now that Henry has finished his roll-call,' Ranelagh said with a certain solemnity, 'I hope that we can learn something more about Kristen. Of course, we are all very worried about her condition. Several of us rang up the hospital and we were told that she wasn't allowed to speak or to receive visitors. But Arthur managed to see her and even to talk with her.'

Seldom looked around the table, scrutinising the expectant faces and I was ready to do the same. At first he seemed to speak only to Josephine and Laura, as if answering them belatedly.

'What you heard is unfortunately true: she underwent a very delicate surgical operation and her spinal cord has been affected. She won't be able to walk again, and her mother told us that she won't be able to have children.'

There was a small horrified shriek, murmurs, gestures of consternation. I swept as fast as I could from one face to the next, not knowing very well what I was supposed to be looking for. After all, response to someone else's misfortune always has a certain theatricality, something of a learned reflex. The two women, following the conventional division of emotions according to the sexes, allowed themselves a stifled cry and even a hint of tears appeared in Laura's eyes across the table. The men also had their conventional gestures but these were reduced to a bare minimum. Only Albert Raggio half-raised his arms and then let them fall helplessly, as if mutely bewailing an injustice. Raymond Martin shook his head and clicked his tongue: those who express themselves through irony are always left bewildered when confronted by raw human pain. As for the rest, all I saw were bowed heads, half-lifted eyebrows and evasive eyes. But on top of all this, to make my task even more difficult, was the fact that they were English, long trained in the art of not expressing emotions. I suppose that any reaction that had gone a fraction beyond what I'd observed would have been considered suspicious.

Seldom let that first moment of shock go by and then fixed his eyes on them again.

'But as Richard said, I managed to talk with her and there's something I need to share with you all about what she discovered in Guildford.'

He then told them about Kristen's first call concerning the item in the catalogue listed as 'Cut Pages in Diary' and the paper she had found in the corresponding folder. While Seldom spoke I saw in their faces deep concentration, amazement, even disbelief. But once again, none of their expressions, their faint reactions, seemed to me discordant or feigned. When Seldom spoke of the paper just as Kristen had described it – somewhat creased, written on both sides, with jottings of dates in Alice's life on the back – no one seemed to recognise it. Seldom interrupted himself to ask the question plainly: had anyone else seen the mention in the catalogue or the paper? No one answered, but now, yes, scrutinising the downcast faces like those of children caught in the act as Seldom looked at them one at a time, I could see unmistakable signs of shame. Sir Richard came to the rescue, taking on his allotted role.

'Arthur told me all this earlier. And though I've been to the Guildford house many a time, I have to confess that I, at least, must have overlooked it.'

A rippling murmur was heard, like a falling line of dominoes, in which everyone seemed to feel relieved in sharing the same fault. Only Thornton Reeves took on a bellicose tone.

'I once sent another student to look through the catalogue. I never saw it with my own eyes. And obviously I was not aware of that paper. But if none of us ever saw it, might it not all be an invention? Or did she show it to you, Arthur?'

'She refused to show it to me, or even tell me what the sentence was, but she had decided to reveal it here, to all of us, last Friday.'

'I went to Guildford as soon as I heard,' Ranelagh interrupted, 'in order to confirm that an item labelled "Cut Pages in Diary" indeed appeared in the catalogue. Kristen had already removed the paper, but I saw the file, just as she described it.'

'And we two,' Seldom said, making a sweeping gesture to include me, 'were able to see a photocopy of the beginning of the sentence. The handwriting is without doubt that of Menella Dodgson.'

Seldom then asked me to explain something of the technical examination we'd undertaken, but Josephine didn't allow me to proceed.

'For God's sake, Arthur! The suspense is killing me! What's the beginning of the sentence?' Seldom waited for a moment, as if silently consulting with Ranelagh, and then enunciated, word by word:

'"L.C. learns from Mrs Liddell that . . . " That is all Kristen allowed us to see.'

'L.C. learns from Mrs Liddell that . . .' Josephine repeated slowly, as if she were a medium conjuring up a ghost, and then shut her eyes so that all the possible meanings of the phrase might converge upon her. The others, too, seemed to be caught up in the same kind of rapture, searching for reverberations and mulling the words in silence.

'We can't get very far with just that,' Thornton Reeves said with irritation. 'I still don't understand why that girl didn't call *me*. I wouldn't have allowed her to withhold that kind of information. Also, it's clearly irregular that she's kept the paper.'

'Perhaps we can't get very far with what the phrase *affirms*,' Raymond Martin observed. 'But there is something that the phrase seems to deny. It's obvious that Mrs Liddell called Lewis Carroll that day to tell him something very precise. And it doesn't look, dear Thornton, like the beginning of a sentence in which Lewis Carroll might ask for Alice's hand, for instance. The phrase, in such a case, would have begun the other way round: "Mrs Liddell learns from L.C. that ... "'

'True,' Josephine said, as if to re-open an old quarrel. 'And as I maintained some time ago: if Lewis Carroll had wished to speak of marriage, it would have been he who'd have requested the meeting.'

'I never claimed that Lewis Carroll would have gone that day to speak of wedding plans *motu proprio*,' Reeves said angrily. 'What I surmised was that Mrs Liddell might have commented negatively on his closeness to Alice and that, within that conversation, to prevent been parted from her for ever, he perhaps proposed marriage *in extremis*. Arranged future marriages were common events. Lewis Carroll himself had a cousin whom he advised to wait to marry an eleven-year-old girl. But I don't think it makes sense to speculate idly about a paper we should all be able to see in its entirety – a paper now held in hiding by a twenty-year-old graduate student! Arthur, how did you let this happen?'

'Yes, indeed, Arthur, how come you didn't grab her by the neck until she spat out the rest of the sentence?' Raymond Martin said, glaring at Reeves with contempt.

'Kristen was afraid that someone might steal her discovery,' Seldom said, looking at Reeves accusingly, in a cold-headed tug of war. 'And we got her to agree that the paper would be put back in its place as soon as we noted it here in our minutes.'

'Whatever she might have feared, nothing justifies the fact of keeping the paper,' Albert Raggio said. 'Just imagine if she'd died in the accident or if something had gone wrong during the operation . . .'

There was a silence during which everyone seemed to sense what no one had said out loud until then.

'Yes: the paper would have been lost for ever,' Seldom said.

'But that could still happen, and any time soon!' Reeves re-launched his attack. 'The paper is entirely in her hands. With the same lack of thought she's shown up to now, she could also destroy it.'

'Why would Kristen do something like that?' Laura said, with a protective attitude. 'According to what Arthur has told us, she's obviously willing to show it to us. And her future academic career hangs on this thread. That's something that must certainly be made clear to her.'

'She promised to show us the paper as soon as she's out of the hospital,' Ranelagh said. 'Arthur, is that not so?'

'Yes,' Seldom said, 'but it might be weeks before she does. Her mother told us that her recovery will be extremely slow.'

'Which brings us to the next question,' Sir Richard said. 'We have on today's agenda the vote for whoever is to publish the diaries. And regarding this question, there's a new proposal that Leonard has just put forward in writing. Arthur and I asked ourselves, when we found out about this paper, whether we should not delay the decision until we're able to measure the impact that this sentence will have on our system of annotations, and on the way in which we have depicted up to now Lewis Carroll's character. But I'd like to hear the opinion of you all on this, because I believe we're all keen to come to a conclusion as soon as possible regarding the question of the contract and the advance.'

'Kristen seems to believe,' Seldom explained, 'that the sentence will lead us to consider a number of questions regarding Lewis Carroll in a different light. She was euphoric when she called me from Guildford. And after we spoke with her at the hospital, she asked me to bring her Lewis Carroll's diaries and his correspondence to go through it in full once again. She's convinced that the paper will have far-reaching consequences. But it's also true – and this is something I've seen again and again – that graduate students, through an excess of enthusiasm, have a tendency to overestimate the value of their first discoveries.'

Though Seldom hadn't looked my way, I felt I was blushing. He was no doubt referring to me, and, unfortunately, not only to my first discoveries, but also to my second and third.

'If Lewis Carroll himself had cut out that page,' Josephine said, 'then we might be able to expect a shocking revelation, the confession of improper behaviour of some sort of which he later repented. But as you'll remember, I was able to prove that in fact the page was torn out by the nieces, after his death. I'm inclined to believe that on that page he set down the essence of his conversation with Mrs Liddell, and that he'd allowed a certain detail to slip in that might have left him in an unfavourable light, a detail he himself might not have noticed. The Dodgson sisters wanted to paint an image of Lewis Carroll that was above all a pious one. You'll remember as well that I was able to prove that they inked out another page in the diary simply because Lewis Carroll had recorded there a moment in which he'd become angry with Alice. I would be very surprised if through this piece of paper there emerged a character very different from the one we've all known.'

'And I don't believe,' Laura unexpectedly added her voice to the discussion, 'that these two women would leave in writing something that would decidedly taint Lewis Carroll's image. In fact, it was in order to avoid precisely this that they tore out the page! And yet, if Kristen is so sure of the paper's reach, it might be possible to infer from the sentence something that may allow us to reconstruct whatever it was they wished to hide.'

'This is a discussion that involves both the whole and the parts,' Thornton Reeves said. 'The whole is the entire corpus of books on Lewis Carroll, the thousands and thousands of pages that we all together wrote on him. Are we to believe that a sentence scribbled by two bigoted sisters can jeopardise an essential aspect of what we already know? This young lady thinks it's no doubt important because it was she who found it. But to all intents and purposes, there's nothing that prevents us from voting right now. I imagine no one is seriously considering leaving the signing of the contract in suspense because of what might be written in that sentence. If need be, we could incorporate whatever little anecdote is revealed in the foreword or in a footnote.'

'I agree with Thornton on one point,' Seldom said. 'At times we fall into a superstitious way of thinking that makes us believe that if something is concealed, it's necessarily valuable. De Santis, the well-known Argentinian scholar, called this 'the theory of the hidden treasure': if something is hidden, it must be a treasure. I too investigated this in my book on the aesthetics of reason. We tend to value the information that's not revealed above that which is, simply because what is unknown has not yet been assessed: it lives like an electron before it's affected by the observer in a limbo of infinite possibilities. However, in this particular case, I also allowed myself to fall under the spell of the suggestion. I think I know Kristen well enough to believe that what she found is important, or unexpected in some way, beyond her personal interest in making a name for herself. But I agree with Thornton as well (and I reach the record of two coincidences in a single session) in that we can carry on and vote, because we'll have all the time we need ahead of us to review whatever may be necessary before the diaries are published.'

Ranelagh scanned the room to make sure no one else wished to intervene. All seemed anxious that no other hand be put up, like a couple about to be married fearing a last-minute impediment.

'Well now, if we're all in agreement ... Could we ask you, Leonard, to please leave the room while we discuss this issue?'

The publisher got to his feet with ill grace, and Ranelagh's eyes alighted next on me. I stood up, feeling rather uncomfortable.

'Thank you,' Ranelagh said, as if he owed me an apology. 'According to the rules, only plenary members can attend each voting session. But Leonard can show you in the mean-time the entire collection of the Vanished Tale titles in our library along the hallway. We'll call you as soon as the voting is completed.'

Chapter 13

We went out into the hallway and the publisher, nonchalantly, pointed out a glassed bookcase in four sections that rose almost to the ceiling. I thought it might show common good manners to pay attention to the titles, so I began to inspect the spines from the top shelf down. I mainly wondered if I would find one of Seldom's books there. Fortunately, the collection had been set up in alphabetical order and I found the book at once: a thin volume with the title *Through Syllogisms, and What Lewis Carroll Found There*. I wanted to find Laura Raggio's as well, but I realised I didn't know her maiden name. I turned towards Hinch to ask him, but he seemed too nervous and lost in thought, anxious about the results of the vote, and not at all interested in giving me a guided tour. I noticed that he kept pulling out chocolates from his pocket and popping them in his mouth. At one point he caught me watching him, his hand halfway to his lips, and tried to apologise.

'It appears that this whole collection is suddenly worth nothing,' he complained with bitterness. He kept casting quick, brief glances at me, all the while keeping an angry eye on the closed door of the meeting room.

'Each one of them, every time they'd finish one of their little books on Lewis Carroll, would come running to me. They begged me, they pressured me, they flattered me. Look at the number of these books, small and large. They'd put any other publisher to shame: books on Lewis Carroll's children's fiction, on his stammer, on the corns on his feet, on his sermons, on his laundry bills, on every miserable Oxford twig he ever trod on. And after that, of course, the second wave: books on the books about him, the catalogue of catalogues. I said yes to all. And when at last there is one book, one, that may allow me to recover some of all that I lost publishing the others, this is how they thank me: into the hallway, like a servant! Do you know that I had to mortgage my house, the only thing I managed to buy in a whole life dedicated to those damn books? And all this, just to match a crazy American offer. It's unfair: an international publisher has all of eternity to recover the investment. I, on the other hand, don't have that many years left to live. However,' he sighed, 'I suppose there are worse things. Just take that poor girl. You went with Arthur to the hospital, isn't that so? Did you see her afterwards? One tends to suppose that young people know each other.'

'In fact, I barely knew her, but yes, I saw her after she recovered consciousness.'

'Is that so?' Hinch said, with a spark of interest. 'And how did that happen? Because I know that some of the lot here tried to see her, but they were told that she wasn't able to speak yet, and that she preferred not to receive any visitors.'

'I accompanied Seldom when she was beginning to recover, and she asked to speak to him.'

'Ah, yes, I see. And you found her ... totally lucid? Years ago, I was struck by a car in London. I fell and hit the back of my head on the pavement. And when I woke up in the hospital, I wasn't able to remember a thing, neither the moment of the accident nor any of the preceding hours. Not even when I returned to that same street days later was I able to

recall a single image. In those days, I possessed an extraordinary memory, and yet that day was altogether lost for me.
Of course, as the years go by, you'll see that you lose almost
all of the days you've lived. But at the time, it shocked me
deeply. I was about to set up this publishing company and I
toyed for a while with the idea of calling it Black Stone Press.
The obvious choice would have been, of course, White Stone,
the symbol Carroll chose to mark his happy days, every
time he met a new girl with whom he became friends. But
what I wanted to name was almost the exact opposite: the
black-out of a memory, the days gone without trace. Finally
I chose Vanished Tale, a name that also stands as a small
homage to Carroll. Even those who keep diaries, even the
most obsessive ones, lose a day from time to time. We have
to resign ourselves to the fact that no human life is all that
interesting always, not even for its owner. But in Kristen's
case, what happened?' His eyes left the door for the first time
and attached themselves to me, expectantly, while his hand
plunged again into the pocket hiding his chocolates. 'Did she
remember everything? Did she remember just fragments?'

'She remembered ... quite a lot,' I said, feeling uncertain as
to how much I could disclose. Hinch seemed to take my hesitation as a confirmation of something else and drew closer,
as if to confide a secret.

'You know what?' he said with a conspirator's look. 'By
chance I found out that they'd placed a policeman at her door.
Don't you think it strange that there should be a policeman
looking after her? We all thought, as Arthur mentioned, that
what happened was just an accident. But I believe there's
more to it. Am I right?' He was staring at me now almost
with amusement, and there was a sly twinkle in his eyes, as
if it were the easiest thing in the world to make me reveal
my secrets.

'You couldn't have found out by chance,' I said, trying to counter-attack. 'Someone must have told you. Or did you go there yourself?'

Hinch looked at me with indignant surprise.

'No, of course not. I didn't know her that well.' And then, as if to show he had nothing to hide, he pretended he was trying to remember. 'It was Thornton Reeves who mentioned it. He was angry at her but at the same time he was her adviser, and I suppose that made him feel somewhat responsible. Even though he was told that she wasn't seeing visitors, he decided nevertheless to go to the hospital and make sure she was being well looked after. He's a very good man in spite of the fact that his manners are sometimes a bit wanting. When he asked for her, they made him wait and a policeman came down to take his name. He didn't seem surprised at that, but it set me off wondering. When someone is accidentally hit by a car one isn't given a policeman to look after one, don't you agree? My whole life, I've been a reader of detective novels, and I have a sort of antenna that makes me pay attention when one of these ... incongruous details appears. So when Thornton told me, I became intrigued. In the papers, all they said was that she'd been hit and left abandoned on the road. But I realised that there had to be something more to this, perhaps something she had said upon waking. Or a witness who might have seen what happened.' He stared at me with an inquisitive look in his eyes, and then, unable to contain himself, he asked: 'What did she tell you?'

His tone, his stare, reminded one of a nosy neighbour trying to find out the sordid details of a piece of gossip. I noticed that once again he slid his hand into his pocket. I heard the crinkling of the wrapper, and then the hungry, furtive movement of his fingers towards his mouth.

'I can't tell you anything,' I said.

'Of course, don't worry,' he said and laughed, rocking his head from side to side. 'If you can't tell me anything, then you've told me everything.'

'No,' I said, feeling furious with myself, trying to remember how much I might have revealed. 'I didn't tell you a thing.'

'Someone tried to kill her, isn't that so? That's the truth. She must have remembered something upon waking, and that's why the police are there.'

I pursed my lips and felt I was blushing under his eyes, as if he had discovered me at fault and could now guess everything by seeing right through me, without even needing me to answer his questions.

'Don't you worry,' he said. 'It's nothing that you've told me: you're transparent because you're young. But if this is something that should remain undercover, I too will know to keep my mouth shut. We publishers are accustomed to keeping secrets.'

At that moment, the door was opened. Thornton Reeves made a welcoming gesture as if greeting a prodigal son, and gave Hinch his hand with a big smile on his face. Hinch made his way back with a dignified and calm air, and when he was once again seated at his place at the table, everyone clapped warmly. Sir Richard, with a satisfied look, allowed the applause to die out before speaking.

'Dear Leonard, I'm pleased to tell you that the vote was unanimous. Each of us thought back to a book of ours published in your series, and we recalled everything we owe to you.'

Hinch nodded, and seemed truly touched, no trace of that anger with which he had spoken to me, like an actor who quite naturally puts on his mask again to take his place on stage. I asked myself if this apparent agreement, the relaxed and friendly faces listening with approval, might reflect the habitual atmosphere of these meetings, the one Seldom wished to bring back once more. When it was his turn to give thanks, Hinch behaved impeccably: he was modest, witty, amiable. He even had a little surprise up his sleeve: he confessed that he had hoped that the Brotherhood would vote in favour of Vanished Tale, and he had taken upon himself to invite a journalist from the University Cultural Channel. If they were all in agreement, he said, now that there was a perfect quorum, he might be allowed to call him in. He had been promised that the news about the publication of the Lewis Carroll diaries would appear on the University channel and also on national television that very night.

There was a chorus of excited mumblings. I leaned over towards Seldom.

'I had a rather odd conversation with Hinch outside in the hallway,' I said. 'I'd like to tell you about it.'

Seldom nodded.

'Wait for me in the Bear Inn; when this is over, we'll talk.' He lowered his voice to a whisper. 'I too have something to tell you.'

Chapter 14

As I went downstairs, I saw two men carrying a camera and a reflective umbrella, and, behind them, the journalist, mic ready in his hand, a tall, very thin man with curly grey hair. He was the same man who'd interviewed me the previous year for the *Oxford Times*, and who'd sniffed around Seldom and myself since the first of those past murders. I tried to remember his name: Anders or Anderson. We stared at each other in mutual surprise.

'I thought you'd have returned to Argentina by now,' he said with a slightly ironic tone.

'I thought you worked for the *Oxford Times*,' I said, trying to imitate his tone.

'Yes indeed, but I work in the crime section and Oxford is after all a village, a peaceful village. I've not had much to do since our last encounter. Only domestic incidents, Japanese students committing suicide, car crashes, that sort of thing . . . A young woman was hit by a car a few days ago, but she wasn't even killed, which makes my job even more difficult. So I'm putting in a few extra hours at the University channel.' He cocked a finger at me pretending to pull a trigger. 'But if you happen to hear of a murder, please let me know.'

I walked down St Aldate's to the almost invisible passage-way off Blue Boar Street, and sat waiting with a beer in my hand, amusing myself by inspecting the wall oddly covered with ties, until Seldom arrived, half an hour later. He was carrying a pile of books that he dropped on the table.

'Sorry I'm late,' he said. 'Kristen asked me for several volumes of Lewis Carroll's correspondence, and I had to fill out the forms to take them out.'

He went to get his own pint at the bar and when he returned, he carelessly piled the books on the floor by his chair to make room for himself and his beer.

'You go first,' he said.

I tried to reconstruct as best I could the main points of my conversation with Leonard Hinch, but when I finished I didn't notice any reaction in Seldom except a slight nod, as if he hadn't caught the punchline. I said it again: 'You see? Thornton Reeves decided to go to the hospital, even though he too must have been told that Kristen wasn't allowed to see anyone.'

Seldom raised his eyebrows and gave my suspicions a second chance.

'You think that Thornton went to the hospital, let's say, in order to finish her off?'

I wasn't sure if he was still speaking in earnest or if he was pulling my leg, like when he'd carry one of my mathematical ideas to their absurd end, in order to point out an error.

'Not necessarily,' I said, 'but perhaps he wanted to find out how much she remembered about the incident. Imagine that it was he who had run her over. At least he'd want to make certain that she hadn't seen him. And after all,' I said, feeling somewhat offended, 'didn't we ourselves call the police because we were afraid that something else could happen to her in the hospital? That someone might want, as you say, to finish her off?'

'You're right,' he conceded. 'But according to what you've

told me, how much Kristen remembers of the incident is something that seems to interest Leonard Hinch, isn't that so?' He remained silent for a moment, in one of his thinking moods, until he looked at me once more. 'You know what's bothering me, deep down inside? I can't manage to see any one of them as the suspect. In detective stories it's easy to believe that every one of the characters could be the guilty party, but in real life the opposite is almost always true: we have difficulty believing that someone we know is a criminal. The police drag off the street a handcuffed man who's buried seven wives in his garden, they unearth the bodies one after the other, and even then, the neighbours say they can't believe it. "He was such a charming man!" they say. "Always saying hello and giving us gardening tips." And I feel much the same about our lot. That's why I wanted you to come with me, someone who might be able to see them with different eyes. When we were in there voting and we unanimously chose Hinch, I felt that my previous suspicions were ridiculous, that everything was normal once again. I've known Thornton and his arrogance ever since high school, and I can very well imagine that he didn't consider himself just an ordinary visitor. It's possible that he thought that if he went in person to the hospital, they'd let him in because of who he was. And I'm still inclined to believe that all he wanted to do was ask her for an explanation, or even to offer his help, because he felt responsible for her, just as he said. But then again, we can't discard anything. It might be useful to find out if anyone else went to the hospital.'

'And what was it you wanted to tell me?' I asked, somewhat disheartened.

'On Tuesday morning, Petersen called me. He wanted me to put him in touch with a mathematician or a physicist who specialised in the analysis of sound recordings. The video camera that recorded the traffic on the Kidlington roundabout also recorded the noise level, because of noise pollution, but the site of Kristen's incident is somewhat further away, and the sound of the impact cannot be heard on the tape. Partly, they suppose, because of the rain that night, but also because of the wall of a tractor plant that stands in the way. Even so, through the opening of a vacant plot, you can see the billboards of British Telecom; they are sufficiently large to hope that the sound might have bounced off them, like a sort of echo. It seems that there was a pioneering study by an Argentinian physicist on the trajectory of echoes in a certain criminal case that Petersen has heard about, and he wants to try something like that here.'

I didn't know anything about that Argentinian physicist, but I had seen in various parts of the city the immense billboards of the publicity campaign of the British phone company, reminding its customers to add a 1 to the beginning of every phone number. Under the slogan 'It's *One* to Remember', they'd dug up the glories of Britain's past, from Vivien Leigh and Laurence Olivier to Jackie Stewart, John Lennon and Winston Churchill. I had even seen in the vicinity of University Park a billboard with Fred Perry holding up his Wimbledon trophy. I tried to imagine how this physics billiard game would be played out with sound waves.

'And what does Petersen expect from such a study?'

'Something akin to a reconstruction of the soundscape. To allow him to pinpoint, if possible, the exact time of the impact, and, above all, to detect if there was a previous sound of a car braking or the screech of tyres. This would be evidence in favour of the accident theory. Or, on the contrary, if it were to reveal the sound of a sudden acceleration, as if someone had been waiting for her ... And also, whatever might be heard from the impact itself: if the car stopped or didn't stop, and in what direction it sped away. In any case, I told him he already had in his staff someone who could perform this sort of test perfectly, and I sent him to see Leyton Howard. And you know Leyton: I spoke with him this morning and he had already been on two consecutive nights to the site in order to record the sounds that can be heard regularly in the evening. He recorded owls and ravens and the barking of dogs in order to have parameters of intensity and height as points of reference. He asked for a squad of men to carry out the topographical measurements. He got a fleet of cars to be brought out, and he recorded the sound of the brakes and the acceleration of several different kinds of motors. He spent yesterday analysing the tape. He managed to filter out the patter of the rain, and he managed to separate the sounds in a time span according to the different frequencies.'

'And did he find anything?'

'At first, all you could hear on the tape, very faintly, was a single sound: the cawing of a raven apparently flying away. But when he studied visually the images of the waves on the frequency detector, he discovered the peaks of two echoes, and when he amplified them, he found something interesting. The first echo was in the low frequencies: it was the repercussion of the impact. The second one, immediately following the first, was the echo of the raven's caw, as if the noise had frightened it.'

'And what conclusion can we draw from this?' I asked, puzzled.

'Very little, but at the same time, quite sufficient. Because when Leyton calculated the distance from the raven to the camera, and also to the billboard, during the time between the audible caw and its echo, he managed to trace a curve of possible points for the location of the raven. And one of those points was at the top of the plant's wall. Indeed, the raven nests in that same street, and furthermore, its caw lies in the same frequency as the expected sounds of a horn or a braking car. Therefore, the raven becomes something like an indirect witness: if those other sounds are not heard, it is not because they were covered, or because they were too weak, but because they never existed. The driver didn't honk the horn, nor was there any attempt to brake. That will be his conclusion in his report to Petersen.'

'That's curious ...' And I tried to shape in my mind an idea not yet fully formed. 'Leyton achieved something similar to what I'm intending to do with the writing reconstruction program. We can't hear the sounds directly, but we still have the echoes. And in the photo Kristen received,' I said, trying to follow the same track, 'we might be able to follow, up to a certain point, Lewis Carroll's movements while setting up the sitter's pose ...'

'Yes, that's true,' Seldom said. 'What is real is always a projection, the embedded trace of something that walked in other dimensions. And as to that photo, it hasn't yielded any new clue. Petersen took the trouble of asking, one by one, all the possible correspondents that Kristen could remember about the photo she received: none admitted having left it.'

'And so? You think that the photo could signal the beginning of a series? That there'll be another ...?'

'I believe,' Seldom said, 'that Kristen should reveal, rather sooner than later, what that sentence says. The truth is that I still fear for her life, and I was asking myself ...' He stopped, undecided how to carry on, as if he felt it necessary to gather his strength before touching on a particularly delicate subject. 'I was asking myself, since we last saw her at the hospital ...' He started again, on the verge of a stammer, shifting his eyes in sudden discomfort, ' ... whether what she refused to tell me, what she refused to tell any of the members of the Brotherhood, she might not feel she's able to tell under certain ... certain proper circumstances, to someone else, someone closer to her own age, someone for whom she might perhaps feel a special kind of trust ...' And he left the sentence suspended, hoping that I would finish it.

'You mean,' I attempted to continue, the image of Sharon fleetingly crossing my mind, 'that she might have a close girlfriend or boyfriend to whom she might have revealed what's in the sentence?'

'No,' said Seldom, somewhat disappointed. 'I'd be very surprised if Kristen had a girlfriend with whom she's close; I've always seen her on her own in the cafeteria, she didn't even have other students with whom to study. Nor do I think she's got a boyfriend: we'd have seen him in the hospital. And you yourself saw her leave the cinema alone. No, I wasn't thinking of someone to whom she might already have told the contents of the sentence, but rather someone to whom she *might* tell it.' And he looked up at me again, as if he couldn't find a clearer way of expressing himself. Only then did I fully realise what it was that he meant, and something in that sudden illumination, as well as the fact that I hadn't burst out laughing, gave some relief to his discomfort.

'I couldn't help noticing,' he carried on, 'that you two seemed to get on together, when we were walking out of the Institute. When I went with her to the bus stop, Kristen asked me a couple of questions which at the time I found odd and unusual for her, until I realised that she had used her feminine wiles simply to find out if you had an Oxford girlfriend.'

I blushed slightly, and for the sake of saying something, blurted out:

'How funny. That same night I wondered, because of the easy manner with which you two left together ...' And here I stopped myself, seeing the astonishment on his face, and wondered how to soften the words that were pouring from my lips. ' ... that ... you might have gone for walks together often.'

'Yes,' he said. 'Of course. We went for walks together a few times, especially when I was her postgraduate tutor. But not in the way I believe you're thinking.' And here he smiled, amused. 'I've never allowed myself anything of the sort with a student. Or, to tell the truth, almost never,' he said, as if remembering a slightly uncomfortable and long-past exception that went against the virtuous principle he had imposed on himself. 'Certainly not with someone this young. And of course, I would not be talking to you in this way if I didn't fear for her life. I thought that perhaps you could approach her, exactly as a friend of the kind she never had. And even if she doesn't tell you anything more about the paper, that would allow us to keep an eye out and make sure that nothing else happens to her.'

We sat in silence. The equivocal mission he had wanted me to undertake had been left floating in the air between us and had begun to unveil a convoluted maze of consequences and possibilities.

'If there were the slightest chance that Kristen might recover,' I said, 'I would surely attempt it, even if there were no mysterious piece of paper involved. In fact, I *had* thought of trying, but that was ... before. Perhaps now things have changed for her as well. When we went to see her and I tried to help her, she pushed me away.'

'Yes, I noticed that too, but I read it as the contrary: that she didn't want to appear as disabled, that she didn't want you to feel pity for her. It was a reflex due to pride, her attempt to show herself still of one piece.'

'But you don't think it would be horrible of me to try, in her present state, to raise ... her expectations?'

Seldom held a hand to his face as if an image had come to him that he wanted to blot out.

'You're absolutely right. It's that I can't bring myself to conceive that Kristen will not be able to walk again. Yes, it would be something terribly cruel. Please, forget the whole thing.'

But the 'thing', now made explicit, refused to disappear so suddenly, maybe because for a moment I had imagined myself to be like the hero of one of Henry James's novels who must subtly seduce a woman in order to gain access to some secret papers in an ancient Venetian palazzo. Or perhaps because, with greater intensity, in spite of everything I wanted to see her again, and thinking of her I too had forgotten that she was condemned to spend the rest of her life in a wheelchair.

'I think I can visit her,' I said, 'and talk to her as much as possible, and help her with everything she might need from outside the hospital, without allowing this to mean anything else ... in whatever other sense you like. Even if she doesn't say anything to me about the paper, at least I might be able to rescue her from the clutches of those Methodist hags.'

'Just for that reason alone it might be worth the attempt,' Seldom said. 'However, I no longer think my idea was a good one, and I would not want to add more suffering to everything she's already enduring. But if you think you can manage it without anyone getting the wrong idea ...' He swallowed the last of his beer and pointed to the volumes of Lewis Carroll's correspondence piled up at his feet. 'I promised to get these books for her and we're still in visiting times. Do you want to take them to her yourself?'

Chapter 15

When I arrived at the hospital and gave my name at the reception, they called Kristen from the switchboard, took down my name and the number of my identity card, and sent me to a room in the step-down unit, one floor above. I noticed that the policeman on guard was no longer there, at least not obviously visible. I knocked on the door and thought I heard a murmur inside that stopped all of a sudden. Kristen's mother opened the door just a crack, and stepped out into the hallway.

'I'm sorry,' she said, 'we were just finishing our prayer with Sister Rosaura and now Kristen wants to freshen up a bit. She didn't know you were coming.'

'How is she?' I asked.

The mother shivered as if struck by an involuntary and painful spasm.

'I think she's reached that stage when the tears dry up and resignation sets in. At least she'll be leaving soon: she's being discharged in two or three days.'

'Will she manage here in Oxford by herself? Or will you take her with you?'

'She certainly doesn't want to go back to Guildford. She's absolutely determined to stay here; she told me that she has a great task ahead. And I can't move in with her: I have to look after my own home and my garden. I fear I'll find an invasion of mice when I get back. But fortunately this angel crossed her path here in the hospital. She'll go and live with Sister Rosaura, at least to start with, till Kristen becomes accustomed ... to the wheelchair. It was a marvellous coincidence: the sister's lease is up and she was looking for someone to share the flat with, because she can't afford to pay by herself what they're asking for in the new lease. And we couldn't afford a nurse to look after Kristen all day long, and I don't think she wants me that close to her. You know: at a certain age, we parents must lose our children.'

I nodded. She looked me in the eye, and suddenly took one of my hands in hers.

'May I ask that you too look after her? I always thought she was very lonely here.'

'Of course, certainly,' I said.

She wrote down on a card Kristen's new address on Headington Hill, and I scribbled for her on a scrap of paper my own address and my number at the Institute. She tucked away the paper as if it were something precious and with some embarrassment she tapped my hand.

'I'll take advantage now that you're here and go and shop for a few things Kristen requested.'

She peered into the room and nodded towards me.

'I think you can go in now.'

I stepped into the room. Kristen was sitting up under the soft, clear light of the window with a couple of big pillows tucked behind her back. I felt, almost like a powerful weight, the sudden, serene and radiant beauty of her face, leaning towards me with a smile, as if she were aware of the effect it had on me. The bruises under her eyes had vanished, her face was luminous, and the only visible trace of the ordeal she had undergone was a small round scar left by the tube in her neck. There was something exposed and naked in that beauty that I read as a challenge or a statement. If earlier, because of her shyness, she had tried to hide her beauty as much as possible, as a sort of unrequested, uncomfortable gift, now, due to a mysterious compensatory law, she seemed to want to display it ostentatiously. I noticed as well that under her thin nightgown, thanks to a perhaps well-calculated error in the buttoning-up, her breasts sent out an equivocal message, hard to ignore. All this, I supposed, must have been a consequence of the struggle in the concealed section of her lower body, the half hidden under the sheets, accompanied by the painful, irreversible note struck by the wheelchair parked under the window. I looked into her eyes once again as if groping for an ancient thread, and it seemed as if those eyes were saying to me, halfway between pride and sadness: *This is all that is left of me.* I might have answered her, without lying, that nothing of all this mattered to me: under her recaptured look, I realised that I was no longer asking myself if I could fall in love with her but rather if I could fail to do so. She was wearing a kind of French beret that covered her head down to her eyebrows but some of her long hair had been saved. Sister Rosaura was standing in front of her, brushing with deliberate slowness the strands that fell from under the beret's rim down to Kristen's shoulders and her back. I stared for the first time into the eyes of the sister and I understood, in a flash of immediate dislike, that she might become a formidable enemy. She was still a young woman, with a resolute look and features that changed quickly from a beatific smile to a bellicose expression. She had the erect carriage of someone accustomed to making sudden practical decisions, and also a faded sexuality, not entirely resigned, that she seemed to sublimate in an excess of positive and optimistic energy. I noticed she was deliberately taking her

whole year typing out bibliographies before they allowed me to attend. Oh well,' she said helplessly, 'I suppose that in a hospital bed it becomes difficult to be informed about all that goes on.'

'It had to do with the publication of the diaries. I imagine you heard about the offer ... '

'Yes, the publishing company in the States. They couldn't stop talking about it.'

'Leonard Hinch managed to come up with an equivalent sum. They wanted to resolve the signing of the contract as soon as possible, and they discussed how much the words on your paper might change their view on Lewis Carroll. They all agreed that it wouldn't be a drastic change,' I said, and waited for her reaction.

I had the impression that she was fighting hard to restrain herself. Her eyes were on fire.

'We'll see about that,' she said. 'It will change things far beyond what they might imagine. It would almost amuse me to let them carry on, let them do their thing, write their little notes and quibbles. But how did the vote go? Did they ultimately give it to Hinch?'

'Yes,' I said.

'Until last week, there were opposite bands. No one objected? Josephine Grey? Laura Raggio? Arthur?'

'It was an absolutely unanimous decision,' I said.

She seemed suddenly saddened or overcome, as if she had been left on her own once and for all. I asked myself what she might have held against Hinch, and if he might have tried something on with her as well. But when she spoke again, I felt disconcerted, because she said with bitter equanimity: 'However, I think it was a fair decision: after all, he's published all of their books. Without exception.'

'Yes,' I said, 'they asked us both to step out while the vote was taking place. Hinch felt it was humiliating to have to wait outside and he told me the same thing: that he'd published every one of them. He also wanted to find out how you were getting on. Even though he said he didn't know you all that well.'

'Not for want of trying, but I managed to keep my distance,' she said with a hint of distaste. 'He's a pig. And Laura at least knows it for certain. However, I realise that rituals can always trump anything. The law of inertia: the first axiom of English science. And what else did he ask you about me?'

'We had a talk about memory. He said he too was hit by a car once and that he lost all memory of that day. He asked me something that I'm also curious about: if you were able to recall anything, if in all these days a detail had come back to you ...'

I saw that her lips trembled slightly as she shook her head. She made a helpless gesture.

'No, the last thing I remember is that conversation you and I had about a second life. I've thought about that conversation many times in the past few days. I would never have imagined that that second life would be a wheelchair for ever. For ever!' And tears sprang to her eyes.

I went up to the bed, sat on the edge and held out my hand. She gripped it, shaking all over, and one of her tears fell on my wrist.

'But perhaps, later on ... Medicine advances every day,' I said, feeling somewhat like a conman.

'That's what Sister Rosaura says to me: that we must pray for another miracle. And that even if that miracle does not take place, in saving my life and leaving me in this condition God surely has a purpose for me. Maybe my mission is to write that book and forget all the rest. Everything else.'

The strictly binary logic of religion, as Seldom would have said: every good thing is a gift, every suffering a test. I held back from telling her my thoughts about a god who would save her life in order to leave her in this condition, and I couldn't help thinking of Stendhal's phrase: 'God's only excuse is that He doesn't exist.'

At that moment the door opened and Sister Rosaura came back in. Kristen withdrew her hand and the sister stared at me with a look of surprise and accusation, as if I, a typical representative of the male sex, were guilty of having made Kristen cry. She chose to ignore me and spoke to Kristen in a tone that was almost a reprimand.

'It's dinnertime already, and missie hasn't had her bath. I think we should allow our visitor to leave.'

I stood up and looked straight at Kristen, seeking out her eyes while she wiped her tears. But I saw that, far from protesting, she calmly put on her glasses, while Sister Rosaura stood by her side like an impatient guardian. I stammered a goodbye and left, upset and furious.

When I reached my room at the College, I tried in vain to concentrate on Raymond Martin's book of puzzles. My eyes landed on one of the March Hare's ironic answers: 'You might just as well say that "I like what I get" is the same thing as "I get what I like"!' I still held in my palm the warm memory of Kristen's tight hand and of her tears. Did I have, or was I about to get, with her what I liked? Above all, could I some day like what I got? I suddenly remembered that the evening news would announce the publication of the diaries, and I switched through the channels until I found the university's. The segment had already started. The journalist – in the end his name was Anderson – was holding his fat mic in front of Leonard Hinch and, behind him, there could be seen all the members of the Brotherhood, looking elderly and frail. Seldom seemed almost a youngster among them. Hinch was talking about how the work would be divided among them, and explained that the volumes would be published one a year, with exhaustive research into all the contemporary personalities mentioned by Lewis Carroll. The journalist, somewhat surprised, asked how many years the entire project would require. 'Nine volumes, nine years,' Hinch said proudly, and the camera swept from left to right, almost ironically, over the bony and wizened faces, as if the cameraman were asking, like I was then, how many of them would live long enough to see it finished.

Chapter 16

During the following week I sent Kristen a couple of emails to ask her how she was doing, but I didn't get an answer. I wondered if she had a computer of her own at home or, like me, and like almost all students at the time, she had to use the ones at the Institute. In that case, I supposed, I'd have to wait a very long while to receive news from her, and I made up my mind to go at some point to the address on Headington Hill that her mother had given me. Nor did I see Seldom during all that time: when I climbed up to his office on Wednesday, I saw a notice on his door saying he'd be in Cambridge for the rest of the week. I knew he was attending one of those scholarly algebra seminars that had become a cloak-and-dagger hush-hush affair. Fermat's last theorem, the white whale of mathematicians, the enigma that remained unsolved for over three hundred years and for which Andrew Wiles had believed he'd found the solution – an announcement that had gone round the world as the triumphal achievement of the century in Mathematics – had twisted itself around one more time like a wounded monster in a B film and, during the period of checking the proof, the specialists assigned to review it had detected a small gap in the calculations that no one had found a way to fill. Months went by and the proof could not yet be published. This was keeping on tenterhooks the other brotherhood, older and vaster, of the Pythagoreans, even though the subject was only spoken about in sheepish whispers. I knew that Seldom belonged to the innermost circle of the peer reviewers, but he never breathed a word about the subject. I decided to take advantage of my week to finish up my scholarship report. I finally set a date with Emily Bronson to tell her about the results I had come up with and to ask her for her signature, still missing on some of the forms, and not imagining the consequences of the trivial conversation I would have with her at the end of our meal. Emily was in excellent spirits. Holding the paper very close to her face, she had scrutinised with her single eye the formulae and codes of the program, uttering under her breath slight grunts of agreement as she proceeded to decipher the instructions. As soon as I started to explain the general idea, she immediately grasped the possibility of a joint paper, and seemed delighted by the copious references to her work in the bibliography. Before ordering our coffee, we had solved all the remaining mathematical questions and she gladly signed the forms. We sat in peaceful silence for a moment and suddenly she seemed to remember something.

'Would you by any chance be interested in purchasing a car for your remaining time in Oxford? There's a visiting professor at my college who's about to fly back to his country and can't seem to be able to sell it. I believe he's lowering the price day by day, and by now it must be dirt cheap.'

'How much is dirt cheap?' I asked with little hope.

'Oh, thirteen or fourteen hundred pounds, I suppose,' she said. 'I think it's a five-door Citroën, which I believe is a very good make, though I know nothing about cars. It has only one catch,' she said. 'It would have to be taken very soon for a check-up; its MOT has almost expired.'

Thirteen hundred pounds was my monthly stipend as a

bursary and it was unthinkable for me to dispose of a sum like the one suggested by Emily, but something in what she had said brought back the echo of a conversation on cars that I'd heard in the visitors' office shortly after my arrival one year earlier.

'Suppose this professor can't sell his car and the day of departure is upon him,' I said. 'This is something that must happen quite often, isn't it? Because the check-up is usually quite expensive.'

'Of course,' Emily said. 'In general, the MOT isn't worth the visitor's investment because afterwards they don't have enough time to sell the car.'

'And what do they do if they can't?'

Emily gave me a puzzled look, as if it were the first time she had been asked to ponder the question.

'Sometimes they ask the professor who has hosted them to try to sell it for a while longer ... Other times they just leave it in the Institute's car park. Or I suppose they sometimes abandon it at the door of the place they've rented.'

Now I recalled with more precision the joking conversation between the two very young visiting professors.

'But isn't there also a place behind the Community Park that is a sort of limbo for abandoned cars that are still in working condition? A place where car-less students sometimes go to try to start them, and take their girlfriends for a spin?'

Emily blushed slightly, as I had mentioned a sinful place, beyond the pale.

'I may have heard of something like that. But you must know that driving a car without its MOT is considered a very serious offence in this country,' she said as a warning.

I laughed.

'Don't you worry, I wasn't intending to do anything of the

sort,' I said, and I thought that what I would do as soon as I returned to the Institute would be to write to Seldom and tell him about this.

I didn't expect him to answer that very same day, but when I checked my emails one last time before leaving, I had a brief message from him in my inbox. He agreed with me that it was a place that should be checked out. He wondered if Petersen hadn't already done so and told me that he had forwarded my email to the inspector, adding a line to pose the question.

On the Monday of the following week, halfway through the afternoon, I heard at last his steps and his voice on the staircase. He was chatting with a couple of students. I waited half an hour and went up to see him. The door of his office was ajar and there were a few more students waiting their turn in the hallway. But when he leaned out and saw me lurking there, he said with a smile that I should wait for him at the Little Clarendon pub, and that he'd have a beer with me as soon as he finished.

I had never been to that pub before. It had a very long counter of polished wood and two or three television sets switched on but muted. I sat across from one that was showing snippets of a tennis tournament and became absorbed by the possibilities of a tiebreak. When Seldom appeared I politely asked him how it had gone in Cambridge.

'Better than we might have imagined,' he said with a mixture of happiness and relief. 'One of Wiles's old students, Richard Taylor, managed to complete the missing link at last. Now we can say for certain that the theorem has been proven and that will finally be published.'

I was thoughtful for a moment.

'How many people in the world would you say might have been able to detect the gap in the original demonstration?'

Seldom stared at me with a puzzled smile.

'Ten or fifteen, I suppose: those present in the classroom the first time he set out his demonstration. And I should exclude myself because nowadays I would not have the necessary concentration to follow all the steps. Perhaps only that group of half-a-dozen referees who were able to read it in detail.'

'And are they not the same six people who will now attest to the correctness of the proof?'

'What do you mean?' said Seldom, somewhat irritated. 'They are all extraordinary mathematicians. The proof *is* now correct. There are no doubts about it.'

I tried to reformulate it otherwise.

'I suppose what I meant is that the very idea of a mathematical demonstration, from the days of antiquity onwards, was imagined in what I would call a democratic way. And not only for extraordinary mathematicians: anyone could be led by the hand, and each one of the little logical steps would become obvious, irrefutable. You wouldn't even require a human intelligence to follow these steps, even a computer might be able to corroborate them. But with the complexity that mathematics has achieved throughout the centuries we now have something like a paradox: in each specialised field there are only four or five people who understand what it's about, and these same people end up corroborating each other's demonstrations by means of peer reviews.'

'The way you say it sounds as if it were a consecrated truth, a fodder of sects and cults,' Seldom said. 'It's not at all like that and you should know it. The demonstration will be written out and anyone will be allowed to tear it apart taking the same logical steps applied to any other. In the future, anyone with enough patience will be able to detect an error if there is one. You yourself, if you gave it a couple of years, might be able to follow it. And in a few decades there'll be many more than five or six who'll understand it. What seems difficult to us now will seem natural later on. However, it's true that soon we are about to suffer from another problem, in all its bewildering breadth: Ulam's dilemma. The incessant multiplication of papers in every field is already exceeding our capacity to peruse them one by one and soon there'll not be enough mathematicians to corroborate the number of theorems put forward in the hope of publication. But as far as *this* result is concerned, you may rest assured: we scrutinised it very carefully, statement after statement, and through all available eyes. Fermat's last theorem has been demonstrated conclusively beyond all reasonable doubt.'

He lifted his pint as if bidding me to join him in a toast.

'And I have another piece of news for you that you'll be interested in: your intuition about the car turned out to be correct. Petersen called me this morning. On the very first day, they checked the place because it's from there that students steal the cars they use to race one another in the outskirts at night. But he decided to go again himself with a forensic team, and they discovered that one of the cars had been thoroughly cleaned. That is to say: what aroused Petersen's suspicions was that it had been *too* thoroughly cleaned. Inside, they were unable to find fingerprints either on the steering wheel or on the door handles, but outside, on the front bumper, they found traces of human skin. The car did indeed belong to a visiting professor who left Oxford almost a month ago. And something else: whoever started it up didn't have a key but jacked the cables.'

'That should tell us something, don't you think?' I said. 'Because it requires a certain skill. I wonder which of the members of the Brotherhood could perform that sort of trick. I can't imagine Josephine Grey trying to jumpstart a car.'

'Until a few years ago you'd have been sorely mistaken,' Seldom said. 'Josephine was one of the first women in England to race professionally. When we go to visit her, you'll see all her cups and medals. And later she became a car collector. But I too asked myself who could have known how to start the motor in that way. During the ride back from Cambridge I tried to remember. Raymond Martin, of course, is one. During the war he was assigned to an armoured division and had to learn to handle all sorts of vehicles. And Richard Ranelagh as well; he received his training with MI5: they must have taught him this kind of trick. And Thornton Reeves surely would know how to do it.'

'How come you're so certain about Reeves?' I asked.

Seldom stopped making his list as if I'd found him at fault. He smiled sheepishly.

'We were fellow students and we jumpstarted his father's car a few times when his father wouldn't give him the keys.'

'So you would also have known how to do it,' I said maliciously, but his face grew dark.

'I never drove a car again after my accident,' he said.

'And the rest?' I asked. 'Albert Raggio? Laura? Henry Haas?'

'I'm not sure about Albert and Laura, though I know they have a car: every summer they take a tour through the Continent. Henry Haas also drove a car in the past, a small Volkswagen, but I think he sold it quite some time ago.'

'And Leonard Hinch?'

'Yes, Hinch as well. I suppose he would know how to do it better than anyone else: his father had a garage and, as an adolescent, Hinch would work with him every summer. I remember he offered to rescue what remained of my car after the accident, to try to see if he could build it up again, but I preferred to let it be turned into scrap metal.'

'That's interesting,' I said. 'Hinch was very keen to know how much Kristen remembered when she woke up, and now you tell me this. Don't you think—'

But I stopped because Seldom was pointing impatiently to the images on the television screen behind me. We both kept silent, simultaneously mesmerised by what we were seeing: on the screen, among the images of the local news, there appeared Anderson's interview with Hinch and, following that, a photograph of the publisher in which he appeared young, trim, with almost all of his hair, and a caption beneath it saying that he had been found in his office, dead.

We asked the barman to raise the volume. Apparently, death was due to some complication of Hinch's diabetes, and the report focused mainly on his professional career, showing a series of images of the books he had published and photos of him standing with some of Britain's best-known writers, as if this were one of the customary obituaries for someone from the local cultural scene.

Nevertheless, Seldom insisted that we leave at once to call on Inspector Petersen.

Chapter 17

'I wanted you to come here because there's something I want to show you,' Petersen said.

We were in his office at the police station. Nothing had changed there since the previous year. The same strict high-backed chairs, the same sturdy metal cabinets and, on his desk, the same silver frame with the photo of his daughter frozen in her childhood. Sunlight was beginning to dim slowly and I thought that, if I looked through the window, I would see the same eternal regatta glide down the same golden river. Nor had the inspector, now that I could observe him in his natural habitat, altered in the slightest, except for the slow progression of his grey hairs. I noticed only one single different detail: when he offered us coffee, he ordered a tea for himself, and told us in a resigned tone that his doctor kept crossing out more and more of the things he enjoyed in life.

'The body was discovered by the cleaning lady who comes in the morning,' he told us. 'Hinch's secretary is on holiday, but this woman has the keys to the office. She found him on the floor next to his desk, as if he had tried to stand up but hadn't managed to reach the door. Hinch wasn't married, and doesn't have any next-of-kin, and fortunately this woman called us at once, without touching anything. The forensic pathologist was puzzled. When he turned the body

over, Hinch's features were distorted and rigid, his mouth
wide open and his shirt still damp, as if he had been sweat-
ing profusely before dying. Because of these unmistakable
clinical signs, the pathologist reached his conclusions immediately, though he's conducting, as we speak, one last blood
test. Apparently, Hinch was poisoned with the chocolates
that were in a box on his desk. The substance used was our
old friend aconite, also known as monkshood or wolfsbane.
It's a very poisonous substance even in small doses: barely
three milligrams are enough to kill a man. A single chocolate
would have been lethal, but aconite also produces a sudden
fall in the blood sugar level. We know that Hinch was diabetic and, according to what his cleaning lady told us, he
reached for one of these chocolates every time his glucose
was low. The box had just been opened and there were four
or five wrappers in the waste-paper basket. The pathologist
surmised that the first poisoned chocolate lowered his blood
sugar and that he probably ate three or four before beginning
to feel the more severe symptoms of the poisoning. Whoever
sent that box of chocolates must have known him well and
hated him intensely. Apparently, it's a rather horrible death:
an unstoppable perspiration that soaks the clothes, massive
cramps, vomiting, a burning sensation on the tongue and in
the chest. And on top of all this, according to the pathologist,
the victim has the impression that his eyes are popping out of
their sockets and that his head is becoming larger and larger,
as if it were about to explode. Fortunately, Hinch didn't share
these chocolates with anyone else.'

'That would never have happened,' Seldom said, and proceeded to tell Petersen about Hinch's *dolce avarizia*.

'I see,' Petersen said. 'Someone who knew him well and
wanted to kill only him. We found this card on the desk next
to the ribbon of the box.' And he pulled out a printed card

inscribed in copperplate handwriting with only four words: 'The Lewis Carroll Brotherhood'. At the bottom there was a picture of the White Rabbit dressed in his chequered waist-coat, consulting his pocket-watch.

Seldom examined it for a moment and pulled from his wallet a card to which he compared it.

'All the members of the Brotherhood have cards like this with our names and Tenniel's drawing,' he said, placing one card on the other to show Petersen the edges. 'Whoever sent this card had only to cut off the top strip with the name of the bearer so that it would seem like a gift from the entire Brotherhood. Hinch probably thought it was a polite gesture to placate the frictions concerning the contract to publish the diaries, and he opened the box without suspecting that anything was amiss. Who received the box? Could you speak with his secretary?'

'Yes, we reached her in Bristol. She seemed utterly dis-traught. She's certain of never having seen or handled the box. But she told us that much of the correspondence that arrived at the publisher's office was simply left in the pigeon-hole at the entrance. Hinch had a pigeonhole installed large enough to receive hefty manuscripts. I suppose he was trying to avoid as far as possible meeting face to face with all those who brought him their works-in-progress.'

'So anyone simply coming up to the office door could have left the chocolate box,' Seldom said in a low voice, as if speaking to himself.

'Yes,' Petersen said, 'I don't think that we will get any fur-ther going down that path. But there's something else that I wanted you to see. When we examined the box, we lifted the plastic bottom and there, underneath it, we found ... this.'

He reached across the desk to show us a photo even more alarming than the first one. It depicted a girl no more than seven years old, totally naked like the first, lying on the grass with both her hands behind her head and her legs slightly drawn up. But this time, the white triangle of the pubis appeared entirely exposed. It looked like a photograph taken in a lonely wood, though I realised that this image too had been cut out and pasted on the painted background. The posture was carefully arranged, the arms were lifted so as to expose the breast and the armpits, the hair had been combed to one side, held behind the head by the small hands. One of the legs was bent behind the other so that the triangle of the pubis jutted forward.

Petersen, with an uncomfortable cough, asked Seldom if this photograph told him anything more. He too, I think, seemed astonished to see with such crudity this dubious aspect of Lewis Carroll.

Seldom made an attempt to think out loud. Both photographs, both aggressions, were seemingly intended to provoke this effect: to bring into the open, in the most strident way possible, with a forceful focus on the murders, Lewis Carroll's inclination, perhaps as a warning not to publish the diaries.

'The Brotherhood has always displayed a rather cautious and benevolent attitude concerning this matter. But apparently someone, perhaps a crusader against paedophilia, is of another mind and wants to make crystal clear with these attacks his or her condemnation of Lewis Carroll's character.'

'Yes, that seems reasonable enough,' said Petersen.

'And yet, I can't bring myself to believe in this fully,' Seldom said. 'I think I know quite well each one of the members of the Brotherhood and I can't imagine any one of them thinking in this primitive, coarse away about Lewis Carroll. And far less, that they might have committed these crimes. Unless there's someone acting as a mole among us, someone who has been putting on a show all this time, in all our meetings and even in his or her own books on Lewis Carroll.'

'Maybe there's some other explanation that might come out of the investigation ... before there's another death, I hope. As for now, according to our official procedures,' Petersen said, 'I have to ask you for absolute secrecy concerning these photographs. For the time being, we will not even say that Hinch's death was murder. On the one hand, we don't want the information about the photographs being leaked to the press, and then having someone getting rid of his favourite enemy by merely placing a photograph by Lewis Carroll on the body. On the other, there's something else I want you to be aware of. I had a chat with Sir Richard Ranelagh and asked him to tell me about the Brotherhood in greater detail, and so I learned that a Royal Personage is your honorary president. You can imagine how this piece of information startled me.'

'It's a merely symbolic position,' Seldom said. 'He has never attended any of our meetings. It was an affiliation that Richard managed to get through his contacts in order to impress our foreign correspondents, and allow us to exchange material with colleges and Carrollian circles around the world.'

'Yes, that's what he told me as well; nonetheless this constrains me to be even more cautious, and I'll have to inform MI5 about the matter. I don't think the Royal Personage would be amused to see himself involved in a scandal of murder and paedophiliac photographs. I'll ask you please not to have any contact with any journalist. I know that one of them, Anderson, was sniffing around yesterday at the morgue.'

With that, Petersen seemed to put an end to the conversation and stood up to accompany us to the door. When he was about to open it for us, Seldom turned round and asked point-blank: 'And what do *you* think about the two cases?'

Petersen smiled vaguely, as if he had not expected such a direct question.

Chapter 18

'Do you have the impression that Petersen suspects Albert Raggio and his wife?' I asked Seldom as soon as we were downstairs.

'No, I don't think he said it with such a literal intention,' Seldom answered. 'Nor do I think that he was referring strictly to a married couple, but perhaps, for instance, to a pair of accomplice lovers.' He added with an ironic smile and a high-pitched voice: 'Darling, you tried it your way using brute force, I prefer to try my own way now.'

'But in that case,' I said, 'the motive would disappear. Why would a pair of lovers confabulate to denounce this aspect of Lewis Carroll? Instead, I can well imagine a married couple, with a small child who's been approached by a paedophile, using the Alice books as bait, or some other of Lewis Carroll's tricks. A paedophile who attacked her and left her with a severe trauma ...'

Seldom stood still and looked me in the eyes.

'Have you been speaking with Laura Raggio, by any chance?'

'No,' I said, surprised. 'I was thinking of a story I read in my adolescence, "If I Should Die Before I Wake". But why do you ask?'

'Albert and Laura had a daughter, many years ago. She was

called Albertina and, as far as I know, she was an intelligent and happy child, charming, and beautiful like her mother. I once saw a picture of her. She was also one of the best students in her school. When she was about ten, she became a fan of Lewis Carroll's books. And one day, the day before her twelfth birthday, she mysteriously committed suicide.'

'Committed suicide?' I repeated in astonishment.

'She threw herself into the river from the bridge. I've always believed that this was the main reason the Raggios approached the Brotherhood. Shortly after I'd met them, they showed me several times the Lewis Carroll books that their daughter had annotated, with the drawings she made in the margins, and they would mention her whenever they could. For a time I thought that the daughter was alive because they always spoke of her in the present, until Richard and Raymond told me the ghastly story. But I never knew the reasons for her suicide. However, I don't think Petersen was thinking of them, even though perhaps he might know something more about it: I believe he was in charge of the investigation at the time. However, I was intrigued by another of his comments. Do you have a moment to go with me into Waterstones? There's a title on my old school reading-list that I'd like to consult.'

We were close to the bookshop and I followed him through one of the corridors that led to the section of classics set up in alphabetical order. Seldom crouched down to look through the 'W's and with a small gesture of triumph extracted Oscar Wilde's *Lord Arthur Savile's Crime*.

'I knew I'd find it here: maybe they still set it as an obligatory text in school,' he said. He started to flip through it from halfway to the beginning, turning the pages quickly, seeking a single word which he knew he'd recognise once he saw it, as if sniffing out a clue, until he seemed to find what he was looking for. He first read silently to himself and seemed somewhat disappointed.

'Here it is, and yet it isn't. Sometimes sentences disappear from books. I remembered that Lord Arthur Savile intended to use aconite to commit his crime. I remembered there was a description of its effects. And yet it doesn't say much ... '

I asked him for the book that he held open in his hand and I read out loud: '*Lord Arthur was a good deal puzzled at the technical terms used in both books, and had begun to regret that he had not paid more attention to his classics at Oxford, when in the second volume of Erskine, he found a very interesting and complete account of the properties of aconite, written in fairly clear English. It seemed to him to be exactly the poison he wanted. It was swift – indeed, almost immediate, in its effect – perfectly painless, and when taken in the form of a gelatine capsule, the mode recommended by Sir Mathew, not by any means unpalatable.* I don't quite know what you're looking for,' I said. 'But perhaps you con- sulted the volumes by Erskine mentioned here ... '

Seldom, with a puzzled look, took the book again and reread the paragraph in its entirety.

'But of course. That must have been it. In those early days I was terribly impressed by things like that.'

We asked one of the attendants for Erskine's *Toxicology*. It had been long out of print, she said, but she guided us nevertheless to the Natural Sciences section and took down from one of the shelves an impressive volume on the history of poisons. We looked in the index for aconite and Seldom followed the description feverishly, as if he felt he was once again on the right track.

'Here it is,' he said and read out loud: '*The victim of the poisoning has the impression that his head grows incom- mensurably; a sensation that then extends to the rest of the body and to the extremities.* That is what Petersen told us. The impression that the body grows large. What does that remind you of? Doesn't it resemble the episode in which Alice nibbles "a very small cake" and suddenly starts to grow and keeps on growing?'

'True enough,' I said.

'And you remember what Kristen told us, that she felt as if she had soared through the air "like a sky-rocket"? I hadn't realised it then, but that's what Bill the Lizard says when he comes down the chimney and Alice gives him a sharp kick that sends him flying.'

'You mean to say that this might be a series? Crimes based on the Alice books? The Wonderland murders? Shouldn't we go back at once and say all this to the inspector?'

Seldom hesitated and slowly closed the book.

'After all, I'm a mathematician. You'll understand that I don't feel very comfortable with an induction in two separate cases.'

I stared at him, scarcely able to believe my ears. I suppose he saw the disapproval in my face.

'Would you rather wait for the next murder to confirm it?' I asked.

'No,' he said somewhat uneasily. 'I would prefer to make some sense of what we know up to now. To try to imagine the motives behind the person who's doing these things. The purpose is to keep something secret or, on the contrary, is it to bring it out into the open? We don't even know this. Is it really a campaign to denounce Lewis Carroll's paedophilia? I don't believe that either. Doesn't it seem somewhat outdated now, a hundred years after the events? Would it not have been enough to publish a sober critical piece in the papers? I'm also concerned by Petersen's strategy. Of course, it seems reasonable to hide the fact that Hinch was poisoned and the appearance of the photographs. But isn't it like a challenge that might lead whoever is behind all this to plan a third and more drastic attack that would be impossible to keep under wraps? I don't know. Perhaps we should go back to the origin of the problem: Kristen's role in all this. Were you able to speak to her about it?'

I was obliged to answer that I had not even seen her again. Seldom became thoughtful.

'But now I think you should definitely go,' he said, 'and take her a copy of the photo we've just seen, and tell her about the circumstances of Hinch's death. She, more than anyone, has the right to know. To know everything.'

'Do you think this might make up her mind to show us the piece of paper?'

'I don't know, but I ask you to do everything possible and impossible to convince her. Now, you must understand, it's truly a question of life or death.'

Chapter 19

The evening had not yet set in and the air, suspended miraculously in the clear sky, had a warm and transparent quality about it. I decided to take a walk through University Park before returning to my room in the College. The tennis nets had been taken down on the grass courts and I crossed, with a touch of melancholy, over the lines painted with lime. In the far background, I noticed a few people sitting at the corners of the cricket field, waiting for the batsman's turn. I walked a little further down a somewhat neglected path and arrived suddenly at a turn where the river came into view between unkempt, overgrown weeds. I followed the edge dotted with reeds, watching the calm, unfazed parade of a number of brown and metallic-green feathered ducks, when I suddenly heard a commotion, stifled cries and an unmistakable curse in Spanish. In a clearing by the river I saw a hefty man hitting a smaller one. The small man had fallen on his knees and was begging for mercy in English, covering his face as well as he could to shield it from the kicks and the blows. A girl not older than ten was trying to tear the furious man away, begging him, in Spanish, to stop, 'Papá, no, please, Papá,' without managing to prevent the man from attacking his victim. I guessed, by the child's accent, that they were tourists from somewhere in Spain. I approached cautiously and saw to my astonishment that the kneeling man covered in blood was none other than Henry Haas. I took one step further until I was next to the aggressor and shouted at him in Spanish to stop. He stared at me, somewhat disconcerted, still blinded by hatred, but for a moment he interrupted the attack.

'Do you really want to kill him?' I asked. 'Look how he's bleeding.'

I knelt next to Haas and tried to stop the haemorrhage in his nose. One of his eyes was shut and bruised, and his nose looked as if it had been broken. He was bleeding from the mouth and there was an impressive red stain on his white shirt. I tried to help him get back on his feet but his knees were trembling so much that he wasn't able to stand up. He whispered to me in English not to leave him.

'I wouldn't care if I did kill him,' the man said. 'The fewer of his kind in the world, the better.'

The child by his side was crying in anguish.

'But Papá, I swear he wasn't hurting me: he only wanted to give me a teddy bear and draw my picture.'

The man looked at his knuckles, which were grazed and stained with blood. He seemed slowly to recover his senses and bent down to hug his daughter. He pointed at Haas and then to a bag lying on the grass, from which the brown head of a teddy bear was visible.

'I went to the toilet for a moment, I left her here feeding the ducks, and when I came back I found this bastard pulling the teddy out of his bag to give to her.'

'I didn't do anything to her, I wasn't trying to do anything to her,' Haas was repeating to me in a pitiful tone, attempting to stop the blood with the hem of his shirt.

With great relief, I saw the man grab his daughter's hand to leave. I pulled out my handkerchief and handed it to Haas, but it seemed like nothing would stop the bleeding.

'I have a disease of the blood,' he said. 'It's something like haemophilia. I need to get back home to take an antifibrino-lytic. Please, help me.'

'Shouldn't we go to the hospital?' I said in alarm.

'No, please, not the hospital. I live very close by and there's a short cut behind the park. It won't take us more than five minutes.'

He stood up slowly and tried to take a first cautious step. He had also received a kick in the ankle and could barely walk. He leaned on me and I dragged him along as best I could. But what concerned me most was the blood that had already soaked through my handkerchief and was starting to drip down my shoulder. I felt that Haas's strength was seeping away and I was afraid that he would faint. He was now a dead weight that I was obliged to carry. Fortunately, he weighed very little; he had the bone structure of a child. We crossed from one end of the park to a short curved lane and he pointed to some steps that led to a red double door. I heard him rummage about in his pocket for his keys, which he handed to me. When I opened the door, he tried to get in front of me to prevent my going in, as if he felt suddenly ashamed or didn't want me to look inside. He thanked me, he told me that his medicine was in the bathroom and that he'd manage by himself. But as soon as I let go and he tried to take a first step, he crumbled on the threshold. In despera-tion, I patted his face and asked him to tell me where I could find the medicine. With a weak gesture he pointed towards the hallway. I stepped over his legs and pulled him by his arms into the hall. Leaving him with his head propped up against the wall, I ventured into a dark corridor. I opened the first door I found and I heard a furious roar coming from behind me, as if Haas had found the energy for it in the spasms of agony.

'No, not that one!'

But thanks to the cone of light coming through the open door, I had already seen inside the room a patchwork of tiny portraits, a bewildering collection of miniatures that covered all four walls.

I shut the door, stunned, not at all sure what I had seen, and opened the one next to it. I searched in the bathroom cabinet until I found the antifibrinolytic. I took the toothbrush out of its glass and filled the glass with water. I returned to Haas with the pills and looked in the kitchen for tea towels to stem the bleeding. Haas took two pills at once and seemed to revive with the first sips of water.

'You saw them, didn't you?' he asked, his eyes still turned towards the ceiling, as his blood soaked through one tea towel after another.

'No,' I said, feeling frightened. 'I didn't have time to see anything.'

'Yes,' Haas said slowly. 'Yes, you saw them, even though you didn't manage to do more than glance at them perhaps. But you got the wrong impression. I want you to go in again. Please. Turn on the light and look carefully at them. After all, you've just saved my life, and I think you might understand. You are young and kind; you seem like a good person. Look at them. But look at them carefully. And when you come back, you'll tell me what you saw.'

Still full of misgivings, I returned to the corridor, opened the door and switched on the light. I saw a bare room, like an open space in an art gallery, with all four walls covered with small pictures almost superimposed one upon the other. They were all portraits of little girls done in pencil but with such incredible precision that the faces had a disturbing verisimilitude, as if they were living creatures in there, waking all at once when the lights went on. I moved from one face to the next. The girls were between six and ten or eleven years old. Mostly they looked ahead, as if caught in an emotional rapture, with a clear and intense look in their eyes. A few details of the hair and the outline of the face were barely sketched out, though an indubitable mastery made the childish features appear vividly, lending a radiant and immediate quality to their expressions. *Look at them carefully*, Haas had said. And when I stopped to look, I thought I could indeed identify something recurrent but fleeting in all the faces. They seemed frozen in time, caught in a kind of exultation, about to receive or accept something important, gripped in an intense emotion that elevated them to a different plane. As if they had made an intimate decision and something of that decision was flowing out, unstoppable, through their eyes. I thought it resembled the look I'd seen in some adolescent girls in the moment of the happy expectation of an imminent granted kiss. Was it that, then? I kept on looking at the pictures, trying to make out the meaning of their expressions by means of an uncertain key. I felt I was at the edge of the truth, just on the point of discovery but, even then, missing one essential step. All these faces seemed to be saying the same thing, over and over, at different times, certainly throughout many years. What was it, exactly? I asked myself how old Haas was now and when he might have started his collection. Nor could I be certain of the order, if there was one, of their places on the walls. Which was the first portrait, which the last? I looked at two or three more of those little faces that seemed to exult each in their own tiny secret, and I went back into the corridor. Haas had managed to stand up and was now sitting on a kitchen chair, drinking a glass of water with slow steady sips.

'Now, yes, now you've seen them,' he said with a touch of pride, as if he were an artist intimately certain of his worth, an artist who had long been keeping himself in hiding and could at last show himself in public. He seemed almost happy that someone had finally discovered his sanctuary.

'You're the first person to have seen them. And if you looked at them carefully, you will have discovered *the truth*. I don't know what that madman who attacked me in the park told you, but I have never laid a finger on any of them. Not one of them. Never. I would never do that. I only want that which you saw in there. Just that moment, just that look. But to understand me fully, you must know that there is yet another room, with almost as many portraits as this one. A room I call the Room of Scorn, Mockery and Pity. As an adolescent, I was unable to grow taller than the height I am now, while around me all the boys and girls grew as if they were eating Alice's small cakes by the handful. Nevertheless, I tried to do what my schoolmates did, to approach this girl and that, and the response was always the same. In their eyes, in their smirks, in their answers: scorn, mockery, pity. Every time I received one of those looks it felt like a red-hot iron burning my skin. I held on to those looks, I couldn't make them heal. It was then that I started to draw the pictures of each of those rejections that I carried engraved in my mind like on a photographic negative. And all by myself, I discovered that I had this gift: the possibility of conjuring up, from the slop pail of my memory, not only the features, not only the gestures, but the emotion itself, still burning bright. I don't really know why I did it, because when each portrait was finished it hurt me once again. Until one day, a miraculous day, a day I should mark with all the white stones of the Roman Empire, a little girl approached me while I was doing one of these drawings. It was very near to where you found me today. When she saw me finish it, she told me that she thought it was a very pretty picture. I answered, without really thinking, that it was the portrait of a girlfriend who had left me, and that explanation seemed to move her. She asked me to do her portrait as well. We spoke, I made a few jokes while I drew her, and proposed also a few of the word games that appear in Lewis Carroll's books. She laughed, and she also tried to tell me the jokes and games she knew. I made more jokes to hear her laugh but, at the same time, I realised, because I was sketching her portrait, that something in her was translating itself into an intimate conviction, a certain resolve. She suddenly told me that I should no longer be sad because she would love me. She promised she'd love me more than all those girlfriends of mine. And then she became serious. And I saw how it came to the surface . . . for the very first time . . . that thing which I capture and preserve for myself in each of the portraits. That which peers out of the eyes of girls at that age and gives them a gleam like a fluid, the first colostrum of love, the pure substance not yet contaminated by fear, defence mechanisms or calculations. That primordial element that springs naturally in every girl when one learns to play for them the two or three necessary notes. Those looks are all I collect. I don't want anything more for myself. I have never laid a finger on them. Though I know I could have. And in many cases, believe it or not, they themselves tried, or prompted it. But I never felt attracted to them in a *physical* sense. In this I'm even more innocent than Lewis Carroll was. I only took those tiny offerings of love that kept me alive all these years. If it had not been for these little girls, for this infinitesimal mercy that life granted me, I would have committed suicide many times over. And now that you know everything about me,' he said brusquely, 'please go. The monster will heal himself alone in his lair.'

*grateful to you if you could possibly visit her and
reassure me on this. I'll always remember your kindness
and that of Professor Seldom during the difficult days
I spent with her. If ever you come to Guildford, I'd be
more than delighted to welcome you in my house and
serve you an English tea. Kristen must at least admit
this about her mother: that she makes the best scones
in the entire county. I've just sent her a batch by parcel
post. Hopefully she'll invite you to taste them!*

I had thought of postponing the visit to Kristen until the
weekend but her mother's letter made me decide to go to
Headington that same afternoon. I climbed the hill under
a merciless sun, trying to seek a brief refuge in the uneven
shade of the trees. Upon arriving at the top, I found the name
of the street I'd jotted down, and I looked for the number
zigzagging from one side to the other, trying to make sense
of the maddening English street-numbering system. At last I
found the house: it was divided into flats and surrounded by
a white picket fence from which one could see a gravel path
that led to the back garden. There were a number of bells with
names and initials, and on one of them, which appeared to
have been written in more recent ink, I saw, with a stab of
jealousy, the letters K and R. I rang the bell once and then,
after a long wait, I tried again. I guessed what flat was hers
by listening in the afternoon silence to the echo of the bell,
and I thought that I saw someone spying on me from behind
the curtains of one of the windows. I supposed it was Sister
Rosaura and that she could easily lie to Kristen, and tell her
that it was only a travelling salesman. Or perhaps the two
were discussing whether to let me in or not. I rang the bell
a third time, somewhat more insistently. Finally, the door of
the small flat opened and I saw Sister Rosaura come down

the stairs, patting her hair into place and making signs for me to come in through the fence.

'Oh, I thought it was you, but I couldn't make you out without my glasses. I suppose you want to see Kristen: you'll find her reading in the garden. Carry on to the end of the path. She prefers to stay in the veranda while I have my nap. I work nights at the hospital; this is the only time when I can sleep,' she said in a tone of reproach.

I apologised as best I could and carried on down the path to the back of the house. It led to a surprisingly large garden, spread out in progressive wilderness with a few low trees at the back and beds of colourful flowers along the veranda. I found Kristen sitting in her chair, which she had wheeled up to a glass-topped table. She was leaning over a sheet of paper, making notes from a book, and she couldn't conceal her shock when she saw me appear at her side. I noticed a glimmer of joy stifled at once by concern or alarm, as if she suspected that I hadn't come merely to see her and feared a different, hidden motive. She managed, however, to give me a warm expectant smile, pronouncing my name with something of a delayed pleasure. She reached out her hand, but I preferred to kiss her on the cheek in the Argentinian manner. I briefly saw, as I leaned over her, a thin gold chain hanging from her neck and, behind a loosened button on her blouse, some sort of locket. When I stood up I could see she was blushing and that she had lifted a hand to tidy her hair with a nervous gesture. In the past few days, I had forgotten the powerfully seductive effect her face had on me. The sun had given her skin a golden colour and her deep blue eyes, magnified by her glasses, were fixed on my mine and seemed pleased to hold my gaze. Her smile deepened as she asked me to sit by her side, on one of the iron armchairs of the veranda.

'What an ... unexpected surprise,' she said teasingly. 'Were you strolling through the hills?'

'Last week I sent you two or three emails to see how you were doing. But I never got an answer.'

'I'm sorry,' she said. 'And thanks for your concern. I must have a pile of emails that have been accumulating these past days. Since I left the hospital I haven't been back to the Institute. I suppose I missed all the news. I'm trying to advance as fast as possible with this,' she said, pointing proudly to a bundle of sheets next to the books.

'That's what I imagined,' I said, 'and that's why I decided to come in person.'

'Well, as you see, I'm trying to catch some sun and I think that here I'm safe from danger. The most serious thing that's happened to me is that I broke several nails trying to do a bit of gardening.' And she stretched out her hands to show me.

I took one in mine to inspect it closely, and I saw that indeed a couple of the nails were broken. When she tried to pull her hand away, I kept it in mine, and for an instant our eyes locked, our fingers still touching.

'No,' she said. 'Please don't do that.'

'Do what?' I asked, not letting go of her fingers.

'Don't touch me like that, don't look at me like that. I can't allow myself . . . ' she said with a stifled moan, and once again she laid her hands on the table, away from me. 'I can't even think about it, it makes me far too sad. I feel now as if I were living in another world. Even what my eyes see makes me believe that it's as if I had been shrunk to the height I was as a child. For many years I felt an absolute aversion towards the whole idea of English gardening. I suppose it was in part because my mother loved her garden and spent so much time there. But now that I too am almost level with the ground. Everything in me has changed. As if I had been torn away from my previous world and were unable to know what will emerge from this one. If *anything* is to emerge some day,' she said sadly, in a whisper. 'All I can go on doing is this.' And she pointed to the pile of sheets. 'I realise it can seem like a sort of madness, but it's the only thing that separates me now from real madness.'

I measured with my thumb the pile of sheets.

'And have you proven what you really wanted to prove?'

'Without the slightest doubt,' she said with that touch of pride that I had so often seen in the eyes of mathematicians. 'I don't yet have a few of the final details but even if today I were to be struck by lightning, let's say, anyone else would be able to fill in the blanks. The essential question has been dealt with.'

'How curious that all these pages were born from that single sentence,' I said.

'It's that the sentence opens a whole new world: something that has always been there but that no one has had the wits to see.'

'Now that I'm here,' I said, looking around me at the garden, 'and that you've told me about your new horticultural passion, I can't help wondering where you might have buried the piece of paper with the sentence.'

'Cold, cold,' she said. 'It isn't buried. At the very most, you could say that it's sunk. I'd never hide it right here, in this almost public garden.'

I stood up and stepped back, as if I could reach the window of her flat.

'So it could be up there, guarded at all times by the fierce Rosaura?'

'Cold,' she said, 'and you have an unjust idea of Rosaura.'

'But let's see ... If it's not in the garden and not in the flat ...' I drew near her wheelchair and placed both hands on the arms.

'Warm,' she said in a low voice, holding back a smile.

I extended a finger towards her neck and lifted the gold chain a little further.

'Burning,' she said, serious and expectant.

I lifted the chain a bit higher and I felt that something was caught inside on the button of her blouse. I looked at her again and put my hand forward to loosen it.

'No,' she said, and gently stopped me. As I looked on, she pulled aside the cloth of the blouse and I saw, for a dizzying second, the steep slope of her breasts and the sudden tracing of the taut blue veins. She raised her chin slightly, freeing with light movements a long glass capsule in the shape of an elongated cylinder. She showed it to me for a second, holding it between her fingers. Inside one could make out, rolled up like a delicate papyrus, a yellowish piece of paper. She made the capsule sparkle in the light. 'It was a gift from Rosaura. I was supposed to carry an olive twig inside,' she said, as if to apologise for the substitution. 'However, I can now always have it with me.'

Quickly she let the capsule fall into her blouse again. She seemed to regret having shown it to me.

'I'll ask Rosaura to bring us something to drink. And you should taste the scones my mother sent me. I haven't offered you anything ...'

'No, please, don't call her. We wouldn't be able to go on talking.'

'You shouldn't be so hard on her: she's giving me a hand with everything; I don't know what I'd do without her. She's even offered to take me to the Institute and go and collect my emails, but I prefer to be here on my own, at least in the beginning. As you understand, I don't want to be overwhelmed with the demands of the Brotherhood. Or Arthur's. At first, when I saw you, I thought it was he who had sent you.'

'But then, you haven't heard what happened? You haven't heard that Leonard Hinch is dead?'

'I heard that he had died, yes. I saw it on the news a few days ago, something to do with diabetes, right? I can't say I was heartbroken.'

I shook my head slowly.

'He was murdered. Poisoned. Only the police are not saying anything for the time being. The murderer sent him a box of chocolates poisoned with something called aconite. And inside the box was another of Lewis Carroll's photos.'

I let Kristen absorb what I had just told her. She seemed bewildered, as if a number of alarm bells had started to ring inside her head, and something she had until then only imagined as a remote possibility sprang back to hit her with brute force. She sat speechless for a moment and I could see in her darkened eyes the swell of fearful conjectures.

'What photo was it?' she said at last.

'One of a naked little girl lying in a forest.'

She looked through the books on the table. She opened one and went to the back, to the appendix of photographs, until she found the image that the inspector had shown us. I nodded. She stared at it for a moment, though it seemed to me that she had merely found a place on which to fix her eyes. Her hand on the page was trembling and suddenly I heard the small sound of a tear hitting the paper. I looked at her with astonishment and saw that she was taking off her glasses and lifting a hand to her eyes.

'I thought it had been a natural death,' she murmured. 'That's what they said on the news. But now, what you've told me makes all the difference. All the difference in the world!' she said with a whimper.

'They haven't made it public because they fear that a scandal about the photos might somehow tarnish the image of the Royal Personage.'

'The image of the Royal Personage,' she repeated in

disbelief, as if things had reached a point out of control. 'What sense does that make? What would it all have to do with royalty? Will the Queen of Hearts make an appearance now as well?'

'I thought you knew. This Royal Personage is the honorary president of the Brotherhood. They don't want him involved in a matter of murders and paedophiliac photos. I imagine they're holding back the information as long as possible until they find out who sent the box of chocolates. And the person who hit you with the car,' I said. 'This seems to confirm what Seldom was thinking. If he was worried before, now ...'

But before I could finish my sentence, she lifted her eyes as if something had scorched her.

'Did Arthur say anything more to you? Now I understand. He sent you to get the paper, didn't he?' she said suddenly, as if an old suspicion had flared up again.

'No, please, not that,' I said, almost in despair. 'I wanted to come and see you from the very first day. I sent you several emails the first week; you'll see them eventually.'

My words didn't seem to convince her entirely, but she did drop her angry look.

'What I can't understand,' she said, 'is why Arthur thinks that revealing what's in the paper might explain anything of what's happened. Before I was run over, only the three of us knew that the paper even existed. Isn't that still the case?'

I said to myself that it was time she was told everything.

'From the very beginning, no, that wasn't so,' I said. 'Seldom had told Sir Richard. But I suppose there's something else he's afraid of. Perhaps another member of the Brotherhood had read the paper in Guildford and didn't want its contents to be revealed. I'm certain that Seldom only wants what's good for you. He thinks you'll be safer once everyone knows what the sentence says.'

'So Richard Ranelagh knew,' Kristen said, as though that was the only thing she'd heard. 'And you both lied to me in the hospital.' Her face had changed and she was staring at me almost with aversion. 'I can see it all now: you did what they asked you to do, you came as their ambassador. Fine,' she said icily, as if she'd made up her mind. 'My message to Arthur and Ranelagh and all the rest of the Brotherhood is that I'll give them the damn paper only when I decide to. Perhaps never. Don't ever come back here. My God,' she said to herself, 'to think that I almost allowed you to ... I almost believed ... And now,' she said, as if fighting against her indignation, and lifting a blank distant face to signal me the way out, 'I want to be left alone. Please.'

Chapter 21

I walked down the hill with huge strides, mortified as well as
furious with myself. I couldn't stop thinking of how close I'd
been. Why, I reproached myself, must I always say a word too
many and make a gesture too few? And now, in all likelihood,
everything was lost. I had seen suspicion in her eyes, a glint
of loathing even and, above all, disappointment, the kind of
look that denotes an adamant rejection. I was wrapped up
in thoughts of this kind when I was obliged to step aside to
avoid another person climbing up the hill and showing signs
of weariness. Something about the unkempt figure and the
curly hair made me lift my head. Anderson also stopped in
his tracks, surprised by the coincidence. We were the only
two creatures alive in that long street under the midday sun.

'I think I'm going to the place you just left,' he said. And
then, with a mocking tone of reproach: 'I asked you to let
me know if you heard of another murder. You seem to have
a divining rod for getting yourself involved in crimes.'

'What crime?' I asked, with badly disguised innocence.

'*Crimes* in the plural,' he said. 'Because this girl, there
was an attempt on her life as well and you certainly knew
that when we last met. I heard that she was under police
protection at the hospital, and now I intend to ask her a few
questions. Fortunately, I have good friends at the morgue: I

know about the poisoning of Hinch. And I even know about the photos.'

I stared at him, this time with real alarm. I couldn't imagine who might have told him all this.

'What photos?' I asked cautiously.

'Aha, they didn't tell you that, did they?' And he laughed out loud. 'Consider it a news flash: they've discovered in Hinch's desk masses of pictures of naked little girls. At first, they thought they were photos from Lewis Carroll's time, from the early days of photography, a private vintage collection. But in fact they are pictures taken in our time with the same camera used by Lewis Carroll, treated with chemicals and hand-painted as in his day, to make them look old. It's not clear if Hinch sold them as antiques, or if it was a way of disguising them in order to sell them to paedophiles. They also found the list of customers who bought them, in a separate accounting book. They must be distinguished clients, even though the names are not yet known: they're written out in some kind of code. I don't think that either you or I will ever lay eyes on the list.'

I thought of Hinch as I had seen him last, in the hallway with his books, wearing two of his masks. I would never have imagined this third one, which he had managed to keep hidden up to his death. I asked myself if his whole publishing enterprise might not have been from the very start a meticulous screen for this other secret business, and I imagined him receiving and delivering envelopes under cover of darkness, or even perhaps in plain daylight, by means of a network of inadvertent messengers. Maybe he had also used some of the photo albums compiled by Lewis Carroll himself and, here and there among the pages, were these recent photos of little girls of a hundred years later, identical in almost everything except the watermarks of time. The similar hidden in the

similar. Was it not, in its own way, like a version of the paradox in 'Pierre Menard, Author of *Don Quixote*', that I once
discussed with Seldom? The same photos that, a century earlier, Lewis Carroll could parade in polite society without (as
Borges put it) 'a warning to the future', using girls of the same
age and identical smooth childish nakedness, transformed
now in their opposite, in infamous travesties. As I tried to fit
this new piece in the emerging puzzle, I consoled myself with
the thought that at least Anderson had not found out about
the *other* photographs.

'You still can't believe it, eh? *Do ut des*,' Anderson said,
and seeing my blank face he explained: '"Tit for tat". A little
Kidlington birdie, or rather a raven on a wall, told me that
this young lady has a piece of paper stashed away that everyone wants to see. What do you know about that? I can tell
you're quite good friends with her and I imagine she's told
you something.'

'No, she's told me nothing,' I said. 'And I think you should
leave her alone. She's suffered enough because of that piece
of paper: she's in a wheelchair now.'

'So? Is it true that she was hit by a car because of that
mysterious paper? Don't get angry, I won't say that it was you
who confirmed it. I hope you'll agree with me that it's best if
these things come out into the open. Are you not a mathematician? You must prefer the Enlightenment to the Dark Ages.'
He raised a hand to wave goodbye and quoted in a mocking
tone: '"We must know, we will know."'

I went a little further down the hill asking myself if I
shouldn't go back, maybe through a side street, to warn
Kristen about Anderson's visit. I didn't know if Inspector
Petersen's warning had reached her about keeping the
matter of the photos secret, and I feared that she might show
Anderson the one she had found in her pigeonhole. At the

same time, I realised that, with or without that piece of information, Anderson had decided to reveal what he knew, maybe in just a few hours. I thought that at least Seldom should be informed about all this and I decided to go and see him. He wasn't in his office but Brandy, the Institute's secretary, told me to look for him in the seminar classroom: he had still half an hour of class left. I went up to the classroom but decided not to interrupt him. I entered as silently as possible through the back door and sat down to listen to him from one of the last rows. Seldom raised a questioning eyebrow when he saw me and I signalled to him that I wanted to talk to him later on. On the blackboard there was written the name of Willard Quine and the sketch of a rabbit.

Seldom was telling his students the mental experiment on translation designed by Quine. In his quick handwriting he jotted down two lines outlining the essence of the situation:

A scrupulous English anthropologist arrives on an island of aborigines who have never been in contact with outsiders. A rabbit runs by and one of the aborigines points at it and says: 'Gavagai'.

Seldom paused, read aloud the two sentences and then wrote the crucial, apparently innocent, question:

What should the anthropologist write down in his translation notebook?

I, who had already attended the class, could see how everyone held back from giving the most obvious answer, as if they realised that the question was in some sense a devious one.

'The key fact here,' Seldom said, 'is that our anthropologist is really scrupulous and only allows himself to jot down "rabbit" provisionally, because he realises that the aborigine might also be saying "food" or "animal" or "plague" or "big ears" or "white" or "quick movement" or "hunting season". Or it could happen that, on this island, rabbits might be sacred animals and that *"gavagai"* is a religious invocation upon meeting a rabbit. And it could also be possible that on the island the rabbits were only a handful and that each of these rabbits had a name and that *"Gavagai"* was the name of that particular rabbit. Or, on the contrary, that there could be countless rabbits and to distinguish them they had a meticulous classification, like the Inuit to distinguish different kinds of snow, and that *"gavagai"* was a word that meant "white-rabbit-alive-and-running" but that they had a different word for "white-rabbit-dead-on-dish".'

Now that I was hearing him again I asked myself if the choice of Quine's running rabbit among several other possible examples was not a small homage to Lewis Carroll, and I promised myself to find out at the end of the class. Seldom carried on to the crux of the problem.

'Our anthropologist then decides to discard progressively the false meanings till arriving at the true one, and spends a great deal of time trying to understand what are the words or the gestures of these aborigines to say "yes" and "no". But even when he thinks he has succeeded, even when he has managed, with a certain degree of confidence, to point at different things and animals and colours, and ask each time *"Gavagai?"* and receives answers to all his questions that he can translate as "yes" or "no", he soon realises that he's as far from the truth as he was in the beginning.'

While Seldom was discussing the successive misadventures of the anthropologist's attempts, something of that discussion echoed in me, faintly but with the insistence of a jingle. Was it not the same problem of the logical series in search of the clue?

In a way, yes: each new attempt by the anthropologist was yet a new term in the series that allowed another inference, but he was never able to be perfectly certain of having reached the 'true' meaning. Seldom was saying something similar: even when the aborigines answered 'yes' every time the anthropologist pointed at a rabbit, and they answered 'no' every time he pointed at one of the thousand other things on the island that were different from a rabbit, how could he tell if 'gavagai' was not merely a word they said out loud, perhaps superstitiously, every time they saw a rabbit? And so the aborigines would laugh every time the anthropologist would point at a rabbit and say, 'Gavagai', and would make grand affirmative gestures, happy for the recognition and understanding, while they perhaps whispered among themselves that at last this poor fellow understood that we say 'gavagai' in the same way that the English might say 'bless you' every time someone sneezes.

But this, I suddenly realised, exactly this same thing, could be happening to us with the photos. I thought I understood now Seldom's caution. What was the true meaning of the series that had, for the time being, only two terms? Had we inferred too quickly, and perhaps erroneously, that 'gavagai' meant 'rabbit'? I tried to establish another kind of pattern for the photos. Kristen had received hers before she was attacked, as a caution or a warning. But Hinch's was hidden, to be discovered only *after* his death. Did this small discrepancy have a particular meaning or intention?

I saw that Seldom was ending his class and I approached his desk before another student could intercept him. He greeted me with a hand white with chalk and signalled that I should wait for a moment until he finished wiping the blackboard. As he was about to erase the drawing of the rabbit, I asked him if Quine might have chosen this example from among so many others as a homage to Lewis Carroll.

'I truly don't know,' Seldom said in a tone of surprise. 'It's possible; we should ask Raymond Martin who knew him quite well. However, if Quine had wished to allude to Lewis Carroll, he would rather have chosen an egg. There's a discussion with Humpty Dumpty on private language in the second of the Alice books that relates much more directly to this question.'

'It also occurred to me,' I said, 'as I was listening to you, that the anthropologist's problem is ultimately the same one you and I discussed several times about the continuation of a logical series: each of the anthropologist's questions is a new step that appears to bring him closer to the meaning, but he can never infer that it's the only solution.'

'Yes, true enough,' Seldom said, 'because, if the anthropologist is a stickler for truth, the discarding operation is potentially infinite. For that reason there's no hope to send a human language into space with the assurance that it will be understood correctly. I think that in the end, what we call "meaning" is a happy and unexpected consequence of a failing in logic in our species: induction in a few cases, a conceptual inference stemming from the first examples, a certain sufficient coincidence in this initial approach, all a bit rough and tumble. But even the attempts at later refinements, which seem subtler to us, can also prove insufficient. That's what Quine's experiment ultimately shows.'

'I was thinking that the two photos that have appeared up to now also denote a meaning that must be translated, as if someone were repeating "*gavagai*" each time, to make us understand something.'

'Carry on,' Seldom said, as if he had suddenly become interested.

'Well, I wasn't able to go much beyond that. I tried to imagine another pattern, something that wasn't the more obvious one of "rabbit". I only came up with this: Kristen received her photo before she was attacked, as if it had been left on purpose for her to see. But in Hinch's case, the photo was hidden underneath the plastic sheet for it to be discovered *after* his death.'

Seldom remained lost in thought, unconsciously rubbing a chalky finger on his forehead.

'I think—' he said, and stopped, caught in a thought. 'I think that what you've just said is quite extraordinary. You're absolutely right,' he observed, and his look turned blank, as I'd noticed a few times before, tightening his features as if struck by sudden blindness while inwardly pursuing a slippery idea. 'I believe it's just as you say. "*Gavagai*" does not necessarily mean "rabbit", even if we are told the word every time a rabbit runs by. What is the true consequence of all this? That we don't yet know, even if ... perhaps ...' He came to himself all of a sudden, as if emerging from a trance. 'But you didn't come here to tell me just that, did you?'

I then explained about my failed visit to Kristen. And immediately after that, in order not to reveal the painful way in which I'd been dismissed, I told him about my meeting with Anderson and what he had mentioned about Leonard Hinch and the secret business of paedophiliac photographs. Seldom became pale, unable to take in the revelation, caught between incredulity and consternation.

'That's horrible,' he said. 'Horrible,' he repeated to himself. 'And it will cause untold damage to the Brotherhood: we will all be under suspicion. We should let Richard know, unless he's already aware of this.'

'That's the reason I came here to see you. Anderson knows that Hinch was murdered and that Kristen was run over with the intention of killing her. And he wants to publish a piece revealing all.'

'Then I think we should go to see Richard at once. I know he's still acquainted with certain people who might be able to convince the editor to delay the publication for a few days. Even if, at this point,' he said, 'it might be better to reveal everything. I wouldn't want us to be accused of covering things up.' He picked up the small pile of books that he had used in class. 'I should return these to the library, but I'll do it tomorrow. I think that at this moment we can find Richard at The Eagle and Child.'

I followed Seldom along the hallway between classrooms and down the stairs to the entrance hall. Seldom went to leave the books provisionally in his pigeonhole and came back walking slowly, as if he were carrying an explosive in his hands. He was holding a white envelope glued shut. He inspected the front and then the back: there was no inscription. He opened it carefully, not wanting to handle it more than was strictly necessary, and allowed the white rectangle it contained to fall out. The photograph showed Lewis Carroll and young Alice, on their own, in a lovers' embrace, about to kiss on the lips, or just afterwards. Even though there was no naked skin exposed, the image was much more disturbing than the two previous ones. It looked like a picture taken with the camera at close proximity, automatically. Alice could not have been older than ten; Lewis Carroll was over thirty at the time. But in the photo he appeared as a soft, delicate youngster, looking like a Romantic poet, the hair carefully parted with ringlets on both sides. Alice, in his arms, was the size of a doll, and seemed to be standing on tiptoe, half lifted by his arm and stretching towards his mouth. She was dressed like a bride, all in white, her head turned sideways, her hair falling over her shoulders. Her left arm was stretched towards his neck, while his open hand held her firmly by the waist. Both had their eyes closed and their lips were almost touching. Her mouth was slightly open, suspended in the infinitesimal instant before or after the kiss. Could it be that they were merely play-acting, as in a game? Pretending to be sweethearts, bringing their lips together as closely as possible? But even if it were only a game, there was nothing innocent in the picture. The intensity of his absorption, the way in which his hand held her tight from behind, her closed eyes, her abandon, all seemed to point in only one possible direction.

Seldom had remained silent and was staring at the image from a distance, as if it had an awful power of both attraction and repulsion.

I looked into his face to see if I could detect a sign of fear or concern, but I could only notice his knitted brows, as when he felt troubled by an incomprehensible step or a loose end in a problem of logic.

'I suppose this means,' he said, 'that I am the third term in the series.'

Chapter 22

Walking into the pub we recognised the small egg-shaped head of Sir Richard Ranelagh at one of the last tables in the back. A man seated with his back towards us was talking to him at close quarters, as if telling him something confidential, and Sir Richard was nodding gravely with a worried expression. There was something in the man's girth that felt familiar and as we drew near, I saw that indeed the man was Petersen. I asked myself what might have brought the inspector to this place: he would not have dropped in casually for a beer. When they noticed that we were approaching, they cut short their conversation. Seldom excused himself but Sir Richard at once signalled to us to join them.

'It will only take a moment,' Seldom said. 'And in fact, it's lucky that we found you here as well,' he added, looking at Petersen. 'It's about Anderson.'

He briefly told them about my encounter with Anderson and of the journalist's intention to break the news of what he had discovered about both cases.

'And what did Anderson find out about Hinch?' Petersen asked, staring at me with an indignant look, as if I were the guilty party. 'What exactly did he tell you? I think I'll have to fire someone, or even *everyone* in the office.'

I repeated what Anderson had told me about the photos in the desk and the list of clients with their names in code.

Petersen shook his head wearily and Sir Richard looked at Seldom with a bitter gesture of despair.

'The inspector just told me. I still can't believe it. All these years ... And we never suspected anything. This might mean the end of the Brotherhood,' he said.

'In any case,' Petersen said, 'even if we can't stop Anderson from publishing, it would certainly be important for us to have a few more days' grace. Sir Richard, show them what you just received.'

With slow gestures and trembling fingers, Ranelagh pulled out from one of his pockets a white envelope, opened it carefully and showed us the photo of another naked girl, with long old-fashioned ringlets and painted cheeks. She was sitting on a rock on a beach, caught in profile, deep in thought. One of her legs was bent upwards exposing the thigh and part of the deep shadow close to her groin.

'I don't know if it will serve as consolation,' said Seldom, 'but I too just found one in my pigeonhole.'

Neither Ranelagh nor Petersen showed surprise.

'I believe everyone in the Brotherhood received one,' Ranelagh said. 'Thornton Reeves called me, he was baffled. And I got an email from Henry Haas. Before coming here, I called Raymond Martin and he also found one this morning, slipped under the door of his office. None of them knows yet what the photo might mean: all were surprised that the envelope was blank, and at first they thought it was some kind of announcement for a Brotherhood event. I only need to find out whether Josephine and the Raggios also received one. I haven't been able to get in touch with them. I wanted to ask you to go to Josephine's house and ask her, I'll deal with the Raggios. The inspector and I were saying that they all deserve to know what's happening. I will call a special meeting for the day after tomorrow.'

'Please show us the one you received,' Petersen said to Seldom.

Seldom, as if he were matching a bet, placed on the table the image of Lewis Carroll with Alice in his arms.

'Interesting,' said Ranelagh, holding it up slightly. 'Because this image is a fake.'

'Fake?' Petersen said, astonished. Seldom, too, seemed surprised.

'When Henry Haas assembled his collection of Lewis Carroll's photographs, there appeared several of these counterfeit images. I believe Lewis Carroll's anonymous detractors were responsible for circulating them. Or perhaps simple pranksters. This one was cobbled together from a real self-portrait of Lewis Carroll on which they pasted a cut-out of Alice from another photo. And the hand behind her back has been added; if you look closely you'll notice it. Henry published this image and the way it was made in one of the chapters of his book on apocryphal photos attributed to Lewis Carroll.'

'I'm beginning to regret never having opened the book,' Seldom said. 'But what does this mean for us, that the photo is a fake?' he asked, almost to himself.

'Whoever is sending out these photos wants to malign Lewis Carroll as much as possible, even with fake pictures,' Ranelagh said angrily. 'Or perhaps it's someone who doesn't know much about Lewis Carroll, someone from outside the Brotherhood.'

'And concerning the photos the others received?' Petersen asked. 'Could you find out anything?'

'According to what they told me, they are all images of naked or almost naked girls, taken by Lewis Carroll at different times. We could ask the members to bring them to the meeting. Perhaps a clue will emerge from a discussion between us all.'

'I'll need to have them analysed before the meeting; I'll send one of my men to collect them. And I'll take these two with me. But you, as Lewis Carroll experts, can't tell me anything more right now?'

'I already told the inspector that the girl whose photo was in the box of chocolates was Evelyn Hatch, aged about six. She was the sister of Beatrice Hatch, who posed for the first photo and also for the one that was sent to me. They are part of a series of hand-coloured photos that were inserted into paintings of different landscapes.'

He stopped to let Seldom speak, but Seldom seemed unwilling to do so. To encourage him, I asked him to repeat for the benefit of the inspector the sentence that Kristen had mentioned to us from the Alice books, and the effects of aconite that we had discovered, reminiscent of Alice's growth after eating the little cake. In my hasty English, I realised that I had ended up telling the story myself.

'I hadn't decided to tell you that,' Seldom said, casting a reproachful glance in my direction, 'because it's the sort of association that's so vague that it seems ridiculous as soon as it's mentioned.'

'And yet, I find it interesting,' Sir Richard said thoughtfully. 'The car that hits you and sends you flying like a sky-rocket, the poison that makes you grow. What's next? What will it be when my turn comes?' And he seemed for a moment lost in weighing up possibilities, as if the illustrations of the Alice books were parading before his eyes. 'The problem is that there are too many deaths hidden in Wonderland. Although that's not a bad thing,' he said with philosophical detachment. 'There should be enough for all of us, like Alice's comfits.'

'I'm not altogether convinced. Nevertheless, just in case, I'll look through the books once more,' Petersen said. 'It will be a curious way of revisiting my childhood.' He made a sudden gesture of apology with his hand because his phone was ringing inside his jacket. He pulled out the hefty instrument and went towards the door in search of a better signal. Seldom took advantage of the inspector's retreat to lean towards Ranelagh.

'I think it's important,' he said, 'that Kristen also attends the meeting. After all, she was the first to receive a photo. I'll go to her house and let her know. I still believe that only when she reveals what's on that paper will we reach the bottom of this madness.'

'Of course,' Sir Richard said. 'The fact that we'll all be murdered is not a reason to stop insisting that the girl show us the paper and return it to Guildford. She still owes us that, and if she refuses to come, perhaps it's time we sent a different kind of emissary.' And he nodded towards the inspector, who was speaking by the door, walking about in worrying circles.

'I hope it doesn't come to that,' Seldom said. 'I have something to say to her that I believe will persuade her. I'll go now to see Josephine and then I'll climb the hill to visit Kristen.'

Petersen returned to our table with a worried look on his face.

'That was Buckingham Palace. Following the security protocols, I was obliged to let them know, and this morning, going through the correspondence at the entrance desk, they found that someone had managed to leave a blank envelope there. It contained another of Lewis Carroll's pictures. So now the Royal Personage has a picture of his own.'

There was a shocked silence, as if we all had conjured up an image of fanfares, banners and red carpets.

'Do you think we should invite him to our little gathering?' Sir Richard asked with a weak smile.

'No,' Petersen answered in all seriousness. 'I don't believe he'd honour us with his presence, but I asked that they send us the photo. And most certainly, as you well know, they'll also want to send someone from MI5. Now more than ever we need to stop Anderson.' And he turned to Ranelagh. 'Can you pull some strings?'

Sir Richard appeared doubtful, and said he couldn't promise too much.

'I'll do what I can with the people who still remember who I was.'

Out on the street, as we were saying our goodbyes, I asked Seldom if I could accompany him to Josephine's place.

'Certainly,' Seldom said. 'I'm sure she'll be pleased to see you again, since almost no one comes to visit her any more ...'

I walked by his side, trying to keep up with his long strides. He seemed to be thinking intensely and was barely aware of the crossings, of the people around him, of me by his side.

'Can I ask you something?' I said nevertheless.

He seemed startled upon hearing my voice, as if I'd torn him away from some faraway place.

'Of course,' he said with a faint attempt at politeness.

'What came to your mind when you saw the envelope with the photo in your pigeonhole?'

'You mean to say ... before we crossed over to the pub? Before learning that all had received one?'

I nodded.

'I thought that it was a sort of ironic punishment, even just in a certain sense. To die within a logical series. You already know why: I suddenly remembered last year's murders. But I also thought that if I really am to be a logical term in the series, I want at least to understand what the key is. The fact that the photo was sent to me ... It made no sense.'

'But it makes even less sense that a photo was sent to *all*.'

'I won't deny that I felt relieved,' and I saw a fleeting smile cross his face, 'because if we all received a photo it's as if no one had received one. I was reflecting on that just now. Don't you think there are almost *too many* photos? We only had two at first, but then the ones printed by Hinch appeared and now there's a deluge of them ... even a fake one, and one for the Royal Personage. It's like a trip of stampeding rabbits.'

'You mean, an attempt to add many footsteps in order to hide one?'

'I don't really know what I mean,' he said with a helpless and bewildered gesture. 'I can't even say whether we are faced with someone too inept or too astute.'

We walked for a while in silence, until I decided to ask him another question, which was in fact the one that puzzled me the most.

'When you told Ranelagh that you might convince Kristen to come tomorrow ... what are you thinking of telling her?'

'That it no longer concerns an academic credit but a human life. If I can't appeal to her reason, I'll try to appeal to her new religious side: the Christian obligation of caring for others. Because if at first I feared for her life, now I fear for that of someone else.'

'And who would that other person be?'

'I'm not sure, but when you told me today about your encounter with Anderson, I had an intuition, maybe a mistaken one. Consider this: when was Kristen attacked? When she was about to show us all the Guildford paper. And when was Hinch attacked? Shortly after announcing that he'd publish the diaries in their entirety. In both cases, it seems that someone wanted to avoid, by the most drastic means possible, that something – we don't yet know precisely what – come out into the light, to be seen by all. That's what I thought when you told me that Anderson was intending to publish an article with everything he'd discovered.'

'So ... it's Anderson you're concerned about?' I asked him, and I recalled that Anderson had spoken to me, with ironic pomposity, of the Enlightenment and the Dark Ages. 'It's curious: I didn't mention this before, but Anderson used David Hilbert's words to make fun of me: "We must know, we will know".'

'Anderson was for a time a student of mathematics before becoming a journalist, a somewhat wayward student. He quit in his second or third year; I don't know if he came to learn that Hilbert's optimism would face limits.'

'But if it's as you think, would it not be the messenger who's killed in every case, as Petersen suggested?'

'Precisely,' Seldom said. 'You see, killing the messenger is an act as cruel as it is stupid, once the news has arrived. But what happens if you succeed in killing the messenger *before* the news arrives? It's still cruel but not necessarily stupid. Imagine for a moment, like in a version of the Chesterton story of "The Three Horsemen of the Apocalypse", that a general wants to send the king the recently discovered name of a spy who has infiltrated the highest circles of the court. Imagine that he has only three messengers with swift enough mounts, and that on the road to the palace the spy, aware of this, sends a sniper to kill one after the other.'

'The name, or the news, would never be known,' I said. 'If that's what is happening, it would be a good thing to know at least the number of messengers: I hope it's not everyone who has received a photo.'

Chapter 23

'Yes, it was put through the letter box, either last night or very early this morning,' Josephine said. 'It was inside a white envelope; they brought it up to me together with the rest of the post with my breakfast. If this young man were kind enough ...' she said and pointed to a small roll-top desk. 'That's the envelope, next to the glasses case. I was very much astonished and tried to think who might have sent it.'

We were in a room with a varnished pitch-pine floor lit through stained-glass windows, which could have passed for a reading-room in an old, well-preserved library. Shelves completely covered three of the walls, reaching dizzyingly up to the ceiling, with a sliding ladder that immediately tempted one to climb it. From a large armchair set inside a bow window, Josephine had welcomed us with loud demonstrations of pleasure. As soon as we were seated, she ordered her chauffeur Mahmud – who, as he opened the door to us, revealed himself in the ancillary role of butler – to bring us tea, just as Seldom had warned me.

I stood up and handed her the envelope and the glasses case. She put on the glasses with a quick and lively movement of one hand, and with the other pulled out a small sepia-coloured photo from the envelope. She turned it towards us and allowed us to study it on the low black-and-gold Chinese table at her feet.

'It's one of Carroll's favourite girls, and the one he photographed most throughout his life. He name was Alexandra Kitchin but they called her Xie. In this picture she must be about six.'

In the photo one could see a very small girl leaning back in an armchair, her head on a large cushion, half-dressed in a white and strapless light summer frock, her shoulders and part of the breast exposed. The skirt had been rolled up to uncover the thighs. The left leg was bent upwards, the knee raised high, so that the hem had shifted to reveal the hollow of the thigh. The intended image seemed to be that of a woman reclining languidly, with abandon, revealing her nakedness with a sort of negligence. But what most drew one's attention was the girl's expression: in spite of the haircut – an obviously childish short, straight fringe – and her very round face, somewhat like a doll's, her look and the firm line of the mouth had a grown-up determination and seriousness, almost defiant, as if she had consciously taken on that role. Once again, I was aware of how strangely elderly the faces of the children appeared in these old pictures. I had once heard certain explanations of this phenomenon: the facial rigidity due to the long exposures and to the careful preparation of the poses, the early-Victorian repression of the spontaneous gestures of a child, the flattening of the features due to the magnesium explosion. Nevertheless, it never ceased to astonish me, this total lack of a childhood element in the portraits of these children.

Seldom glanced at the image for a moment only, distractedly, as if his mathematical mind had already been satisfied with a theory that benefited little from a new example. I remembered his words: 'Too many photos.' This was merely one more. And I also remembered his advice to graduate students: examples should be few but well chosen, with critical qualities. No matter how large the pot, the soup can be sampled with just a spoonful, according to the Law of Statistics. True: but if it's an alphabet soup, Seldom would warn us, the chosen spoonful has to contain the entire ABC.

Josephine waited for Mahmud to place the teacups on the table and close the door, but seemed to have great difficulty holding back her curiosity.

'I was somewhat intrigued this morning when I opened the envelope and saw the picture for the first time. But I'm much more so now that you are both here. This has something to do with what happened to that poor girl, isn't that so, Arthur? Can you believe that the police came to our house and Mahmud had to open the garage and show them the Bentley? Somehow they found out that Mahmud's son had been involved in an accident that night and they questioned him for hours. Because what happened to Kristen was no mere accident, isn't that so? Neither was it a student car race ... It was all because of that ripped-out page. I had a presentiment from the very first moment, when you went downstairs at Christ Church to answer that call.'

'Nothing is yet clear,' Seldom answered cautiously. 'Everyone at the Brotherhood received a photo like this between yesterday and today. All different girls, but all naked and in ... disturbing poses. But it's true that Kristen received one like this on the morning of the day she was run over.' He didn't seem sure how much he could tell her, and Josephine became aware of the hesitation in his voice.

'And Hinch? Hinch also received a photo, isn't that so?'

Seldom nodded gravely. Josephine made a muffled sound in her throat.

'So it wasn't as they said on the news? You mean to tell

me that he too was somehow *murdered*?' She pronounced the word with horror and also a hint of fascination. The matter seemed to give her much guilty amusement.

'That's why Inspector Petersen wants to get us together as soon as possible,' Seldom said. 'I can't tell you anything more, but Sir Richard and I wanted to make sure that you received the summons.'

I noticed that Seldom had quickly finished his tea in order to leave as soon as possible. Josephine seemed to notice it as well.

'But Arthur, you can't leave just like that; my curiosity will kill me and you'll be responsible. Does this mean we're all under threat?' And she appeared to be considering that possibility for the first time, more in disbelief than in fear. I remembered that this woman had taken part in car racing; surely she'd felt close to death in many a bend, and perhaps the idea of being once more in a dangerous situation did not entirely displease her. 'Tell me at least if this girl Kristen will be at the meeting: I don't want to die before finally knowing what the devil is written on that scrap of paper.'

'She should be, of course,' Seldom said. 'And she should reveal to everyone once and for all what's on the paper. I'll do whatever's possible. We know she's already written almost a whole book on that single sentence. That's all she wanted, she said. Now I hope she'll keep her promise.'

'Since our last meeting, I've hardly been able to think of anything but that sentence. I'll tell this young man, Arthur, if you allow me a pinch of vanity, that I was the first to detect the interference of other hands in the matter of the torn-out pages of Lewis Carroll's diaries. I could reveal what was concealed under a large ink stain with which those hands had tried to hide a whole paragraph, and I also discovered that they'd tried to make up a continuity in the diaries, in a bad imitation of Lewis Carroll's handwriting, to hide the fact that a page had been torn out. But of course, page 183 was the most intriguing. I no longer believed that anything new could be discovered. And suddenly this girl appears with news about that sentence. I can well imagine Menella Dodgson, wrapped up in the Puritanism of an elderly spinster, and convinced of her purifying mission, caught between what she believed to be her responsibility to watch over Lewis Carroll's image and her guilty feelings about mutilating the diaries. And I can imagine her remorse in getting rid of that page. Maybe she thought she'd have one day to account for her behaviour to the rest of the family, or that, when she died, to a Higher Court. She destroyed the page but she nevertheless decided to keep a record of its contents. I can't tell you how many times I cursed myself for not having read that catalogue conscientiously, for not having been able to get hold of that paper. Every day since our last meeting, I have sat myself down right here after breakfast to consider how the sentence beginning "L.C. learns from Mrs Liddell that ... " might carry on. I have not stopped repeating it to myself all this time and I've come up with the most ridiculous possibilities. What does Mrs Liddell tell him that day? What does Lewis Carroll find out?'

All of a sudden, Seldom seemed to pay attention to what Josephine was saying.

'And what would you say is the most likely hypothesis?'

'There could be, of course, several possibilities. At about that time Lewis Carroll was engaged in an academic dispute with Mr Liddell, the dean, who had refused to vote for a project that he'd put forward. But I discard this possibility: the dean had already shown signs of having forgiven him. I have been rereading my own books and my notes on Mrs Liddell, because I think the key to the problem lies with her.

No doubt she was the one who oversaw all family matters and it's clear that her obsession, the one thing that ruled her entire life, were the social stratagems and the marriage prospects of her daughters, as proved years later when she attempted to play all her cards in order to hitch Alice up with Prince Leopold, when he was a student at Christ Church. She had the ambition, impossible to hide, to "place" her daughters with members of the royal family. Maybe there's something in Thornton Reeves' theory: maybe Mrs Liddell had found out that Lewis Carroll nursed the hope of a future engagement to Alice, and, as a precaution, she wanted to put an end to any further contact with her, because she had for her daughter "great expectations", as Dickens would say. After all, Alice, barely eleven, had captured the heart of John Ruskin and of that other professor of mathematics; the mother was surely convinced that her daughter, in just a few years, would make anyone she wanted fall in love with her. And that's why she wished to keep her away from the all-too-frequent company of a man who could give rise to future suspicions and gossip, and lower the value of her merchandise.'

'But if it were only that,' Seldom said, 'it doesn't seem to incriminate Lewis Carroll unduly. Why would the sisters have torn out the page?'

'Yes, I thought of that as well. Possibly because Lewis Carroll might have spilled on that page all his angry or ironic remarks against Mrs Liddell. I don't think he appreciated being kept away from the girls. And Menella might have wished to prevent this bellicose aspect of her uncle being revealed in the future, even if it were just a small dispute. No, I don't think that on that piece of paper is anything too shameful about Lewis Carroll. But curiously, that intrigues me even more!'

'It makes no sense to keep turning this question around,'

Seldom said, standing up. 'I hope that on Thursday we'll know, and in Menella's own handwriting. It will be like summoning up a ghost.'

'Those damn sisters!' Josephine said. 'Can you believe that when Menella was once asked about the diaries' missing pages, she answered that before her death she intended to cut out many more? Unfortunately for us, Lewis Carroll himself already held back far too much: he didn't need the assistance of some bloody page-rippers.'

Chapter 24

On the following morning, when I came down to breakfast in the college cafeteria, I picked up from one of the magazine racks a copy of the *Oxford Times*. I wanted to find out if Anderson had published his article, but there was nothing under his name either on the front page or in the crime section. I imagined that Sir Richard had reached one of his contacts in time to delay the publication for a day or so, and yet I guessed that Anderson was the kind of journalist that wouldn't easily be made to keep quiet, and that he would not rest until somehow or other he'd published his scoop. That reminded me of the curious phrase Anderson had used about the raven on a wall. How could he have found out? I couldn't believe that Leyton would have told him but I decided to drop by his office anyway and ask him.

I found him concentrating intently on what looked like a list of names, but as soon as he heard me approach from behind, he turned the sheet over and quickly put it down on his desk, so that I wouldn't see it.

'What's so secret?' I asked. 'The list of guests for your birthday party?'

'Sorry,' he said. 'I can't comment: it's a classified document.'

'Can I guess? I'd bet it's the coded list of names that was found in Leonard Hinch's desk. And you've been asked to decipher it.'

'I don't know who Leonard Hinch might be,' Leyton said, holding my look with his impassive eyes and tugging at his reddish beard. I knew I'd guessed right.

'And yet, it might be good for you to know,' I said, 'that Hinch was the editor of all the books of the Lewis Carroll Brotherhood. If he'd had to choose a code, wouldn't you think he'd choose the one invented by Lewis Carroll himself? Raymond Martin has a whole chapter in his book on puzzles and riddles dedicated to discussing it. Essentially it's a code with an alphabetical matrix. You only need to find the key word that Hinch was using. Maybe it's worth your while to look for it.'

Leyton stared at me with scorn and mild surprise, as if he couldn't believe that for once I might be able to tell him something he didn't know.

'Thank you, I suppose,' he said sarcastically, and looked up as if expecting me to leave.

'There's a journalist from the *Oxford Times*, Anderson,' I said. 'Is it possible that he came by in these past few days?'

'He was here yesterday, yes,' he said.

'And he asked you about the measuring of echoes?'

'He didn't have to ask me much: it stood in front of his eyes.' And he pointed to the blackboard. I hadn't noticed it as I came in, but there was the drawing, in full sight, clear as daylight for anyone who knew what to look for: the sketch of the billboard, the height of the wall, and a curve of dots and crosses with the inscriptions 'CAR' and 'RAVEN'.

'But did he ask you about your conclusions?' I insisted.

'Anderson's a clever guy: he was a fellow student of mine during my first years here. He put the pieces together and drew the conclusions himself,' he said in a cryptic tone.

Suddenly I asked myself how much Leyton knew about the whole affair, or how much he'd inferred from the work that he was given. I tried once more.

'And what would be your own conclusions up to now? The pieces you yourself put together.'

'I'm not interested in putting together pieces. I think of each job they give me separately. One day I find the proof that a car had not braked, and now, on another day, I'm asked to work on a list of names in code. Of course, I can't help seeing other things.' And he stared hard at me. 'I know, for instance, that one night you borrowed the plaque from here, and that sometimes you don't see what's right under your nose. But as I say, I don't try to put all the pieces together. That could be a dangerous enterprise here: curiosity killed the cat.'

I left with the ambiguous sensation of having been vaguely threatened, and I walked back along the sidewalk to Alice's shop, still mulling over the question. I stopped for a moment in front of the window; the tourists were taking turns snapping pictures next to the life-size cut-outs of Alice and the rabbit in the chequered waistcoat. I mingled among them and glanced unavoidably at Sharon, who was busy inside, seemingly attending several customers at once. The door suddenly opened with a tingling of bells and I was surprised to see the tottering figure of Raymond Martin poking his cane forward to help himself down the small step to the sidewalk. He seemed equally surprised to see me. I helped him climb down and he immediately showed me, like a happy child, the small treasure he had found in the shop. It was a mug with Alice in front of the large tree from which the Cheshire Cat stared down at her.

'The marvellous thing about this mug,' he said, 'is that when you pour hot liquid inside it, the image vanishes and only the Cat's smile remains. I'm thinking of offering it to Josephine as a prize if she beats us in the coffee-with-milk contest.'

The way in which he pronounced Josephine's name, with a

warm and intimate ring, made me see him suddenly in a new light. I think I smiled involuntarily: yes indeed, the tone was unmistakably that of a man in love. I wondered how I could ask the question and decided to use Anderson's method.

'So it's true that you and Josephine ... ?'

He laughed and shook his head.

'It was true, far too long ago. I can't imagine who told you. You should have seen Josephine in those days. However, every so often I like choosing a gift for her.'

I told him then that I was reading his book on Lewis Carroll and that I had not yet been able to solve the puzzle 'To make the DEAD LIVE'.

'You don't expect me to solve it for you, eh? A mathematician should take pride in solving his own problems. This puzzle is especially interesting, because Lewis Carroll had dealings with the occult towards the end of his life. He took part in spiritualist gatherings and he even said he'd managed to photograph ghosts. "To make the dead live."' And he sighed softly. 'At a certain age, you'll see, we all become a bit spiritualist and want to bring our dead back to life. The puzzle is an innocent game of letter substitution, though of course, word games can be very serious as well: to give life to his golem, you'll recall that the Rabbi of Prague wrote *emet* on the forehead of his creature, the Hebrew word for truth. And to turn it into clay once more he only had to erase the first letter: *emet* became *met*, meaning death. And after all, aren't our programming languages the golems of our time, with their instructions BEGIN and END, life and death? Even, seen from the right perspective, our DNA, the code of all biological life, is, when all is said and done, a game of permutations and substitutions of merely a few letters. Therefore, I think it won't be a waste of time for you to carry on looking for the solution to the riddle. But I will give you

a hint.' We'd reached the corner. He stopped for a moment
and tapped me twice on the shoulder, and a cunning glint
appeared in his eyes. 'If you weren't able to get from DEAD to
LIVE, maybe you can try inverting the order and turn LIVE
into DEAD. It's very difficult to bring the dead to life again,
but not that difficult to turn the living into the dead. That's
known as *murder*.' And seeing my bewildered look of alarm,
he cackled with laughter, well pleased with himself.

I returned, walking slowly. As I crossed the pathway among
the tombstones of the Church of St Giles towards Banbury
Road, I couldn't stop thinking about what Leyton had said as
if it were a warning, and about the vaguely sardonic manner
in which Raymond Martin had uttered the word *murder* like
a sort of private joke. But did any of this make sense? I tried
following the combination of the new hypotheses that kept
popping up, which I was forced to toss aside almost immediately as absurd. 'For he who doesn't know where he's sailing,
no wind is favourable.' But it was also true, unfortunately,
that for he who doesn't know where he's sailing, the slightest
breeze seems to show the way.

Once in my room at the College, I tried my hand at the
puzzle again, turning it around as Raymond Martin had suggested. With no more luck than before, I filled several more
pages of failed intents. At a certain point, feeling defeated, I
dropped the scribbled pages on the bed and grabbed a handful of coins to go to the laundry-room in the basement and
wash my accumulated clothes. Back in my room with the
clothes all washed and dried, I turned on the TV to watch
the evening news. The first image to appear on the screen
was the face of Anderson with his eternal ironic smile and
his unkempt grey curly hair. He hadn't returned home since

the previous day and they were anxiously searching for him throughout the town and in the Oxfordshire surroundings. The last thing that was known was that on the previous day he'd left his office at the *Oxford Times* at six in the afternoon. So he went back to the paper after our encounter, I thought. Beneath the photo was a number to report any information. I asked myself if I should call and recount the conversation I'd had with him. But, I reminded myself, Petersen knew about it already. I remained motionless, void of thought, while on the screen they were showing the rest of the news and the weather report for the region.

I glanced at the list of words I'd written a few hours earlier, as if I were a writing-machine gone mad. I crumpled up the sheets and threw the shameful lot into the waste-paper basket. But even with the lights switched off, and perhaps because I'd skipped dinner, I was needled by this small riddle inside the larger one. Was it possible that I couldn't solve even this? I finally turned on the light, pulled the papers out of the basket, and flattened them again on the bed. Some of the papers of the previous day had become mixed with these new ones. Trying to go from DEAD to LIVE I had written:

DEAD

LEAD

LEND

LAND

And beginning from the opposite end, in one of the several attempts I'd just thrown away, I had written:

LIVE

LINE

LANE

I put the two pages together and laughed out loud. The riddle, I thought, had solved itself inside the basket. I took a clean sheet and copied out, one after the other, all the words,

and the riverbank. I got into my sneakers and tennis shorts. Outside, the sudden and unexpectedly cold morning air made me speed up with quick stabs on my back. I ran up Banbury Road and soon left behind Cunliffe Close where I'd lived the year before, past the door of the small shop with the same taciturn Indian dressed all in white at the cash register. At the edge of the road to Kidlington, I faced the stream of traffic pouring into Oxford. I felt, as my breathing became more rhythmic and my body, carried lightly by my legs, seemed to drift away from me, that my thoughts too were floating upwards beyond my reach, as if my animated surroundings made it impossible for them to find a hold. I saw the large billboards in the roundabout proclaiming 'It's *One* to Remember' and, going around it to return with the flow of the traffic, there appeared before me, tall and stark, the long wall of dark bricks of the tractor plant. I looked up to try to make out the raven's nest, and I recalled another of Lewis Carroll's riddles that I'd seen in Raymond Martin's book: 'Why is a raven like a writing desk?' Indeed. Why was the raven on the wall like Hinch's desk? In that Anderson knew about both, might be an answer. I remembered the sardonic look on his face as he told me about the contents of Hinch's desk and how he'd asked me about Kristen. What had he managed to get out of her? I tried to swipe away the insidious web of thoughts that dragged me back to the same tried-out paths. I was no longer accustomed to running and, as I entered University Park, I started to feel cramps of fatigue in my legs. However, panting a little, I managed to cross the park until I reached the other end at the edge of the river. By the fountain where I'd met the battered Henry Haas, I stopped for a moment to recover my breath and stood there watching the calm gliding of the rowing teams and the synchronised swirl of the oars. I walked a little further along the riverbank towards a spot in the distance that looked like a jetty, with signs announcing boats for hire. At the edge, an elderly couple appeared to be arguing as to whether or not to climb into one of the boats. As I approached, I was surprised to see it was the Raggios. I remembered that Ranelagh had planned to reach them and I wondered if they'd been told about the Brotherhood meeting. I waved at them. They took a moment to recognise who I was but, as I came closer, Laura opened her arms as if she saw in me an unexpected but welcome presence. I asked them if they were aware of the afternoon meeting. Of course, they told me; they had both received photos in one single envelope, and they were as puzzled and surprised as the others. They wouldn't miss the meeting for anything. I saw on the boat's seat a bunch of white flowers, and Laura followed my glance.

'It's a marvellous coincidence that you should have appeared just now,' she said. 'Today's the anniversary of our daughter's death and every year we come here to remember her. It was her favourite spot in all the world. From the time she started to explore everything she could about the Alice books, she'd always ask us to take her on the boat trip to Godstow, just as Lewis Carroll did with the three Liddell sisters. Since her departure, we row to the bridge and throw the flowers into the water there where—' Her voice broke but she managed to recover quickly. 'But Albert has sprained his wrist just now as he was dragging the boat.'

'I was telling her that I can row nevertheless, only that perhaps for a shorter stretch,' Albert said with hurt pride while he carefully probed his wrist with two fingers. 'The wrist would have to turn clockwise and that's a movement I can still manage.'

'And I was telling him that in no way do I want him to force it. It's an old lesion that flares up at the end of every summer with any wrong movement. But now, fortunately, maybe you can assist us. I thought of going on my own, but I was afraid of not being able to row against the current on my way back.'

'Certainly,' I said. 'And if we both row, all three of us might be able to go. I think we'll manage somehow.'

Albert shook his head.

'Not possible,' he said somewhat crossly. 'It's forbidden for more than two adults to go in these small boats. But that's not a problem: I'll stay and wait for you here.'

As soon as we'd left, after the first few strokes and while we still could see Albert on the shore rubbing his wrist, Laura winked at me with tolerant scorn.

'Sometimes he behaves like a pig-headed child,' she said. 'It's just stupid male pride. And then I have to button up his shirt, and he can't even write out his prescriptions. He behaves as if he really believes in his theories and his poultices, and that he'll never grow old. As if he's not already grown as old as one can be!' she said, appalled, and then immediately, with natural coquettishness: 'He's ages older than I am, even if perhaps it isn't all that noticeable any more.' And she lifted her face, challenging me to judge. 'He was one of my teachers at college.'

I assured her in every way that my garbled English allowed me that it was so very noticeable that no one could possibly doubt it.

'For how long have you been married?' I asked.

'For more years than I'd have wished for,' she said, as if making a bitter joke. 'When Albertina died we were on the point of separating.' She paused and her face changed, as if she had decided for the first time to speak in earnest. 'But I realised that Albert, who adored her as much as I did, was the only person with whom I could still speak of her. The only one with whom I could share my memories of her. And I suppose it was the same with him, even if we never put it into words. In a certain sense, between the two of us we keep her alive, however morbid this might sound. Every year I pull out her book of drawings and writings, and we look at it together.'

'Can I ask . . . how it happened?'

'It was suicide, however unbelievable it might sound. One day before her twelfth birthday. She threw herself from the bridge and even though two or three people saw her fall, there was nothing that could be done to help her. The current dragged her away.'

'But did you manage to find out why?'

'We had . . . some hints. We were able to reconstruct part of the story. We think she'd fallen in love with a man. In one of her notebooks we found a picture of Lewis Carroll and another one of Alice, glued one next to the other. She had drawn arrows pointing to the figures and had written 'ME' and 'HIM'. I had noticed that she seemed increasingly troubled as her birthday drew near, and we couldn't understand why. We thought it had to do with the loss of childhood, or the typical hormonal chaos at the start of puberty, when the body suddenly starts growing. But afterwards, when it was too late, we found out that she'd read in secret a biography of Lewis Carroll that she'd found on our shelves. On one of the pages, she'd underlined a sentence that said that he would abandon his little friends when they turned twelve. Maybe this man, this monster, had also said something like this to her. We didn't see the signs. The previous night she had wanted to read out loud to me the chapter in which Alice almost drowns in her own tears, and I wouldn't pay attention to her. I told her she was old enough to read on her own. I'll never forgive myself for that.'

'And about this man, did you manage to find out anything at all?'

She shook her head.

'We suppose it was someone she met when she started to go out alone on her bicycle. Oxford seemed to us a safe place, more so at the time, and she would sometimes go out on her own for an hour or two. Or maybe she met him here, in the park. She liked sitting and sketching by the river.'

'You think it was something platonic, or . . .' I was unable to finish the sentence.

'When we discovered the pictures with the arrows, we took the notebook to the police, and Inspector Petersen insisted that an autopsy be performed. No one had interfered with her. But there are other ways to interfere deeply with a girl her age,' she said and I could see tears beginning to show at the corners of her eyes. 'However, justice is not concerned with those other ways. There was no investigation. We tried by every means possible but we never managed to get beyond what I have just told you.'

'And if you were to find out one day who that man was . . . ?'

'I'd kill him,' she said with finality, as if this were an unshakeable decision she'd taken for the rest of her life. 'I'd kill him if it were the last thing I did. Many times, in all these years, I found myself imagining several ways in which I could murder this man if we found him. I never talked about this with Albert, but I'm sure he thinks as I do, and that, in the end, this is also something that keeps us together: the hope of finding him. It doesn't matter what I now think of Albert, I know I could count on him. I know we'd help one another kill him.'

She said this and then remained silent, as if she felt severed from the world and human law, and didn't expect me to understand.

'May I see a picture of her?' I asked.

'Of course,' she said and the shadow in her eyes lifted. 'I always carry with me a photo of the three of us together.'

She gathered the oars and rummaged in her bag. She held it up to me so that I could carry on rowing. In the picture, Albert still had all his hair, and Laura looked radiant by his side, blazingly young, her own hair long and loose. They were holding by the shoulders a girl smiling radiantly, unaware of what would soon happen.

I tried to make out in the features, somewhat blurred by the movement of the smile, any trace that might remind me of Henry Haas's photos. But the proliferation of the faces on the wall, the sheer number of them, had cancelled them all in my memory.

'She was very beautiful,' was all I felt able to say. 'And she had your eyes.'

She turned the picture towards her and stared at it intensely, as if to take in something of that image from the past. We had reached the bridge. Laura put the photo away, bent over to loosen the ribbon that held the bunch together, and spread the flowers on the water around the boat. We watched them float away slowly in the current, gradually drifting apart one from the other. Following them with my eyes, I noticed that the regatta boat had stopped by the bank of the river under a few trees whose branches were sunk in the water. The oarsmen were waving their arms and seemed to be calling for help. We rowed as fast as possible towards them until we saw what they were pointing at, emerging from the water between the leafy branches with the horribly slow movement of a floating buoy. It was a human head, its grey-ish tangled hair dripping water. Its eyes were closed and the skin was ashen blue. With disbelief, I recognised the features, now forever motionless, of Anderson. At the same time, two policemen had arrived, running down the bank, climbing on the branches to raise the body from the water. One on each side, they sunk their arms into the river, and then they too began to shout with astonishment and horror. The head appeared loose, without a body underneath it. One of the policemen seemed at last to recover and grabbed the head behind the ears, lifting it carefully through the branches, as if it were a fragile vase.

I looked at Laura Raggio. She seemed to have fallen into some kind of trance. Her entire body was shaking and her teeth were chattering. She gripped my arm convulsively and begged me to take her back to her husband. The two of us rowed with a primitive impulse, terrified, as if we could escape the awful image by merely getting away. When the boat reached the shore and Albert extended a hand to help her, she collapsed weeping in his arms. I decided to leave and let her do the explaining: I needed to find Seldom as soon as possible. I ran to the Mathematical Institute and climbed the stairs two steps at a time. The door was ajar. Seldom was staring with rapt attention at a formula on the blackboard. My face must have shown the horror since he looked at me with astonishment. I said with breathless excitement:

'You were right! Anderson has been murdered. He's been found in the river. They cut off his head!'

'Cut off his head?' Seldom said in disbelief, not certain of having heard me correctly, or fearing some kind of macabre joke.

I told him about my encounter with the Raggios, and the boat ride to the bridge, and Anderson's head caught in the branches.

'You were right twice,' I said. 'The following victim was Anderson and he died a death from the Alice books.'

Seldom shook his head brusquely, to stop himself from shivering.

'No,' he said. 'It's the other way round. I've been mistaken from beginning to end. I wasn't right about anything. About anything!'

I had never seen Seldom in such a state. He seemed both terribly worried and disgusted with himself, as if he were, once again, somehow guilty of the unforeseen path the events had taken and which he hadn't been able to predict. He let himself drop, weary and defeated, in his chair.

'Please leave me,' he said. 'I need to think. I need to think things over from the very beginning once more. I hope I can make some sense of it all before this afternoon's meeting.'

Chapter 26

I had hardly shut the office door and was running down the stairs, when I realised that, anxious as I'd been to give Seldom the news, I hadn't asked him if he'd succeeded in convincing Kristen to come to the Brotherhood meeting. I was about to turn back when I remembered the unmistakable gesture with which Seldom had signalled to me that he wanted to be alone. I thought that, after all, I would find out in just a few hours. I returned to the College and, while I undressed to get into the shower, I turned on the TV and switched it to the news channel. A woman reporter standing next to the trees by the river was interviewing one of the oarsmen, and repeated over and over, in a voice that could barely hold back her excitement, that this was the very same place in which Anderson's severed head had been found, but that there was no information yet concerning the rest of the body. The images showed teams of police frogmen plunging into the water, and then the camera returned to the studio where they were reviewing, illustrated by the cyclical return of the same three or four images, Anderson's journalistic career. Curiously, they kept repeating that one of Anderson's last investigations, not yet published, concerned the cell of Serbian spies in Oxford, but they said nothing about Hinch's death or the pictures of the naked girls. I skipped lunch and during the next few hours

I remained glued to the screen. I used the remote to jump through the local channels, hoping that there would appear at any moment even the tiniest extra detail. I switched the TV off when it was time to leave for the meeting. Once on the street, I was mildly surprised to see that the afternoon was as quiet as ever, that the students passed me peacefully on their bicycles, that there were no groups at the corners commenting on the case or on the matter of the Serbian spy cell, and that there were no throngs of journalists at the entrance to Christ Church, on the alert for Petersen's arrival. On the news, they had promised again and again a few words from the inspector, but in all that time no one had been able to reach him. However, something had changed at the College after all: standing next to the pigeonholes and the porter, I saw a uniformed policeman who asked me where I was going. Fortunately, Inspector Petersen had been able to spell out enough of my name for me to be identified on the list and be allowed to enter.

Reaching the Brotherhood room, I found the inspector and Sir Richard Ranelagh were seated at the head of the table, talking quietly between themselves. Almost all of the others were also there, still standing, slowly drifting from the coffee urns to their chairs. Neither Seldom nor Kristen had yet arrived. Once again, I took a seat opposite the Raggios and asked Laura if she felt better. 'Of course,' Albert answered for her, 'I made sure to give her a tranquilliser'. Something in his tone made me think that he didn't approve of my approaching her directly, or that he felt I was somehow responsible for the incident in the boat. Laura smiled at me weakly, unable to gather the strength to do more: she seemed to have withered alarmingly in only a few hours. At the other side of the table, Josephine was the only one showing some animation. She was dressed entirely in pink and had obviously been to the hairdresser's: her white hair, held lightly upright, looked like candy floss. I managed to hear her enthusiastically repeating to Henry Haas all the truculent details that the newscasters had revealed about the findings in the river. Thornton Reeves was listening in silence, half-attentively, with a slight gesture of disgust.

'Isn't it odd for Arthur to be so late?' Raymond Martin said, pointing to the empty chair by my side. 'Did you see him at the Institute?'

I shook my head and said I too found it strange, and that I hadn't seen him on my way here. Sir Richard glanced at his watch and then cast his eyes around the table.

'We'll give him one more minute,' he said. 'And speak of the devil . . . '

Seldom walked in with a quick step. He merely nodded a greeting and made a vague gesture of apology with his hand. His face bore a troubled expression that I recognised from previous times, and which I'd also seen on the faces of other mathematicians: the expression of someone who has not quite succeeded in ridding himself of the torture of a calculation that isn't yet right, of a loose end standing annoyingly in the way of the full demonstration of a theorem. I guessed that Seldom hadn't left his office since he'd closed the door behind me, and that until the last minute he'd been sitting in his armchair in pursuit of a thread of thought that escaped him again and again. Some of that mental irritation stuck with him even now.

'Now I believe we're all here at last!' Sir Richard said. 'But . . . wasn't Kristen Hill supposed to be here too?' And he gave Seldom a questioning look.

There was a pause and all of a sudden Seldom came out of his reverie.

'I wasn't able to convince her to come,' he said, 'but she

promised to send us the paper with a note of apology. Has it not arrived?'

'Not yet,' Ranelagh said. 'However ...' He consulted Inspector Petersen with a glance. 'I suppose we can begin anyway.'

'Of course,' Petersen said, placing a brown paper envelope on the table. 'The most important piece of evidence, which the young lady gave me in the hospital, is here: the first of the photos.'

He pulled out the hand-coloured miniature of Beatrice Hatch leaning against a tree, and all the faces bent forward in an effort to have a look.

'This picture,' he said drily, 'reached Kristen Hill on the day she was run over. It came in an unmarked white envelope. We have good reason to believe that what happened to her was not an accident.'

Before anyone could put in a word, he showed them the next photo, that of little Evelyn lying in the forest.

'And this second photo,' he said, 'we found inside the box of chocolates with which Hinch was poisoned.'

Shock and a wave of murmurs spread around the table.

'Yes,' Petersen said. 'We concealed the real cause of death as a precautionary measure, as far as our protocol would allow it, but now you must know the facts: Leonard Hinch was poisoned with chocolates sent to his office, a box with a card from the Brotherhood, and no name attached. Anderson, the journalist that you all knew, found out about this a few days ago thanks to someone from the morgue leaking the information; he was going to publish an account in his paper. You will have heard, no doubt, that Anderson's head was found in the river this morning. What you will not know is that during the autopsy, when the jaw was prised open to examine the inside of the mouth, we found a ball of paper pulp, as if before being killed he had been forced to chew one of the photos. We weren't able to reconstruct it entirely, but some of the fragments seem to indicate that, like the others, it was a photograph of a naked girl. We also have – and this is the reason why I summoned you all here today – the other photos you yourselves received.'

Petersen slid his fingers once more into the envelope and spread out on the table a series of small rectangles one after another.

'I had them examined in the lab but unfortunately we weren't able to find any clues that might effectively assist us. They seem to have been cut out from the same book of photographs: a hardback copy of the entire collection put together by Henry Haas.'

The inspector waved his hand towards the place where Haas was sitting; all eyes converged on him and we saw him blush suddenly. Few traces of the attack remained on his smooth, strangely infantile face. He picked up a couple of photos within his reach and pointed to the thickness of the border.

'I told as much to the inspector,' he said, as if feeling obliged to prove his innocence. 'Even the photo that I received was cut from my book. Hinch always used paper of the same weight, and the quality of the printing is unmistakable.'

'Yes, indeed.' Raymond Martin sighed quietly, as a small posthumous act of recognition. 'In spite of everything, Leonard always used the very best paper.'

'My men are scouring the bookshops in Oxfordshire to find all those customers who have bought the book using a credit card. But most probably, whoever is behind this would have paid for his copy in cash, and we'll be obliged to appeal to the memory of the booksellers. We don't have many clues,' he admitted, somewhat despondently. 'That is why I wanted to get you all together, as the major experts on Lewis Carroll, to see if you can tell me something more about what these photos might mean. Or you may be able to infer, from what I've told you, something that is escaping us.'

Sir Richard looked at him, as if seeking permission to add something more.

'Perhaps we should let everyone know about a rather startling coincidence that Arthur pointed out: the car that struck Kristen popped out of nowhere and made her fly in the air, just like poor Bill in Wonderland: "All I know is, something comes at me like a jack-in-the-box, and up I goes like a sky-rocket!" And in the second attack, the poison chosen for Hinch's chocolates was a substance called aconite. It has a horrible effect but curiously similar to what Alice experienced after eating the little cake: the victim feels his head and limbs growing and swelling as if about to explode. And finally, in Anderson's case, I hardly need to say, the murder was the most brutal but also the clearest of all: they cut off his head. "Off with his head!"' as the Queen of Hearts commanded.'

'We'll need to reread the Alice books to find out what sort of death awaits each of us,' Josephine said in a humorous tone that no one seemed willing to share.

'We're also attending to that,' Petersen said. 'I mean that I myself am rereading the books and have very seriously jotted down several possibilities. But I'd be grateful if for now, to begin with, you'd look at these photos and tell me whatever explanation occurs to you.'

Everyone leaned over the table to look at the images with curiosity. I noticed that even Seldom was coming out of his lethargy and was inspecting the row of photographs, as if seeking something that was readily apparent. Or, as I quickly realised, he was merely counting them.

'Which is the photo that was sent to the Royal Personage?' he asked abruptly.

'You mean to say that one of these was sent to the Royal Personage as well?' Josephine asked with growing satisfaction.

There was an expectant pause and Petersen looked at Seldom with severity.

'It's not here. And we had agreed not to say anything about this,' he said indignantly. 'However, since you mentioned it, I can tell you it was one of the most famous ones: the portrait of Alice as a beggar-maid.'

'The Prince and the Pauper?' Josephine said, making her associations out loud. 'It would make sense. After all, Mrs Liddell had aspirations for her daughter to marry Prince Leopold at the time. And it was the photo of which Lewis Carroll was the proudest. It seems like the right choice for a royal gift.'

Petersen spoke again, in a vaguely admonishing tone.

'There's deep concern at the Palace about these events, and what the surfacing of these photos could mean for the Royal Personage's public image, especially when the tabloids begin to divulge the fact that he's the honorary president of the Brotherhood. The Palace is following very closely every one of our steps. Today they were going to send to Oxford someone very high up in MI5, but then someone in command remembered that they couldn't do better than appointing Sir Richard to do the job. And now,' he said, pulling out his small notebook, 'I want to hear what you all have to say.'

objection. Curiously, the Victorian Age, so reviled for its rigid morality, was not as concerned with infantile nudes as we are today. It was common for children to run about naked in the presence of adults, and they found it amusing to strip during the photo sessions when in costume. In his diaries, Lewis Carroll himself comments on this in passing. Even so, and in spite of the easy confidence, shall we say, of the parents at that time, the photos of complete nudes, or, as he called it, 'in dress of nothing', are very few. It was not at all something to which he devoted himself systematically, or that he constantly sought out and, even less so, something he wanted to hide or that anyone would have felt ashamed about. I think that on this table – but Henry might be able to clarify this later – are *all* the photos of naked children that Lewis Carroll took throughout his life. They're barely a handful. All the girls who posed for him, as well as their parents, wrote about their relationship with him and never mentioned a single impropriety. On the contrary: Lewis Carroll exhibited some of these pictures publicly and proudly. When at long last he met Tennyson, his most sought-after celebrity, he brought as an offering the photo of Alice as a beggar-maid, and he wrote with open pride in his diary the comment he received from the Poet Laureate: "The most beautiful photograph I have ever seen." It's only since the fifties that we began to wonder if Lewis Carroll's interest in little girls might not have been entirely innocent. I believe that we here know all this, but naturally, if these photos come to light all together, we can't expect that ordinary people outside our circle won't think along the prejudices and gut reactions of our time and jump to the coarsest conclusion, ready to lynch Lewis Carroll as an abject paedophile. I imagine that when these photos surface in the midst of all the blood and scandal, no one will stop to consider that subtle thing we call the truth. As to the murders, I suspect that they're nothing but what they seem to be: a foul way, and in these times perhaps the only effective one, of making oneself heard to the sound of a gong calling people's attention to these images. However, why someone would want to attack in this manner Lewis Carroll, or our sad huddle of ancient bookworms, is something for which I cannot imagine an answer.'

He looked both ways, expecting someone to second or refute him. I saw with mild surprise that Inspector Petersen had put on a pair of thick glasses and was making notes in his book, like a conscientious but somewhat slow student.

'I agree with almost everything Raymond said about the nudes or semi-nudes of the children,' Thornton Reeves declared. 'And yet ...'

He picked up the trimmed photo in which Lewis Carroll was embracing the young Alice and held it up so that we could all take a second look. 'And yet, I believe that this fake photo captures better than any of the real ones in our books, Lewis Carroll's relationship with little girls: intense, passionate, a fraction away from becoming carnal. Unlike other child-worshippers, Carroll was strictly heterosexual. He said once: "I'm fond of all children except boys", and in the notes he sent to the mothers to arrange a meeting with their young daughters he would insist, with a frankness that today would be considered alarming, that they should come to see him alone because, he said, only in that way "one could find out their true nature". I believe that photography, which had then just been invented, offered him the ideal instrument to approach them physically to the utmost permissible limit. The preparatory ritual, the careful arranging and rearranging of the pose; was it not, in his view, a natural alibi, an irreproachable justification to get near, to reach out with his hand, to lift or take off the clothes and, above all, to *touch*? It's when he starts to take the pictures of the Liddell sisters that, as we can see in his diary, his self-recrimination increases, as do his pleas to God to forgive him, his feelings of remorse. I even prepared a mathematical curve that shows the increment of his prayers as he recorded them, the highest number appearing in the period during which he's kept away from the Liddells. At the time, as Raymond pointed out, the idyllic nakedness of a child was deemed acceptable, supposedly echoing that of the Garden of Eden, if that state of things ever existed, stripped of all ulterior motives. However, and this is the paradox, the same century admitted that an adult might fall in love with a child, with a marriage planned for the future and the disturbing prospect of an early consummation. Lewis Carroll himself had a troubled cousin who wanted to marry an eleven-year-old girl, and he writes him a prudent letter advising him to stay away from the girl and wait a year more before the marriage. Was he also able to restrain himself? We have a fair number of love poems that he wrote to the girls at the time, sometimes on the back of the photos. They can perhaps be excused as an excess of lyrical rhetoric, but read today, they seem quite risqué. Did he truly stay within the limits? Perhaps yes, perhaps no. We don't have a clear answer to this question.'

'I, however,' said Josephine, 'would differentiate between periods. I'm interested in the period when he's already a celebrity and goes back to taking pictures of naked girls. You'll recall that he negotiated a rather complicated agreement that allowed him to set up a private studio above his college rooms. Why would he want such a private space if at the time he wasn't even taking that many pictures? And yet, he was only able to use the studio for a very short time because of certain ugly rumours that began to spread, saying that he was taking liberties with his young models. True or false, these rumours made him decide to give up photography for ever.'

'I have the impression that this is quickly becoming a trial of Lewis Carroll himself,' Albert Raggio said. 'And even though he loved trials and rarely missed one, and even included a satirical trial in his Wonderland, I don't think he'd have enjoyed sitting in one of our docks today. But I suppose that what the inspector expects from us is some sort of clue about what kind of person might be sending these photos, rather than disquisitions about the sexual mores of the Victorian Age. I think it's important to go back to Raymond's question: why would someone want to bring to light this aspect of Lewis Carroll in such a ... strident manner? I can suggest two kinds of person or, rather, personality, almost opposed to one another. Of course, it could be someone who as a child became the sexual victim of an adult with similar characteristics to those of Lewis Carroll, a similar charm and a similar wit. Someone who has suffered in silence for many years and saw in Lewis Carroll, and also in our Brotherhood – we are, in a certain sense, the custodians of his name – the perpetuation of impunity towards these kinds of crimes. Someone who's found out that we're going to publish the diaries, and that Lewis Carroll's love story with Alice, this indulgent version of his relationship with little girls, would be shown once again in a benevolent light. And his fury thus exploded. My wife and I might be excellent candidates for this kind of hate because our daughter, as you know, was one of these victims: how, we don't yet know. But I don't need to tell you this: it was also through our daughter that we came to love Lewis Carroll, or at least his books, and we are perfectly aware of the differences between our centuries. As far as we are concerned, and the inspector can write this down in his notebook: we want to settle the score with just one individual, unfortunately of our own time. We wouldn't waste time on other murders. As to the other possibility: let us imagine a man with the same leanings as Lewis Carroll, but born in our day. Let us also imagine that, just like Lewis Carroll, our Citizen X was torn away from a happy childhood in a pious atmosphere and thrown as a pupil into one of those atrocious schools for boys. And that he was someone of a weak constitution and stunted growth who was not able to defend himself from the beatings and the sexual humiliations. Let us imagine the fierce contrast between his still childish sensibility and the brutal initiation rituals to which novices were subjected until quite recently. The sordid violence, the vileness associated with everything erotic, provoke in him an endless trauma that makes him regress to his lost paradise, to the memory of his childhood routines and games. As an adult, he engages in other games: mathematical puzzles perhaps, or logic, or maybe magic, bridge, Scrabble, chess, games admitted in adult society, but still in the end, games. Of course, women don't notice him because of his childish manners and possibly also because of his morbid shyness. But remember that our man, like Lewis Carroll, is heterosexual. Consciously or unconsciously, he begins to approach little girls and discovers, maybe by acci-dent, that with them he does indeed have a chance, that they appreciate his type of humour, or his games, or his aspect of a child grown prematurely old and sad.'

I couldn't help but look towards Henry Haas, who seemed petrified, hunched down in his chair, his eyes on the ground. I asked myself if Raggio wasn't now speaking to him directly and, for a moment, I lost the thread of his argument. We all, Seldom included, were enthralled by Raggio's gestures, which seemed to have conjured up a convincing creature about to stand on its feet and take its first steps.

'Our man,' Raggio continued, 'doesn't think he's doing any-thing wrong. He loves the girls immaculately, his behaviour towards them is innocent and perhaps quite truly he wouldn't touch a hair on their heads, because, let us remember, he rejects anything that might lead to physical contact and the idea of sex because it brings up the memory of his awful years. But, unfortunately for him, parents in our day aren't as trusting as those in the days of Lewis Carroll. Now an adult who stops to speak to a child is immediately suspect. It's possible that more than once he's been pointed out, accused or threatened. And of course, our man can't talk to little girls in broad daylight, as Lewis Carroll did, and he certainly cannot take them on their own for a boat ride down the river. Perhaps Lewis Carroll is his secret hero and, at the same time, he feels daily an injustice that torments him: why was Lewis Carroll allowed these things and he isn't? Why was Lewis Carroll forgiven and even justified? Why was he allowed to take pictures of semi-naked girls and display them for the great English poets, while he, who asks for so much less, is tarred and feathered? No monster wants to be alone: even the most abject of creatures feels intimately justified and seeks his mates, a confirmation in others that he too belongs to the human race. Our man senses that Lewis Carroll was someone like himself, and he wants to show this fact in black and white to our society today, in a way that will be memorable. And when these crimes are published tomorrow in the papers and Lewis Carroll's photographs enter every household and are seen by thousands and thousands, he'll feel somewhat less alone and will believe, in his own way, that some justice had been done.'

'Do you really believe this?' Inspector Petersen asked in a slight tone of amusement, lifting his eyes from the notebook. 'Don't you think it's all somewhat twisted?'

'It's a conjecture,' Raggio said, a little annoyed and hurt in his pride. 'As to twisted, my dear inspector, it could be said, misquoting Lenin, that the human psyche is not Nevsky Avenue.'

'Perhaps the intention behind the photos is something different,' Henry Haas said suddenly in a timid voice. As if astonished to be speaking out loud but now not able to stop himself, he went on in the sudden silence of the room. 'Perhaps the intention is exactly the opposite. Almost without realising it, we in the Brotherhood have fostered the need to excuse Lewis Carroll, to hide or disparage as far as possible that aspect of his life: for instance, in our effort to maintain that his pictures of naked girls are barely a handful of the immense number of pictures he took throughout his life. This is true, of course. Lewis Carroll maniacally kept a record of his work as a photographer, which we were able to reconstruct, so as to prove that there were a total of only eight naked sessions during twenty-five years of photographic endeavours. On this table, we have almost all of his photos of naked children, at least those that might be seen as ambiguous in a certain sense, because he also took pictures of babies! As you can see, these nudes are far from being scandalous. But if you want to be suspicious, even the question of the number of pictures can be judged otherwise. When Lewis Carroll started with his photographic explorations and took his first semi-nudes, it was considered in good taste to emulate classical paintings with the models dressed in robes that allowed you to make out the female form. In those years, the English Crown gave its blessing to nude photos of children and cherubs taken by Oscar Gustav Rejlander, and even purchased some of his work for the royal collection. Lewis Carroll, therefore, could imitate Rejlander and feel safe, protected by the unimpeachable backing of high art that royalty favoured. But only a few years later, with the development of commercial photography, everything changed, and Victorian society began to impose severe restrictions on the photos and postcards shown in public. The Society for the Suppression of Vice was created, and its members patrolled the streets to requisition from shop windows and display cases any image that might have shown even a partially clad figure. We will never know if perhaps, during this period, Lewis Carroll might have wanted to pursue his interest in nude pictures and didn't dare. However, a few years later, in yet another change in social mores, the child nude came back in an unforeseen way: in the images of Christmas cards and the fantasy world of Gertrude Thomson and her graceful drawings of fairies and angels. As soon as Lewis Carroll saw that this possibility had arisen, he tried contacting Thomson, because he saw in her a twin spirit in her way of thinking about children. He decided to get to know her and, not only did he do so, but they hit it off so well that they ended up collaborating in photographic sessions together. And then he produced, in quick succession, almost all the pictures of naked girls that we know of. What do I mean by this? Maybe Lewis Carroll's nudes were few because it was a double-edged activity, censored for a good part of his life as a photographer. But the number doesn't change, in my opinion, the essential question: that for Lewis Carroll a child's nudity was an emblem of innocence and the purest form of human expression. Some of his pictures have been obviously interpreted in the wrong way: that of Alice as beggar-maid is always shown on its own, but it is part of a diptych with a moral intention, as was customary at the time. There's another photo of Alice dressed in her best get-up that complements this one, like two sides of a coin. And above all, as Raymond has pointed out, Lewis Carroll was terribly proud of his pictures of naked children: there's no guilt attached on his part to these nudes and semi-nudes. And for that very reason, we shouldn't be quick to attribute to sexual disquiet the remorse and prayers expressed in his diaries. It seems much more likely that they rather concerned his lack of dedication to his academic duties and to the crisis of faith surrounding his ordination. For all these reasons, I say that whoever sent these photos understands Lewis Carroll better than we do and is perhaps thinking in a way contrary to ours. Maybe, just like the nephew did in the first biography, he wishes to exalt and make relevant again the beauty of the pure childish form to remind us of what childhood is. Perhaps he is not an envious disciple but an authentic admirer of Lewis Carroll who wants to re-establish a relationship of captive contemplation, someone who also sees children as angels and wouldn't dream of ever laying a hand on them.'

Haas suddenly stopped talking, as if in his ardour he had gone too far and something intimate and secret about himself had come out into the open. There was an uncomfortable silence. Petersen raised his eyes from his notebook and flipped back a few pages.

'Let's see what I've been able to learn so far,' he said with a touch of irony. 'According to my notes, we know that Lewis Carroll made barely a handful of photos of naked children but that he might have wanted to take many more; that he stopped taking them during periods of censorship and went back to trying once the climate had changed. That he took these pictures in the presence of the girls' parents but sometimes alone, and that he arranged to have an absolutely private studio above his college rooms. That his photographic activities with children was utterly honest but that at the same time during this period he recorded his most intense avowals of remorse in his private diary. That these self-recriminations might well be of a sexual nature but at the same time might not be sexual at all but simply concerned with failing in his academic and theological duties. That there's no registered evidence from the girls he dealt with nor from their parents regarding unseemly behaviour, but that at the same time he was allowed to rearrange the girls' clothes and undress them, and get them to adopt all kinds of poses while they were naked. That the child nude corresponded in his time to an Edenic ideal, but that those same girls could be wedded at twelve, or promised in marriage at an even younger age. That his relationship with the girls was described as mere friendship, but also that he would fall in love with them and that he'd write passionate love poems on the back of the photos. That he wrote "I'm fond of all children except boys", perhaps as a joke, perhaps not. That only since the fifties was Lewis Carroll suspected of being a paedophile, but that he stopped taking pictures because of the rumours concerning his private studio. That he took a picture of Alice half-undressed, showing one of her nipples, but that it must be seen in context with another one where she's dressed up as a rich girl. And as for the profile of the possible murderer, he could be someone who either hates Lewis Carroll to the point of loathing or admires him to the point of envy.'

'I think it's a fair summation and we shouldn't be surprised by the contradictions, Inspector,' said Laura Raggio in an unexpectedly firm voice. 'Human law is not "this or the contrary" but made up of simultaneous opposites within the same person, sometimes seeking precarious balances, sometimes tearing the individual apart from within. Freud hadn't yet arrived and sublimation hadn't been identified nor defined. But in a letter to the father of one of the girls that Lewis Carroll was to photograph naked, he wrote a curious phrase that now seems painfully transparent to us: "If I did not believe I could take such pictures without any lower motive than a pure love of Art, I would not ask it." He was fully conscious that his motivations might be improper and, above all, that others might see them as such, and of course while he required Art, written with a capital A, he required no less the Edenic ideal, the Bible and Paradise, the girls portrayed as angels and winged fairies in Gertrude Thomson's work. He required the nude models of Greek art and the pioneering photographs of Rejlander. Because he could never admit to himself a lower motive. He needed his relationship with the girls to be seen in the most harmless and pure light. And yet, even so, the nights remained. And that is why he recriminated himself in his diaries, not daring ever to say clearly on the page that which he wasn't able to confess to himself. Sublimation is a form of contradiction and when it isn't met with social resistance it can last a lifetime.'

'I too think it's a well-balanced summary,' Josephine said. 'I would just add that there was indeed someone who suspected early on that something was not quite right in Lewis Carroll's pictures of children. That someone was Mrs Liddell when he took the first pictures of Alice's older brothers. On a certain occasion, she forbade him to take photos of Ina when alone, and he wrote this down resentfully in his diary. That was the first disagreement between the two of them. But instead of keeping on our discussion of Lewis Carroll, should we not proceed as they do in detective stories? Aren't we supposed to ask ourselves whom does this series of crimes benefit? Tomorrow, as Albert said, these murders will be the main national news. The photos will appear again and again in the papers and on TV. And there will certainly be a prurient curiosity about Lewis Carroll's child nudes. Yes, our century, apparently so liberated in all matters concerning sex, has turned the naked child once again into something taboo. And where will they run to, those who want to sniff out that aspect of Lewis Carroll's life? To our books, indeed, but above all to one: to a high-quality compilation of children's

portraits that will be rediscovered and sell in the thousands.
Don't you think?' she said with feigned innocence.

Henry Haas seemed to slowly become aware of the innu-
endo and he smiled a nervous and involuntary smile.

'But in that case, Josephine,' he said softly, 'I'd at least have
taken the precaution of not murdering our publisher, who
was the one supposed to pay me.'

Inspector Petersen stared at Haas with mild surprise and
uncomfortably cleared his throat, as if about to say something inconvenient.

'But regarding that book, were you not trying to get out
of the contract with Hinch? Isn't that true? As you'll understand, we've had to investigate each of you and according to
my information, you, Haas, had a talk with Hinch in order
to free up the rights.'

There was a different kind of silence, as if all suddenly felt,
for the first time, what the true reason for this gathering was,
and that the amiable man speaking in a low voice was, after
all, a police inspector. As they turned to look at Petersen, I
sensed that they were all thinking of themselves and of how
much they were supposed to say from now on. Haas stuttered
a little, and seemed more offended than intimidated.

'That's true. I decided to rescind the contract, but it was
for the most banal of reasons, which, I think, concerns us all.
Hinch never paid me what he owed me.'

Petersen nodded without saying a word, but as if the
answer only half convinced him.

'He never paid and you truly needed money, isn't that so?
Because you had to make steep monthly payments to a certain
person. Someone who knew a secret that you didn't want
revealed for anything in the world. Someone who leeched you
month after month like a vampire. Am I mistaken in saying
that that someone was Anderson?'

There was an oppressive silence. I saw that all eyes had turned once again to Haas, who was clutching his hands in despair. We saw him put his head down.

'You are not mistaken,' he said with deadly deliberation. 'But it wasn't me! It wasn't me!' he murmured in dismay to himself, as if he knew that no one would now believe him.

'No,' said Seldom unexpectedly, 'of course not. Of course it wasn't Henry.'

Chapter 28

Seldom shifted forward a little in his chair. His eyes were still turned inwards, feverishly searching for the right words, as if a host of events, small details and conjectures were all struggling in a boiling magma, half-coalescing in his powerful mind. He picked up the first photo, the one Kristen had shown us.

'I think the best thing to do is to start at the beginning, or what we believed was the beginning,' he said. 'And that's the extraordinary meeting we all attended right here, waiting for Kristen to arrive with a paper she'd found in Guildford that would enlighten us, for the first time, about the talk Lewis Carroll is said to have had with Mrs Liddell in 1863. As all here agreed, it was a paper that would at most correct a few lines in the established biographies, or appear in a footnote in the future edition of the diaries. However, Kristen never managed to get here. She was brutally run over and left lying on the road, almost dead, on the night before the meeting. That first night, it was still reasonable for us to assume that it had all been an unfortunate coincidence, that Kristen had been in an accident, that soon the guilty driver would be found and that it would turn out to be a drunken student. But I found it difficult not to see here a question of cause and consequence. Arriving at the hospital and seeing Kristen

still unconscious, forced to spend the night alone with her
mother, I felt concern for her and decided to call the police.
It was a mistake. A regrettable mistake, thanks to which we
now have two more deaths that might have been prevented.
However, because of this decision, I could almost have patted
myself on the back during the following days, because when
Kristen woke up she remembered something else: that she had
received this photograph in an unaddressed envelope on the
morning of the day she was run over.'

Seldom lifted the photo of the naked Beatrice Hatch,
her small white body cut out against the coloured pastoral
background.

'This was the first photograph. Very soon, Inspector
Petersen, after interviewing all of Kristen's habitual correspondents, discarded the possibility that any of them might
have sent it. This lent weight to the theory that she'd been
deliberately run over and that the photo was a sort of warning or announcement. When we first spoke with Kristen at
the hospital she couldn't remember anything of the moments
prior to the attack and she made that curious association with
poor Bill, the lizard in *Alice in Wonderland* that Richard has
already mentioned. Shortly afterwards, Leyton Howard, an
old student of mine who works as an expert for the police,
was able to prove, with a geometric study of the echoes of
the crash, that the car had not attempted to brake. In all
probability, the driver was lying in wait in order to hit her:
therefore, it hadn't been an accident but an attack with criminal intent. This forced us, of course, to ask ourselves what
was the meaning and purpose of this photo. It was difficult to
know without any other elements. The most obvious explanation seemed to be the first one given here: the intention of
recalling and exposing, in the crudest possible manner, the
paedophiliac inclinations of Lewis Carroll, either to tarnish

his figure or to cause damage to the Brotherhood. But it was of course too early to be sure. Inspector Petersen prudently decided to keep this information secret and not to reveal the existence of this photo. A few days later, the Brotherhood made the announcement that Lewis Carroll's diaries were going to be published. You'll remember that Anderson then interviewed Hinch and that the interview, with all our faces in the background, appeared on the local television channel. That day, as I listened to Hinch talk euphorically about his plans, I wondered what the person who attacked Kristen might be feeling. If his intention had been to threaten us in order to prevent or delay the publication of the diaries, surely he'd be even more furious now, especially because Beatrice Hatch's photo had not been made public. Remember that in the press, Kristen's case had been treated as if it had been a vulgar traffic incident. However, certain people *did* suspect that someone had tried to murder Kristen thanks to the policeman standing on guard at the hospital, who didn't allow Thornton to come into her room when he came to visit.'

'I went to see her with the best intentions. I merely wanted to find out how she was doing and to offer any help she might need,' Thornton Reeves replied indignantly. 'I'm her thesis director and I also felt somewhat responsible for her. I knew she was all on her own here.'

'Of course. I'm certain that's how it was,' Seldom said. 'But Hinch found out, asked himself why a policeman would be standing on guard at the hospital, put two plus two together and, during a conversation with our young Argentinian friend here, managed to get him to confirm the truth. And then, only a few days later, Hinch was poisoned. Someone who knew him well sent him a box of his favourite chocolates with a card from the Brotherhood from which the bearer's name had been snipped off. The chocolates were left in the letter box of the publishing company and Hinch no doubt thought that it was a gift from all of us, perhaps as a sort of apology for having negotiated behind his back with the other publisher. Except that inside the chocolates was a very powerful poison. And also, hidden in the box, a second photograph.'

Seldom took the photo of Evelyn Hatch and held it in his left hand next to the first.

'This second photo seemed to suggest a series. But what series? At first sight, it seemed to confirm the intention of revealing, or rather denouncing, even more emphatically, Lewis Carroll's relationship with little girls. If the first photo might still have been seen as artistic and defended as it was defended here, this second one, of an even younger girl with her pubis exposed, was far more explicit and awkward. Also, the chosen method, poison, was more drastic: in this case, the intention to murder couldn't be concealed or doubted. In that sense, Hinch's death seemed to dispel all possible ambiguity, and one could imagine the murderer rubbing his hands and saying to himself that now finally the crimes and the photos would be all over the media. And yet, once again, it was not to be. Because going through Hinch's desk, the desk of our old friend Leonard, the police discovered that he was in the business of peddling photos of naked girls, photos that might also be seen as "artistic", except that the models were contemporary. These were photos carefully taken in the same style, the same composition, the same feigned innocence, perhaps even with the same old camera, photos that can't be told apart from those of Lewis Carroll. They were almost a mockery, asking us, "Why was it OK then and not now?" Apparently, Hinch distributed them to a secret group of high-society members, their names concealed in code. And here the police had to make an inquiry. It's a fact at once known and neglected by us all that the honorary president of our Brotherhood is a Royal Personage. He has never attended any of our meetings and I don't think we've ever used his name, except when we resort to the royal coat of arms in order to request a certain publication from a foreign university. Certainly, the appearance of this paedophile cabal and the close relationship of Hinch with our Brotherhood are liable to turn this murder into a scandal for the Crown of unforeseen consequences. So as to save time in the investigation, the death by poisoning was concealed or, rather, the first public version of the facts that attributed the death to an illness was never corrected. And of course, neither was the second photo made public. Nevertheless, a series had been established. Two attacks, two photographs. But what was that series? What was the pattern we were supposed to look out for? Both attempts, when closely scrutinised, revealed marked differences between them. Initially even the inspector, as he told us, was inclined to suspect that the author of the first crime was a man, and the second, the poisoning of Hinch, a woman. Could there be two different individuals, one for each case? Or was it a couple acting in tandem? Petersen also let us know that the poison was aconite, and that raised yet another possibility. Hearing the name of the poison, I had a flashback to my adolescent years when I used to read detective novels. I went and checked a medical encyclopaedia and found the odd coincidence already mentioned by Richard: the effects of aconite, the feeling of sudden growth, are similar to those experienced by Alice after eating her little cake. Then was the pattern that it related to instances of death found in the Alice books? Were they Wonderland murders and were we to look at the Alice books to find out what fate awaited each and every one of us? And yet, there seemed to be even a third possibility: maybe we should examine the succession of *victims*? Kristen was attacked when she was about to reveal something we ignored in the Lewis Carroll diaries. Hinch was murdered shortly after announcing that he would publish those diaries. Was the series someone's repeated and desperate attempt to kill the messenger before the news was delivered? I was inclined towards this hypothesis, and that is why, when I discovered that Anderson wanted to publish an article in the *Oxford Times*, I became immediately afraid for him. But then something even stranger happened: I myself received a photo in my pigeonhole. And before I managed to make sense of this, before I could get over the impression that this caused in me, I learned that every member of the Brotherhood, the Royal Personage included, had received a photo as well. This avalanche of photos seemed to sweep away every imaginable avenue. We know that the logic series 2, 4, 8, 16 can be continued with 32. And also, after Lagrange and Wittgenstein, we know that in an equally logical manner it could be continued with 31 or any other number that we might want to put forward.[1] But we would certainly not expect the continuation of a series in which all the numbers appeared *simultaneously*. That put into question, for me, everything I had previously thought. And made

---

1   To continue the series 2, 4, 8, 16 with 31 it suffices to count the segments into which a circle is divided joining up the lines between the several points, as shown in the figures below.

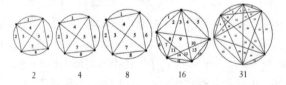

And to continue the series 2, 4, 8, 16 with any number *n*, Lagrange's interpolation theorem states that there is a polynomial $P(x)$ so that $P(1)=2$; $P(2)=4$; $P(3)=8$; $P(4)=16$; $P(5)=n$.

me wonder if we were not facing someone who was either out of his mind or far too astute. Or perhaps, it was a desperate act. Could it be that our Citizen X, as Albert called him, wished to wipe us all out in one fell swoop? Let's say, a bomb right here under the table where we take our tea? This could still make sense if I could imagine X twice foiled, planning now something like a grand finale that nothing or no one would be able to conceal. But I couldn't truly believe in this idea, even though I would not have believed earlier on that our own Leonard Hinch had run an alternative publishing business of paedophiliac photographs. My main problem in all this was that I couldn't manage to see *anyone* in our circle as a possible suspect, someone capable of doing damage on such a scale, planning and carrying out something like that. And yet, Kristen had been undoubtedly run over and Hinch lies dead underground. But let's return to the avalanche of photos. Was there not yet another possibility? Might this frantic distribution of photographs not be the action of some-one else, someone who was in a certain sense the *antagonist* of the murderer, as a way of standing in his path to prevent the next crime? Someone who anticipated the murderer's plan by marking us all with a photograph, so that the photo as a sign in the following crime would be rendered void by over-use? The next murder, even if it were made public, would in this way be detached from the photographic series. I thought it was worthwhile considering this hypothesis. But who might this adversary be? It had to be, of course, someone who knew about the photos beforehand. And yet the information about the photos had been zealously kept secret, and very few of us were in the know. It was not I, of course, and I don't think it could have been my young Argentinian friend. Only two names remained: Richard and the inspector himself. Both of them had certainly almost equal reason to prevent a new

Chapter 28 (cont.)

Seldom swept a hand over the photos Petersen had distributed, with the firm gesture with which I'd seen him wipe a blackboard clean of complicated sums that had been proven wrong.

'What I can tell you,' he said, 'is nothing but conjecture, what we mathematicians call a plausible argument. Even though I think it explains most of the facts. Let me go back then to these first two photos, which are the only ones that really matter. Regarding these two, I wasn't able to decide which, of all the possible patterns, was the hidden one. As I've said, I was inclined to choose that of the messenger who was intercepted again and again. But the message that was supposed to be intercepted kept changing in a most irritating manner. Was it the words on Kristen's piece of paper? Was it the publication of Lewis Carroll's diaries? Each possibility seemed reasonable in and of itself, but I wasn't able to lend it a convincingly definitive sense. I was stumped. At this point, I was supposed to deliver a lecture on Quine's anthropologist and the elusive meaning of the word "*gavagai*".'

'"*Gavagai*"?' Petersen asked, puzzled. 'Anthropology? I always thought your classes were in mathematical logic.'

'Yes, "*gavagai*".' Seldom sighed. 'But no matter. I'll tell this in a different way. You must have heard of the Prosecutor's

Fallacy. If someone is guilty, it's logical to suppose that all proofs must point to that person. But the fact that all proofs point to one person doesn't mean, *ipso facto*, that that person is guilty, as prosecutors infer, alas, far too often. There's a version of what we may call common sense on the same question: if an animal has four paws, a nose, wags its tail and barks, it must be a dog. But for mathematicians, this is not necessarily the case. An animal with long ears, white fur, big front teeth and a fondness for carrots may be *something else* than a rabbit. And this is what our young friend reminded me of, just in time, at the end of the class in which I had been speaking about rabbits as the most obvious animal in the world. It was something he said to me about the photos, something that had been all the time in front of our very noses. In essence, that we should not look at the photographs as such, but only at the subtle difference between the first photo and the second: that the first one arrived *before* the attack, and therefore could be interpreted *a posteriori* as a warning or a sign that anticipated the crime. However, the second photo was hidden in the box of chocolates and could only be discovered *after* Hinch's death. Was this distinction meaningful? I thought, yes. Why, I asked myself, did it go so long unnoticed? Because Kristen, in spite of everything, had managed to survive. And recalling the morning before the attack, she was able to tell us about the photograph. Furthermore, we only found out about that photo because the first attack of Citizen X *failed*. And yet, no doubt the car was driven against Kristen with the intention of killing her. That she survived was almost a statistical miracle. Now let us imagine for a moment that Kristen had been killed that night. What guarantee, what assurance, could the murderer have that someone would notice the photo? In all likelihood, that connection would never have been made, because

Kristen's death would be put down to an accident, unexplainable perhaps, but an accident nonetheless. That is to say, if the photo was meant as an intentional sign, a warning, a message, if that first attack had been successful, paradoxically we would never have received it. But that is absurd. If the murder had been planned as a sign, it made no sense that this sign should have reached us only because of the remarkable chance that Kristen hadn't died. This left me with a disturbing question. Had Kristen somehow lied to us about that first photo? Certainly they had attempted to kill her; she could not have feigned that. But could she have made up, as soon as she was beginning to recover, the story of the photo? This was hard to believe, above all because Kristen had always seemed to me someone naturally inclined towards the truth, someone who would find it very hard to tell a lie. It occurred to me that perhaps she *had* told the truth, but not the *whole* truth. Or maybe, due to the traumatic experience of the accident and the hospital, she had an incomplete or mistaken memory of events. Even though I knew that the police had already spoken to Brandy, the secretary of our Department, I decided that I'd conduct my own investigation. I asked her first, as the inspector's men had already done, if she had seen someone leave a blank envelope in Kristen's pigeonhole. She said no, as she had told them: anyone could come and go without her noticing. But then I remembered that Kristen had been in Guildford prior to that evening and that therefore she might not have checked her post on the two previous days. I decided to ask the question in a different way. Brandy had given her answer to a couple of policemen, and I was sure that the presence of the uniformed men alone would have made her think exclusively of odd or suspicious characters. I asked her to make a further effort and try to remember if anyone else had asked for Kristen, or left something for her on the previous days. Almost immediately she remembered that at the beginning of the week, towards midday, a plump little man, very courteous, had been there and had asked where he could leave a note for Kristen. Brandy had pointed to the pigeonholes in the entrance. She had seen this man before in the department, in the company of Raymond Martin, and maybe once with me. She remembered him distinctly because it had been lunchtime and she was feeling hungry, when the man suddenly pulled a chocolate out of his pocket. I asked a couple more questions to confirm that the man had indeed been Leonard Hinch. It was as I had imagined. I guessed that he had spoken with Kristen before the first meeting – because you'll recall that he was here, even though he was not a member and I had not sent him an invitation. But now I could be certain: the envelope that Kristen found that morning was in all probability the message Hinch had left for her a few days back. But this led me to a new conundrum, because it didn't seem that Hinch had in any way attempted to conceal his identity. Brandy remembered seeing him with an envelope in his hand, but she couldn't say whether his name was on it or not. Now I couldn't help wondering if Kristen hadn't lied to us about the envelope and also about the photo. But once again: why ever would she do a thing like that? Why lie to us about this, especially after having been attacked in such a brutal manner and when she could still believe that her life was at risk? Here I suddenly remembered what my young friend told me in the hospital. He had met Kristen coming out of the cinema that evening, shortly before she was struck down. And she seemed saddened by something. Something had happened to her that day, and it had dimmed the euphoria caused by her discovery. I started to conceive yet another possibility. I imagined that Hinch had indeed left in her pigeonhole the photo she had shown us, but perhaps with a very different motive. Hinch, as we later learned, had a network set up to distribute his photographs, but he had made sure to proceed with extreme caution, so that the photos, if discovered, could be taken for old postcards from the Victorian Age, relics of a lost and fleeting art. Perhaps he wanted to take these precautionary measures a step further and it occurred to him that if a researcher of indisputable integrity like Kristen examined these photos, he could find out if they might pass muster under expert eyes. This would grant him a final certificate of innocence in case someone were to discover the truth. He could then always show in his defence his correspondence with Kristen, and demonstrate that he had always sought from irreproachable researchers the assurance that the photos were true antiques. Or perhaps the photo was a sort of bait to approach Kristen. Well, it is possible that in his note he summoned her to his office to ask her for a report on the photo he'd left in her pigeonhole. He had chosen a day on which his secretary was away on holiday and he would be alone. Here I tried to imagine the scene. Maybe Kristen discovered something of the true nature of Hinch's dealings with the photos. Or maybe something else took place between them, something that we'll never know. But without doubt, because of what happened afterwards, at a certain point of their meeting she threatened to denounce him. Remember that Hinch had just mortgaged his house, the only property he possessed, in order to equal the offer from the American publisher. He also knew that the vote of the Brotherhood was a tie. All it needed was a word from Kristen, for Kristen to tell just one of us what had happened, for him to be ruined for ever. Hinch realised that he had to act immediately. He knew that, close to the Kidlington roundabout, in the direction of Kristen's lodgings, students often raced their cars at hospital, as I clearly remember, was whether I had revealed in my emails the existence of the paper. When I told her I hadn't, I believe she discarded in her own mind all the members of the Brotherhood *en masse*. Why should they attack her, she obviously thought, if they don't even know what the discovery was? She realised then that it must have been Hinch. At that moment, she put her plan in action, and she showed both of us, and also Petersen, the first photo. Of course, she didn't tell us that it was Hinch who had sent it because, for what she was planning, she meant to hide the connection between them both. Perhaps she took only the first step, one that might be attributed to a slip of memory, waiting for a confirmation. Then, on the following days, she received almost simultaneously two devastating pieces of news. She learned, thanks to Leyton Howard's calculations, that indeed someone had wanted to murder her. And she also learned that she would never walk again nor be able to have children. She also found out then, in case there was still something missing to dispel her doubts, that Hinch had sought to know how much she remembered of the previous evening. If earlier perhaps she only wanted to hand Hinch over to the police, now that she knew she was going to be left disabled for life, she decided to seek her revenge. The game was afoot. Inspector Petersen and I, without realising it, had helped her set it up.'

With no little help on my part, I thought bitterly while I looked at the faces held rapt by the story.

'Our first conjecture,' Seldom went on to say, 'was that some kind of crusader against paedophilia wanted to prevent the publication of the diaries. Kristen only had to feed that conjecture. As part of her plan, she had already introduced in our first conversation the words of Lizard Bill from *Alice in Wonderland* so that I would recall them at the right moment. She had probably already thought of using aconite, confidently hoping that someone in the Brotherhood, among those who can recite the complete works of Lewis Carroll by heart, would establish the link with the magical little cake in the book. All she had to do now was to lay her hands on the poison, but inside the hospital, I suppose this was quite easy. That is why she accepted and encouraged the company of one of the Methodist sisters, someone whom everyone trusted and who could have access, like a nurse, to the medicine cabinets. And someone who would be able, when the time came, to walk for her and leave the chocolates in the publisher's letter box.'

'But this story you're telling us,' Petersen said in a tone of disbelief, 'is it only a theory or is there proof of some kind?'

'I wish it were only a theory,' Seldom said glumly. 'And in fact, if I didn't arrive earlier to these conclusions, it's because something in me refused to think that Kristen was able to come up with something like this. And yet, at the same time, it seemed to me that this was the only hypothesis that accounted for all the facts. Kristen was perhaps too intelligent in formulating her plan: for instance, her way of introducing the sentence about the lizard and the space-rocket, so that I would recall it later. It was she, I realised afterwards, who suggested the allusion. When I could no longer refuse to see the possibility of all this, I went to see her. I told her everything I've just told you. At first she remained silent and then she burst into tears, still without saying a word. Then she asked me what to do, as if I were her father. I told her, of course, that she should go to the police and confess. She promised she would, and also that she'd send a letter to the Brotherhood together with the paper "to take all that weight off her shoulders". I'm surprised,' Seldom said, looking at his watch, 'that the letter hasn't yet arrived.'

'But even then, even if she were to confess everything you've told us, we'd still need to explain the murder of Anderson, isn't that so?' Petersen asked.

Seldom seemed about to answer, but at that moment we heard a few discreet knocks and the very young policeman whom I'd seen at the entrance put his head through the door. He approached Petersen and whispered a few words in his ear. The inspector nodded and gestured to someone outside to come in. We saw Sister Rosaura, tall, pale and dressed in brown, appear. She had a letter in her hand that she gave to Sir Richard.

'The messenger has come,' Seldom whispered softly to me.

Chapter 29

Sir Richard took the letter and lifted his eyes to thank Rosaura and dismiss her, but the woman remained stolidly by his side, watching his every move as he handled the envelope.

'If it doesn't inconvenience you,' she said, 'Kristen made me promise that I would stay to make sure the envelope is opened and the letter read. She asked me please not to leave until you've reached the end.'

Sir Richard arched his eyebrows and gave the inspector a questioning look. Petersen nodded in response.

'This is somewhat irregular but, oh well, we were all waiting for this letter. Please take a seat and don't worry: I'll read it without omitting a single word.'

Rosaura sat down next to me, her back rigid against the chair. Sir Richard drew out from the envelope several sheets neatly covered in lines of cramped handwriting. He put his glasses on and his voice underwent a strange transformation as he began to read. It was as if Kristen had become suddenly present in the room and had taken her place among us.

I'm writing this letter at the suggestion – or should I say insistence – of Arthur Seldom, both as an explanation and as an apology to the Brotherhood, though not to all of its members. Perhaps it would be best to start

*with my excursion to Guildford. You'll recall that
we had allotted for my journey two consecutive days
during which the museum would be closed so that I
would be able to work in peace and quiet; Sir Richard
had given me the key to the place with all kinds of
recommendations and precautions. When I arrived, I
found a kind note from the librarian explaining how
the photocopying machine worked and giving me
permission to go through the archives and the boxes
and to examine anything I might find. I spent the first
day there going through the contents of every page in
the diaries, from the first to the last notebook, and
checking that each photocopied page was sufficiently
legible. Once this first part of my work was finished,
on the second day I went through all the books, albums
and papers that were on the open stacks. Then I started
opening the desk drawers, which the librarian had left
unlocked for me. In one of these drawers I found the
catalogue that the members of the family put together
when the Guildford museum was set up, with all the
items they had managed to gather, classified for the
exhibit. One of the lines in the listing, incredible as this
might seem to you, as it did to me at the time, read: 'Cut
Pages in Diary'. I read this in a shocked state of surprise
and disbelief. What might this refer to? At first I thought
it might be some sort of Carrollian joke by a member of
the family, because I couldn't, of course, expect to find
there the actual pages ripped out and lost for ever. Even
so, hardly able to contain my hopes, I went or rather ran
to the shelf marked in the catalogue and I opened the file
numbered accordingly. In it was a single sheet, or less
than a sheet, half a page, seemingly torn out in a hurry,
with writing on both sides. I recognised the handwriting*

at once: it was, no doubt about it, that of Menella
Dodgson. I had previously read most of her letters, and
her handwriting was to me unmistakable. On one side
of the paper were written a few dates and remarks, in
ink of various colours, referring to Alice Liddell's adult
life: her wedding, the birth of her children, her death.
On the other side was the number of the page that had
been torn out from the 1863 diary; and after that, one
could read, also in Menella's hand, a two-line summary
of what had been written on the torn-out page. I'll
transcribe it here just as it appears on the paper:

L.C. learns from Mrs Liddell that he is supposed to be
using the children as a means of paying court to the governess. He is also supposed by some to be courting Ina.

That was all, and at first glance, this meant very little.
Barely a concern over a rumour that might affect the
reputation of Mrs Liddell's eldest daughter who was
already fourteen, an age when she could expect to begin
receiving marriage proposals. Something of far less
weight than what we might have imagined, of such little
import that it didn't seem to warrant the drastic decision
of eliminating the page. But then, why had it been torn
out? It could be, I thought at first, because from that day
onwards Mrs Liddell had kept her daughters away from
Lewis Carroll, and perhaps on that page he had vented
his fury and frustration in a particularly disagreeable
way that made him look bad. But this didn't seem to me
altogether convincing: Lewis Carroll had, on other pages
of his diary, asserted his dislike of Mrs Liddell, and all

those pages survived. And what Mrs Liddell told him could not be all that hurtful, because on the following week he returns, offering to take the girls on an excursion once again, as if it had been nothing more than a passing tiff. It must have been something else. But what? The part referring to the governess, to Miss Prickett, could not be very significant: I remembered well that in other sections of his diaries Lewis Carroll referred to these rumours, and that he and Mrs Liddell had both laughed them off. The only important part of the sentence, therefore, was the ending: the fear of having people believe that Lewis Carroll was courting Ina. This seemed to make complete sense. On the previous afternoon, Mrs Liddell herself, surrounded by her friends, had almost certainly seen Lewis Carroll behaving somewhat too intimately with her eldest daughter, who was at the time quite tall for her age and fully developed. And maybe she'd heard someone else's comment about this relationship.

I remained all afternoon at the museum reflecting on this, and flipping through the pages of the diaries in search of a new clue. And suddenly I had something like an epiphany: I remembered that the first person who expressed concern over Lewis Carroll's photos, the first parent who forbade him from taking pictures of her children when alone with them, was Mrs Liddell, after he had chosen Ina as the model for his first photographs. I went through the many instances where Ina is mentioned in the diaries, at the time and throughout the following years, while Alice's name barely appears at all during that same period. I recalled the intriguing letter that Ina sends Alice when both are adult women, in which she tells her that she's had to write, as a 'made-up excuse' to explain the interruption of Lewis Carroll's relationship with the family, that he had become 'too affectionate' with Alice, who was fast growing up. Actually, this was only partly made up: Lewis Carroll had not become 'too affectionate' with Alice but with Ina herself! And I remembered that there were four handwritten notebooks that never survived, in which the early years of his relationship with the Liddells were set down. All censorious actions on the part of the family belonged to those years: the last was regarding the page torn from the 1863 diary. For an uninformed reader, that page of the diary, on its own, would probably not reveal anything improper, but for Menella, who had read the diaries in their entirety, it was the last trace of a story that had at all cost to be suppressed. I knew then what it was that Menella had tried to hide by ripping out that page: that Lewis Carroll's first child love had been for Ina, not for Alice. Both Menella and Violet had been given, like their father Stuart, the chance to read all of the diaries. And maybe through intuition or a keener perspicacity, they were able to read between the lines what their father missed in those four volumes: a story of forbidden love. Probably what Lewis Carroll exposed in the story told in the diaries was, in his own way, 'blameless' and sufficiently disguised to escape the benevolent eye of his nephew. But Menella perhaps feared that someone else might discover what she and her sister had discovered, and decided to get rid of those four notebooks for ever. However, in the 1863 diary, a last vestige of that love story had survived, on the page that reported the talk with Mrs Liddell. Menella then tears it out as well but, in a pang of remorse, decides to write a few words summing up its essence. That last sign, that miraculous piece of paper, might have been like the Rosetta Stone for whoever might be capable of deciphering it. I suppose I should have communicated this discovery at once to my thesis director, Thornton Reeves, but, I don't mind saying this now, I decided not to: I was convinced, knowing him as I did, that as soon as he'd lay eyes on the paper he'd find a way to appropriate it and claim credit for its discovery. I realised that I'd found, in the most unexpected way, a small hidden treasure, and I was afraid that someone else, as soon as the museum reopened on the following day, might also come upon it. I made up my mind, then and there, to hold on to the paper and call Professor Arthur Seldom in whom I had absolute trust. He promised me that he'd do whatever possible for the credit of the discovery to be mine, and I gave him my word that I would put the paper back in its place as soon as I'd had the chance to show it to everyone at the Brotherhood meeting. I returned to Oxford with the paper well hidden.

During the train ride from Guildford I thought of all the possible ramifications. There appeared, or were compelled to appear, a multitude of fragments of the thousands of pages I'd read on the life of Lewis Carroll, and fragments of his correspondence, that could now be seen in a different light. I realised that, rather than a simple article, I would be able to write a whole book if I managed to disentangle sufficiently that single thread. I won't conceal the fact that I felt euphoric and perhaps too proprietorial about my finding. I was aware that it had been an extraordinary stroke of luck that no one had previously set eyes on the paper and that it fell on me to write that book, and I wouldn't allow anyone to take this away from me. As soon as I arrived in Oxford, I went, as I did every morning, to the Mathematical Institute, to see if I had any correspondence in my pigeonhole, and I discovered the envelope with only my name on it. Intrigued, I opened it.

Inside was a photograph of a young girl in a forest setting that at first glance I thought I recognised as one of the pictures Lewis Carroll took of Beatrice Hatch, and then sent to London to be hand-coloured. Together with the photo was a note from Leonard Hinch. He wrote, in his amiable tone, that he was interested in whatever I could tell him about the colouring technique, the approximate year, the camera and chemicals Lewis Carroll might have used. And he gave me his phone number. I took it as a sign of fate. I was thinking of writing a book and suddenly, as soon as I arrived back in Oxford, the foremost publisher of all the books about Lewis Carroll wanted to see me. I phoned him at once, because the letter had been sitting in my pigeonhole for a couple of days. I thought that the question about the photo was a good excuse to talk with him and propose the idea for my book. I knew enough about this series of photos to discuss them whenever he wished. He laughed when I said that, and suggested I come to his place that very afternoon, at a time sufficiently advanced 'to have a little drink of something'. I explained to him that it couldn't be too late because I was going to the cinema later that evening, and we agreed for me to come to his office at six.

When I hung up, I examined the photo more carefully and suddenly I had the feeling that there was something odd about the image, though I couldn't say what. Perhaps something in the girl's expression seemed to me different from the one I remembered. I went up to my room and pulled out Henry Haas's book where there was an excellent reproduction of that same image. I discovered then something that seemed very strange. There were a number of tiny differences between both pictures. The posture was somewhat more hunched, and the length of the hair seemed different. Even the grass was not exactly the same. For a moment, I thought it might have been a different take on the same day with slight variations of light and camera angle. But then I looked more carefully at the girl's features and realised, unlikely as it might seem, that it was another child. I remembered that Beatrice had a sister, Evelyn, who looked very like her. I wondered if Lewis Carroll might not have tried to photograph both girls in the same pose. I searched for other images of Beatrice and Evelyn. And though I couldn't at first quite believe it, I was forced to conclude that the photo Hinch had sent me was of neither of the Hatch sisters. It was a third girl, one who was not among the child models I was aware of. However, the photo appeared to have been taken at the same time as the others in the series, with the same kind of technique. The only hypothesis I could come up with at the moment was that imitators of Lewis Carroll had appeared during his lifetime. I spent quite a few hours that afternoon trying to search through the bibliography of that decade to see if there was any mention of possible imitators. At six, I went to see Hinch with a preliminary report on what I had discovered. I was surprised that he himself opened the door. He apologised for the disorder of accumulated correspondence on the reception desk, and he explained that his secretary was on holiday. I wasn't pleased to hear this, because I had heard rumours about Hinch and wasn't eager to spend time alone with him. But he welcomed me cordially, above all suspicion, and we went into his office. He had on his desk one of his habitual chocolate boxes and, as soon as we sat down, he offered me one. I knew the joke that went around about Hinch's chocolates and I thought I should feel proud of being an exception to his rule, but I nevertheless refused. He then

with the Liddell family. He heard me out attentively, and stood up as if, infected by my enthusiasm, he were considering the possibilities of such a book. I now believe that he pretended to be more enthusiastic than he really was but, unfortunately for me, at the time I believed him. Even a possible title came up for the future book: Ina in Wonderland. He made me promise that I'd give it to him before anyone else. I was utterly delighted and, of course, said yes. Then he poured out another glass for me and one more for himself, because he said that a toast was always the best way to conclude an agreement. Unfortunately, I accepted that second glass. He insisted I empty it in one go, like he did, at the count of three, and I did. Then he took both glasses, put them on the desk, and tried to embrace me. For a second, I thought it was just his effusive way of celebrating the future publication, equivalent to a handshake, and I didn't immediately reject him. But then, feeling encouraged, he tightened the embrace and tried to kiss me. I pushed him away in disgust and tried to free myself, but he struggled and tried to get to my face, blind to my rejection. I gathered all my strength and gave him a shove that landed him on the floor. During the struggle, I had ended up behind his desk. And he, getting back on his feet, barred the way out. I was afraid that he would once again launch at me, and I pulled out one of the desk drawers as a weapon to defend myself, thinking that, if necessary, I'd bash his head with it in order to get to the door. I pulled the drawer out from its coasters and all its contents spilled on to the floor. I then saw, spread all over the place, dozens of photos of naked girls in all kinds of poses, some in black-and-white and some coloured, pasted on to cardboard cut to the size of the one I had been studying all day long. Both he and I stood there motionless. And then, as he was standing up, he begged me in a whining voice to forgive him and not to tell the Brotherhood what had taken place between us. He realised that I was only looking at the door behind him and he opened to let me out. He told me that he'd never thought of doing me harm, and that it had only been a regrettable mistake on his part. I didn't stop to listen to him: I merely grabbed my bag and the photo he had sent me, and left without looking back. I sat in a coffee-shop and had a good cry, and for a second I thought of calling my mother, but I realised it would be no use. She would somehow blame me for having agreed to have a drink with him. Nor did I know whom I could tell within the Brotherhood: there were too many rumours about Hinch for me to say that I hadn't been warned ...

'Excuse me,' Sir Richard said. 'I need a sip of water before proceeding.'

'Poor child,' Laura Raggio said, clearly moved. 'If only she had said something to me ... '

'For God's sake, Richard, just carry on,' Josephine implored.

Chapter 29 (cont.)

Sir Richard took a sip of water from the glass someone had passed to him, coughed discreetly to clear his throat and returned to the reading.

Once I felt somewhat calmer, I decided to go to the cinema anyway. The film I had chosen, Seconds, *made me even sadder. It told the parable of a man who tries to live a second life and is given a younger body, a lovely house and the chance to dedicate himself to painting, something he had always dreamt of. But even then, in this second ideal life, everything becomes increasingly horrible for him. In the cinema, I burst again into tears, several times. On the way out, I ran into that Argentinian student of Professor Seldom, whom I'll call G because I don't know how to write his full name. He came up to me when he saw me crying and said a few kind words. His face in the entrance hall of the cinema was my last memory of that night. When I woke up in the hospital, my mother was there by my side. She told me that a car had hit me on the road by the plant, close to the Kidlington roundabout, on my way home. She told me that the police thought it had been a drunken student. She, and a doctor later on, asked me to try to remember what had happened. At first, only a few images and snippets of the film I'd seen came back to me. I didn't seem to manage to go either backwards or forwards, after the very brief conversation I'd had with G as I was leaving the cinema. All that night I felt frightened, thinking that like the character in the film, I too had undergone an operation and I was now someone very different inside the same body. But the next day, gradually, when I was left once again alone, the images began to flow back. First of all, I remembered the Guildford paper, and where I had hidden it. Then I remembered the photo in my pigeonhole and the phone conversation with Hinch in the morning. I remembered that in the afternoon I'd been with him in his office. And that he'd poured me a glass of wine to celebrate the future publication of my book. And then I had a confused memory of struggling with him because he was trying to kiss me. The last image I had was of his terrified face looking up at me from the floor, begging me not to tell anyone what had happened. Of course, I wondered immediately if it might not have been Hinch who had hit me with the car. After all, Hinch knew I was going to the cinema that evening and that no one would be accompanying me back home. All he had to do was to follow me in his car to Kidlington and wait for when I turned the corner on a solitary street. And yet, I couldn't quite believe it: it seemed to me excessive, maybe because I had never seriously thought of denouncing him or telling anyone about the disagreeable incident between us. I myself had felt somewhat ashamed and I blamed myself for having been so naive, and for having accepted his second glass of wine. But even if I couldn't quite believe it, neither could I dismiss the thought from my mind. Then I found out that Arthur Seldom also had his suspicions and believed that someone had wanted to kill me, and that this was why he had requested a policeman to stand guard at my door. I therefore asked to speak with him before the arrival of Inspector Petersen, and to see G once more, in case I remembered something else. I realised at once that Arthur believed that the attack was related to the Guildford discovery. I asked him whether he had told anyone else about the paper, and he denied it, telling me that in the email he had sent to the Brotherhood, he hadn't even mentioned it. As a result, I could eliminate from my list of suspects all the members of the Brotherhood, because we three were the only ones who knew about the paper: Arthur, the Argentinian student and myself. Or that was what I believed at the time. Only Hinch remained, even though I couldn't, at least for the time being, simply come up and accuse him. However, just in case, I decided to set a modest plan in action. I showed them the photo Hinch had sent me, without mentioning his name. I allowed myself a white lie and told them that I had received it in a blank envelope. Nor did I mention what I had discovered about the photo. My intention was to send Hinch a warning, a sign telling him that I was able to remember everything. I took only that first step, from which I could still retreat, hoping that the person who had run me over would be found and that everything I believed about Hinch would fade away. I spent the following day in suspense, waiting for more news. I couldn't imagine that the worst news of all would come from within the hospital: the doctors who performed my operation came to tell me that I would never walk again and that I'd be condemned to a wheelchair for the rest of my life. Nor would I be able to have children. Even though deep down inside me I might have guessed something like this, because I had not felt my legs since the attack, during those first days of waiting I had given myself over to the idea of a miracle, a second miracle for which I was secretly praying. Something essential in me changed when I heard the news. I don't mind now putting it in writing. As I promised Arthur, I intend to tell the whole truth. I wept, and inside me I howled in despair, but I felt that what finally emerged was above all hatred, a seething hatred that I had never felt before for anything or anyone. Now all I wanted was a sign that indeed it had been Hinch, but merely to be able, impeccably, to kill him. And on the next day I received not one but two indications. Leyton Howard's report showed that the car had not intended to brake as it came upon me. And more importantly, thanks to G, I found out that Hinch was interested in knowing how much I remembered when I woke up. I don't mind confessing that I heard this as an answer to an unavowable prayer. Now I felt free of any guilt, partly because I understood that it would have been useless to denounce him to the police. If I accused him, I myself would become his alibi. He could turn everything around: if I revealed that he had sent me the photograph, he would simply say that he had wanted a professional opinion. And what had taken place between us – that, too, he could explain in his own way. If he had been sufficiently careful with the car, there would be no traces remaining to incriminate him. So I would live for the rest of my life in a wheelchair, and he would remain scot-free and would publish Lewis Carroll's diaries and, on top of*

everything, he'd make tons of money. I couldn't bear
that. I'd been rereading with Sister Rosaura the old
biblical texts that my mother would recite for me, and I
recalled, again and again, like a prayer within a prayer,
like a whisper repeated in the night, the title of a
detective novel taken from a verse in Ecclesiastes: The
Beast Must Die. Yes. I thought of nothing else: the beast
must die. And even so, I was bothered by the fact that I
didn't yet know what Hinch's true reason was for trying
to kill me. I couldn't believe that it was only because of
the kiss he'd tried to give me and the fear of my
accusation. There must have been something else. But
what? I tried once more to recall everything that had
happened that day, since the moment of seeing the
envelope in my pigeonhole. I remembered that
something in the girl's expression had seemed odd to
me, out of place, and that this had led me to seek out the
authentic photo in Henry Haas's book. I pulled the
photo out of my bag and looked at it again. I
understood at last the hidden and sinister truth: I saw
that in spite of the fact that the camera and the
chemicals must have been identical to those used by
Lewis Carroll, something in the child's features
appeared strangely fresh, alive, contemporary. And I
recalled in a sudden illumination the scene of the
struggle with Hinch in his office, and the photographs
that spilled on the floor when I pulled out the drawer.
Now everything seemed to make sense. There was no
collector of Victorian photographs. It was Hinch, no
doubt about it, who commissioned these photos. Photos
of naked girls, of today, taken with the same Ottewill
camera that Lewis Carroll had used. That was what I
had really seen, without realising it, in Hinch's office.

That was the true motive. I felt a strange calm when I understood that now I could kill him without any remorse. Of course, it didn't seem all that easy to accomplish from this prison that my hospital bed had become. But then fate offered a little assistance. I found out through G the fantastical interpretation that Arthur had given to Hinch's photograph, an interpretation that Inspector Petersen himself was taking seriously: a possible crusader against paedophilia whose purpose was to murder all the members of the Brotherhood. Had I not been, as I was, tied to a hospital bed, I'd have laughed out loud at this, and I'd have made my own list of candidates to offer as suggestions to this honest pipe dream. But as soon as I was left once more on my own, I realised that I'd been served the opportunity I'd been looking for, on a platter. All I needed was to continue with this false conjecture, to add to it a second term. And I would never be suspected, because after all, I'd been the first victim in this imaginary series. In my first conversation with Arthur and G I'd told them that the car had made me fly into the air like Lizard Bill in Wonderland. I wasn't sure that they'd remember this, but I decided to plan Hinch's murder with certain features that would bring to mind some other scenes in the Alice books. I was faced, of course, with the small problem of lying in my hospital bed, but this meant that they were not likely to think of me as the possible murderer. I remembered Hinch's addiction to chocolates and I decided that the simplest way would be to send him a box of poisoned confections. All I had to do was cut off the name of my thesis director on one of his cards, to make it seem that the box was a gift from the whole of the Brotherhood, and to choose another photo of a naked girl to place at the bottom of the box. I asked my mother to buy a box like the one I'd seen in Hinch's office. She would be the ideal messenger, because she lived outside Guildford and didn't even have a TV, only an old radio on which she listened mainly to classical music. Even if Hinch's murder were to make the national news, she wouldn't find out. During a conversation with Rosaura, I was able to introduce cautiously the subject of poisons, with the excuse that my mother never seemed to succeed in exterminating the mice at her place. To my surprise, I discovered that Sister Rosaura was an expert in poisons. I asked her about mercury nitrate because I had read in a book on Alice that the hatters at the time were poisoned by their contact with the mercury that they used to treat the fur of their hats, and that they sometimes suffered serious mental traumas: this had inspired the creation of the Mad Hatter. But according to Rosaura, mercury wasn't absolutely lethal, and I couldn't risk a poison that would allow Hinch to remain alive. But suddenly she mentioned aconite and the strange, agonising effect it produced in the victim: legs, arms and head were felt to expand to the point of bursting. I knew without a shadow of a doubt that this had to be it and no other. Also, aconite was really strong and caused death even in the tiniest doses. I asked Rosaura if she could get enough for me to give to my mother to kill all the mice in her vegetable garden. I don't suppose she fully believed me, but neither did she ask me any questions. Perhaps she guessed that I knew who had been responsible for my attack and what I planned to do. I'll never know, but I want to make absolutely clear that Sister Rosaura was utterly blameless and had no part in

*my plan: I proceeded entirely on my own. Only one
thing worried me when I conceived this plan, and that
was having to face Arthur Seldom. I had the irrational
fear that once he looked at me, he'd know everything. I
wanted to keep him away from me by any means
possible. I knew the aversion he felt for Methodist
nurses as a consequence of his own time in the hospital,
and, in general, of any mention of a God. I decided then
to exaggerate an attitude of religious gratitude, and also
my attachment to Sister Rosaura. And yet that wasn't
enough: he knew me too well to believe in this sudden
conversion, and that was, in the end, the thread that
allowed him to unravel the truth until he reached me.
I'm comforted by the knowledge that I had enough time
to finish my book. You'll find it on my desk with the
title – why not? – that Hinch suggested: Ina in
Wonderland. As to the Guildford paper, you'll have to
forgive me for having decided to keep it. I feel it belongs
to me: it's the only thing in the world that ever truly
belonged to me, and I don't want to give it up. You can
be assured that the words I wrote out are strictly those
penned by Menella. Arthur Seldom advised me to give
myself up to the police after writing this letter, but I
could not bear to double the prison of my body with
another prison. I prefer to apply the old biblical
punishment of an eye for an eye, which seems to me
fairer and more in accordance with my previous
mathematical formation, and drink the same dose of
aconite that I gave Hinch. That is why I asked Rosaura
to remain until the end of the reading of this letter: I
don't want anyone to rescue me at the last moment. As
soon as I get to the final full stop, for want of a
chocolate, I'll inject what remains of the vial into one of*

the scones that my mother sent me in her last care package. I trust that Sister Rosaura wasn't mistaken about the final symptoms. I want to feel, as a last revelation, what Alice felt when she grew taller and taller after nibbling her little cake.

Chapter 30

As soon as Sir Richard finished reading the letter, Sister Rosaura leapt to her feet with a muffled cry. I saw that Seldom was also standing up with the same horrified reaction I'd had myself. But before anyone could take a step towards the door, Petersen's voice was heard, brusque and sharp.

'Please, no one move. Go back to your places. If this young woman did what she said she'd do in her letter, there's nothing that can help her now.'

He held his phone in his hand and, casting his eyes around the table, gave orders that an ambulance and a police car be sent to Kristen's house. We saw Sister Rosaura burst into tears with a long moan of despair.

'I should have known,' she said, 'I should have known . . .'

Inspector Petersen seemed to take pity on her, but only reluctantly.

'It would be better if you leave now, but you'll have to wait for me downstairs, the policeman is still standing guard. Later you'll come with me to the station to make a statement. You'll have to explain about the poison you gave Kristen. I suppose that, as a nurse, you're fully acquainted with the penalties for taking toxic substances out of a hospital dispensary.'

'I didn't take it from the dispensary,' Sister Rosaura exclaimed indignantly, looking daggers at him. 'I grow the aconite root in my own garden: I too have had to exterminate mice a number of times. I never suspected that she wanted it for another purpose.'

'We shall see about that,' Petersen said and pointed towards the door. Sister Rosaura pulled out a handkerchief to dry her eyes, and with a faint nod, took her leave. The inspector waited for the door to close and glanced again around the table.

'Even if everything that the young lady wrote in her letter were true, there's still Anderson's death left unexplained,' he said. 'She says nothing about that, and we know she couldn't have been the murderer. After interviewing her in her house, Anderson returned to his office at the paper and worked at his computer until six. We even have the finished article that he wrote with the intention of publishing it the following day. But you, Professor, had been certain beforehand that it couldn't have been Mr Haas either. Though you never explained why we should discard him from the list of suspects.'

'That,' Seldom said with deadly seriousness, 'is something that Richard should explain.'

There was a murmur of consternation, and Sir Richard lifted his eyes with a stony look. I realised that it was probably not the first time he'd had to give explanations concerning a death, and I saw in the proud expression with which he withstood Seldom's stare and in the sudden stiffening of his aged body, something of a man accustomed to giving orders and taking the consequences.

'Congratulations, Arthur,' he said in a tone that denoted threat rather than contrition. 'I should have known I couldn't deceive you. But take care: sometimes you can be, like that girl, too intelligent for your own good. I'll willingly give you an explanation. However, only to the members of the

Brotherhood, even though I can't avoid the inspector listening in. It's a question that concerns national security and we should ask your Argentinian student to leave the room now. What I'm about to say must remain an absolute secret.'

Naturally, I stood up and left the room at once. All I wanted was to get to Kristen's house as quickly as possible. When I came down the stairs and saw Sister Rosaura surrounded by the police, still sobbing, I realised with sudden and unquestionable conviction that it was too late to do anything. Nevertheless, driven by a desperate impulse, I ran up the hill. When I reached the top, exhausted and out of breath, I saw that an ambulance was parked by the door and that several neighbours were huddled by the fence. Two policemen were stretching cordons over the gravel path leading to the garden. Suddenly there was an excited murmur: the main door of the house opened to bring down step by step, with premonitory care, a stretcher with the body completely covered by a sheet. 'She's dead, she's dead,' the chorus around me was repeating like a monstrous echo, with that prurient excitement, so close to joy, that someone else's death seems to trigger in us.

I walked back home, stunned, void of thought, unable to believe that all was now over. As I passed Christ Church once more, the policeman had left and the hall porter told me that the Brotherhood meeting was over. I went to the Mathematical Institute and looked for Seldom in his office, without much hope of finding him there, and discovered that he hadn't returned. I wondered if someone had let Kristen's mother know of the death of her daughter, and decided to send Seldom an email to find out. When I opened my account, I was surprised to find a message from him, sent a few minutes earlier. He had gone to the Institute hoping to find me. He had something urgent to tell me and would wait for me at The Eagle and Child. He'd be there for another half-hour.

When I entered the pub, I didn't see him immediately in the pale cigarette fumes. I went along the bar to the back-room lounges and there he was, sitting at one of the small tables at the back, a large whisky glass already empty in his hand. He waved at me and stood up to signal to the barman that he wanted a refill. As I sat down, I was taken aback by the changes in his face, now bearing traces of profound sadness. I had never seen him like this, with such a shameful and defeated look in his eyes.

'Please don't stare at me like that,' he begged me. 'Unfortunately, at my age I can't even get drunk. Whisky merely succeeds in numbing me, slowing everything down. I don't seem to be able to advance beyond a couple of ideas. I can't even forget what I want to forget. You realise that Kristen is now dead? *Dead.* You realise that we should never have called in the police? That it was *thanks* to the police that Hinch and Anderson were killed? You realise that over and over ... ? Forgive me,' he said, as if composing himself with a great effort. 'I wouldn't want to burden you with my guilt, because it was all my fault. The fault of this curse that's always inside me. Maybe it is I who should be thinking of suicide.' He took another long sip of his whisky and fixed his eyes on me once more. 'I only wanted to see you to tell you that you should leave, leave England as soon as possible. I've lost a student, I don't want to lose another one. I'd even advise you to start packing your things today. I can help you with the air fare if necessary. Please believe me: your life is in danger.'

It took a moment for me to grasp the import of what he was saying.

'This has to do with what Sir Richard told you?'

Seldom nodded gravely.

'And am I allowed to know at least why? Is it something he mentioned in the meeting-room?'

Seldom nodded once more and suddenly an ill-restrained fury appeared in his eyes.

'I swore like the rest of them not to say anything. But I will tell you, if you promise to leave at once.'

I promised. Seldom gulped down the remains of his whisky to empty the glass, and rubbed his eyes with the heels of his hands, as if he were trying to wake up and rid himself of a nightmare.

'Richard told us that when they opened Hinch's drawers and found the photos of the naked girls, MI5 became seriously concerned. In Hinch's list, just as Anderson had discovered, it seems there were coded names of individuals in the highest spheres of government. Richard received instructions from his old Intelligence comrades to try to prevent the names from reaching the papers. When we met him at the pub with the inspector and he found out that Anderson was aware of that list and intended to publish everything he'd found on the following day, Richard urgently decided to call two men who had worked with him in the past and were to be trusted absolutely, and ask them to "convince" Anderson not to publish. He swore that he had instructed them not to lay a finger on him. But these two men were of Richard's age, and Anderson made the mistake of thinking they were tottering and feeble old men. Apparently, Anderson made fun of them and said he'd include them in his story as a colourful touch. You knew Anderson, he had a sense of humour that not everyone appreciated ... The men grew angry, there was a fight and between the two of them they ended up knifing Anderson to death. Richard feared that this death would make things worse and bring to the foreground MI5's hand in the matter. He went to see the corpse. Anderson's head and features had remained intact. Richard imagined that Anderson's death could be added as the next step in the series, and that the murder could be blamed on whoever was peddling the photos of the naked girls. He asked his men to place in Anderson's mouth one of Lewis Carroll's photos with which Anderson had planned to illustrate his article, and then he gave them the order to cut the head off and to get rid of the body with the stab wounds. In that way, Richard turned Anderson's death into another Murder in Wonderland: 'Off with his head!' He told us that, after all, it was as if our own Queen of Hearts had commanded it. At the same time, he prepared as an alternative version for the press the story of the Serbian spy cell. A head floating in the river could, he thought, be easily associated with the stories of savagery and dismemberment that reached us from the Balkans, and with Britain's recent threats to intervene in the war. He told us that in all delicate Intelligence manoeuvres they always tried to leak two stories simultaneously: one for the press and television, and another, more convoluted, subtly left for conspiracy theorists and for those who always believe they're cleverer than the rest. Two stories, two versions, so that the third one, the true one, remains concealed. When he finished telling us all this, he invoked, of course, the cause of patriotism: for God to save the Queen, he said, men and women too had to play their part. In this case, the part we were asked to play was tiny and the reward enormous. He'd make sure that all the male members of the Brotherhood would be knighted as he was, and that Josephine and Laura would be made dames. All we had to do was remain totally silent about what he had told us. It would never be revealed that Hinch had actually been murdered, and the cause of Anderson's death would

affected. But I think that Kristen's letter did everything to
excuse her. I know it's difficult to imagine that Kristen would
have planned something like that ... I hope that you hadn't
begun to have ... feelings for her.'

I shook my head, uncertain of what to tell him.

'And what she wrote about the Guildford paper? Do you
think that those were the exact words?'

'The Guildford paper ... This must sound incredible to
you, but after Richard told us about his order to cut off
Anderson's head, and after we had voted to remain silent
about the two crimes, he wouldn't allow us to leave before
settling in the minutes the question of the paper. He asked
the same question you did: should we believe that this was
the sentence written on the paper? And here we had another
little surprise: Thornton decided to speak out and confess
that he had indeed seen the paper on one of his last visits to
Guildford. But his book was by then already at the print-
ers and the paper, of course, contradicted his main thesis
concerning Lewis Carroll's quarrel with Mrs Liddell. So he
decided to make a photocopy for his archives but say nothing
about its contents. However, he can at least bear witness that
the words are exactly those that Kristen transcribed. There
was a round of opinions on this and it was decided to commission a calligrapher to copy out the sentence on a piece of
paper from Menella's day. I suggested that Leyton Howard
could do it admirably because calligraphy is another of his
abilities. I know that Thornton agreed to take the photocopy
and a few antique pens to Leyton today, because Richard
wants to go to Guildford tomorrow morning, first thing, and
replace the paper and tie up this last loose end. Or rather,
the one before last. The last, I don't know if you realise it,
is yourself. I didn't quite believe the version that Richard
gave us. I rather think they told him to silence Anderson by

whatever means, and the story of the two little old thugs was a way of making the crime appear as an unfortunate mistake, something that got out of hand. I wouldn't want you to suffer an unfortunate accident as well or to be the victim of a similar mistake in the next few days. Early tomorrow morning I can tell Brandy to reserve a ticket for you. Do you think you could manage to be ready by tomorrow and catch an evening flight home?'

I felt distraught but nodded.

'If I were in your shoes,' he said in a low, urgent voice, 'I'd start packing right now.'

I stood up and he did the same.

'It's best if we said goodbye now,' he told me. 'I don't think I'll go to the Institute tomorrow, but I'll certainly talk to Brandy as early as possible.'

I thought I might never in my life see him again, and for a brief moment felt the impulse to hug him. But Seldom, placing one hand on my shoulder, stretched out his other hand and shook mine with the appropriate degree of effusion, perhaps because he truly thought that we would cross paths again in the near future.

'Carry on working on the subject of logic,' he said, 'and we'll certainly meet again in our itinerant circus of conferences. I hope that the next time, murders will be absent.'

As I left the pub, still feeling bewildered, I went by the Alice shop, hoping to see Sharon one last time. But the shop was already closed. I carried on for another block until I got to the corner of the police station. I didn't want to run into Petersen, but apparently everyone had left: only the entrance booth was lit and also the attic room I had shared with Leyton. I decided to go up. After all, there were a few of

my books there, and papers of my program that I wanted
to take back. I found Leyton practising calligraphy under
an examination lamp. He looked up at me with as much
surprise as his face would allow. I told him I was leaving the
following night and started to gather my papers. He made
no comment: he seemed completely wrapped up in marking
short strokes on a paper, gradually trying to gain speed. I
couldn't help approaching his table and he raised his eyes
when he noticed me next to him. On a board he had laid out
the photocopy of the Guildford paper and on the table were
several sheets on which he was writing at various speeds with
an old-fashioned fountain pen.

'What are you doing?' I asked, as if I knew nothing.

Leyton raised his eyebrows but barely glanced at me.

'I suppose someone lost a paper and they want to replace
it, based on this photocopy. The handwriting is meant to pass
a calligraphic examination.'

He showed me a rectangular piece of yellowish paper, one
side of which seemed torn.

'The problem is that I won't have a second chance: they
only gave me this one piece to try it on. And I don't have long.
They're coming for it in a little while.'

I picked up a sheet on which there were a number of
try-outs: the similarity with Menella's handwriting was
extraordinary. Yes, evidently Leyton had a gift for this as
well. I told him so admiringly and he merely shrugged.

'The important thing is to find both the speed and the
intensity of the stroke. I'm thinking of using your program to
calibrate myself. And now,' he added, 'if you don't mind, I'd
like to be alone. I'm not yet ready to perform in public.'

I went down the stairs into the bare lonely night of Oxford.
In a daze, I thought about the next day: about Emily Bronson
and the excuses I would have to make concerning my grant;

Epilogue

'But how did *you* find out?' Kristen's mother asked me, still sobbing.

I had arrived half an hour earlier at her small house on the outskirts of Guildford: the house, I thought, in which Kristen had grown up. It had not been easy to find her address, and when I knocked on the door for the first time all the curtains were drawn and I wondered if she might have gone to Oxford and if my trip here had been in vain. But when I knocked again, a little louder, I heard the shuffle of feet within, as if I'd woken her from her sleep. She peered out, trying to cover her dishevelled hair with one hand. Her eyes were swollen, from sleep or weeping, and she seemed infinitely older. She told me that she had received a call from Inspector Petersen the previous night, telling her of Kristen's death, and that she had felt like dying herself. She would have ended her life if only she had found enough sleeping pills. She couldn't even start thinking about the funeral because they had told her that the body would be kept in the morgue until the autopsy was performed. That is why she hadn't travelled to Oxford. Suddenly she burst into tears and told me that the previous morning she had received a letter from Kristen that seemed premonitory, because Kristen had stopped writing to her long ago. She should have guessed, she said. She should have *protected* her. She apologised, and asked me to step in as she reached for a handkerchief.

We were now in the kitchen. Through the window of the back door I could see a porch with a wicker rocking-chair and a fenced-in vegetable garden, beyond which lay open fields. A lithe cat wound its way through my ankles and curled up at my feet. Kristen's mother turned her face towards the stove so that I wouldn't see her crying, and asked me if I'd like some tea.

'But why did you come all this way?' she said. 'You shouldn't have bothered.'

'It's that I'm about to leave the country and there's a question that still puzzles me, a detail in what Kristen told me, something only you can answer.'

I could see, because of the tensing of her shoulders, how she became suddenly wary. She turned slowly and looked at me with an expression of alarm and also, strangely, with a certain relief. The relief, I thought, of knowing that someone else *knew*.

'Ask me.'

I told her what I had imagined and she kept nodding silently, again and again, with a tired expression on her face.

'Yes, it happened just as you say. But it was Sister Rosaura who warned me about what Kristen was planning to do. She took me aside for a moment and asked me if it was true that I needed poison to exterminate the mice. Only then did I understand why Kristen had asked me to buy the box of chocolates. When I went into her room to speak with her alone, she collapsed and told me what had happened with that horrible man in the publishing company. And also of her plan. She had the box all ready and wrapped up. All I had to do was take it to the address written on the parcel. Though weeping and trembling, she wouldn't give up. If I refused, she said, she'd ask Sister Rosaura. She kept saying that she'd be unable to live for the rest of her life in a wheelchair while that man was alive. I tried to convince her to go to the police, but she was sure he'd be let off scot-free because of his contacts. Even so, I couldn't allow my daughter, my little girl whom I'd held in my arms, to do such a thing, and I managed to tear away the box from her. I begged her to pray, just as I myself had prayed for her life, to pray and allow God to decide. I left the hospital with the box of chocolates in my hands and before I could find a place to throw it away, an unknown impulse grabbed hold of me. It was like a diabolical whisper in my ear. After all, why not? I thought. Don't we get rid of the weeds in the garden and the pests in the field? Why should that murderer be allowed to live? Kristen had convinced me that they would never suspect her, because both Inspector Petersen and Professor Seldom thought that the murderer was someone intent on killing all the members of the Brotherhood in a crusade against paedophiles. Her plan seemed to me astonishingly simple and also perfect. I was sure it couldn't fail: Kristen had always seemed to me to possess a superior mind. And in the end, if someone were to discover her hand in this, I would step forward and tell the true story. That I had delivered the box, knowing full well what it contained. And I would be condemned, not her. Because I'm the one to blame, don't you agree?'

I thought that neither Seldom nor I, when we discussed the messages, had imagined this other possibility: that the messenger might be the murderer as well. Kristen's mother approached the table balancing the two cups of tea.

'But you haven't told me how it was that you hit upon the truth,' she repeated.

'When I went to visit her at her house,' I said, 'Kristen truly seemed to believe that Hinch had died from a complication of his illness, just as it had been reported in the news. Maybe she even thought for a moment that, as you yourself said, it was God's answer to her prayers. It was I who told her that he had been poisoned. I was surprised to see her reaction to this: she seemed greatly perturbed, unsettled, and said that it "made all the difference". And yet, afterwards, in the letter she sent to the Brotherhood, she confessed her plan as if she herself had been the murderer. I realised, thinking once more about what she had written, that she described her plan in detail but that she didn't actually say *that she had carried it out*. And furthermore, she had afterwards taken her own life. I guessed that she'd sacrificed herself to save someone else. I didn't believe that she was as close to Sister Rosaura as all that, close enough to die for her. Therefore, that other person must have been you. Kristen didn't want anyone else to bear the consequences. As soon as I told her that the box had, after all, reached its destination, she decided, with her suicide, that she and no one else would be responsible for that death.'

'But you, what do *you* believe? Am I not the true culprit? Shouldn't I go at once and confess everything to the police?'

'No,' I said. 'Don't do that. If you did, Kristen would have died in vain, and that would be even sadder still. I only wanted to know the truth.'

Kristen's mother gave a deep sigh and stood up again to open a small drawer.

'In that case,' she said, 'I'll give you an envelope Kristen sent for you. Careful, because I think there is something made of glass inside. She seemed convinced that you would come here at some point. And she was right.'

She handed me a yellow envelope that had only my initial written on it. Opening it, I saw the glass pendant she was wearing with the little rolled-up piece of paper, together with a handwritten note.

*If you arrived at this point I'll only beg you to protect my
mother. I know for myself what punishment I deserve and
I don't regret ending my life or, rather, that horrendous
second life to which I've been condemned. Like Évariste
Galois, I too could write that 'those who care for me are
few, and I'm disenchanted with everything, including love
and glory'. If I managed to spark in you something worthy
of remaining in your thoughts, please don't think of me
with sadness. I too need all the spiritual strength I can
conjure up to die at the age of twenty.*

*PS: I leave you this piece of paper that was my care and
my curse, for you to keep or destroy. But I hope that it
never reaches their hands.*

I returned on foot, slowly, through the town, fingering in my
pocket the surface of the glass capsule as if it were a talis-
man. I still had another half-hour before the next train to
Oxford. On the High Street, I found arrows pointing the way
to the Lewis Carroll House close to Guildford Castle, above
the town. I followed the signposts and climbed up winding
streets almost without realising it, and I found myself at the
entrance, next to the gardens and the tall and still stately
ruins of the castle. It was a simple two-storey house, with
a wooden door painted blue, separated from the street by a
narrow pathway. An old man, slightly bent over, was leaving
the house between the small stone columns that flanked the
entrance. I managed to make out his features and hid behind
a tree to avoid being seen. It was Sir Richard Ranelagh. He
glanced at his watch and started to walk downhill, towards
the station. I then had a sudden impulse. I walked into the
house and, without stopping to look around, I went straight
to the librarian's desk. Showing her my postgraduate student
card, I asked her if I could see some of the Lewis Carroll

material. She was a very nice woman and nodded affirma-
tively, without stopping to inspect my credentials. I asked
for the catalogue from the time when the museum had been
set up, and then pointed to the item that read 'Cut Pages in
Diary'. She looked at me with surprise.

'No problem,' she said. 'I have the folder right here on my
desk. Another gentleman who just left asked for the same
item. What a curious coincidence!'

She indicated a small adjacent reading-room furnished
with two or three long benches. I was alone, but nevertheless
I pulled out Kristen's paper from the capsule as surreptitiously as I could and ironed it out with my hand. I admired
once more Leyton's handicraft of impeccable virtuosity, and
then replaced the copy with the original. The universe now
had a patchwork over a patchwork, and the authentic document would remain forever concealed under the appearance
of a fake.

I put Leyton's paper in my pocket and returned the folder
to the librarian.

'That was quick!' she said when she saw me leaving.
'Would you care to sign our visitors' book?'

'No, thank you,' I said. 'My name is far too long. And I
don't want to miss my train.'

Acknowledgements

Although this novel has as its inspirational starting-point in actual fact – the playwright Karoline Leach's discovery in Guildford of a paper summing up the contents of pages torn out of Lewis Carroll's diaries – all the events and characters of this detective story are fictitious. In particular, the Lewis Carroll Brotherhood that I've imagined bears no resemblance to the Lewis Carroll Society that indeed published an annotated nine-volume edition of the diaries. This is despite the fact that many of the opinions and points of view of my imaginary biographers may coincide in part with those of some of the biographies and articles I've had occasion to consult while writing the book. I found especially enlightening the ones by Karoline Leach, Stuart Dodgson Collinwood, Morton Cohen and Anne Clark, as well as Martin Gardner's annotated edition of the two Alice books, and Charlie Lovett's *Lewis Carroll's England*. Also, Edward Wakeling's notes to the diaries, and his two books devoted to Lewis Carroll's photography.

In the same imaginative spirit, the city of Oxford I describe is not strictly real and would certainly not pass a topographical test. It is the city I've conjured up in my hesitant memory so many years later, plus a few changes added to the actual scenography. I apologise to all Oxonians for a few hills abruptly added to the suburb of Headington, for a Radcliffe Hospital that has nothing in common with the real one, and for certain fountains and landing-docks of dubious existence.

I particularly wish to thank a number of people who gave me invaluable help in the writing of this novel:

- Physics professor Alberto Rojo, for the geometric exposition of the echo problem (based on the pioneering ideas of the Argentinian forensic physics specialists, Ernesto Martínez and Willy Pregliasco).
- Andrew Longworth of the Guildford Museum, for putting me on the right track to consult the Lewis Carroll papers.
- Isabel Sullivan of the Surrey History Centre, for her recollections regarding the item 'Cut Pages in Diary'.
- Edward Wakeling and Charles Lovett of the Lewis Carroll Society, for granting me access to the complete edition of the diaries and to the essential bibliography for researching the book.
- Alberto Manguel, for his erudite recollection of fiction books associated with Lewis Carroll. And for his superb work in the translation of this novel.
- Carolina Orloff, for kindly sending me various articles by Katherine Leach and Morton Cohen.
- Pablo de Santis, Carlos Chernov and Jorge Manzanilla, for their careful readings of the manuscript, and their astute comments.
- And finally, to Brenda Becette, for her own solution to the puzzle 'To make the DEAD LIVE' that appears in the novel, for her patient reading of the first drafts and for her re-readings of the following ones, as well as for her many comments. For her love and intelligence.